CAROLINE MITCHELL
Gower Peninsula, South Wale
between Monmouthshire and
city life. *Chains of Gold* is her c

Find out more at www.carolinemitchellauthor.co.uk

To Leni
with best
wishes —
Caroline

# Chains of Gold

## Caroline Mitchell

SilverWood

Published in 2020 by SilverWood Books

SilverWood Books Ltd
14 Small Street, Bristol, BS1 1DE, United Kingdom
www.silverwoodbooks.co.uk

ISBN 978-1-78132-946-7 (paperback)
ISBN 978-1-78132-947-4 (ebook)

British Library Cataloguing in Publication Data
A CIP catalogue record for this book is
available from the British Library

Page design and typesetting by SilverWood Books
Printed on responsibly sourced paper

*To my loving family*

# Acknowledgements

Tremendous thanks to the Silverwood Books team for guiding me throughout.

To everyone in the writing groups I've attended in Bristol and especially to my creative writing tutors, Rachel Bentham and Rosemary Dun, for their invaluable advice.

I'm grateful to Jo Ullah and Cathy Waterworth for their unswerving belief in me to get this book out, and particularly to my husband Alastair and my wonderful boys, Finlay, Callum and Rory, for all their love and encouragement.

# 1

Leni glanced across the table. Will's chair was still empty. He'd only gone for some more wine. Was he up to something again?

Bottles littered the white tablecloth and she tried concentrating on her neighbour's conversation but the noise of inebriated revellers at the Christmas work party, combined with the stimuli of alcohol and smell of food, fuelled her queasy misgivings.

Reaching for her quilted bag and dropping her napkin on the plush seat, Leni registered a lustful look from one of Will's work colleagues as she excused herself from the table. She strode across the dance floor in her black Armani figure-hugging dress. The sensual pleasure she derived, as the fabric brushed her bare legs and breasts, was marred by the fact that her husband wasn't around to witness the effect of her charms on other men.

Walking into the hotel lobby, Leni took a sharp intake of breath. *What the hell?* Almost concealed by a large, potted fern, Will's shoulders bent towards a young woman, his head close to her blond curls and his hand resting on her forearm. The pose spoke volumes.

'Will, how's that wine order?' Leni's sharp tone had an

immediate effect. The couple sprang apart, but not before she'd observed an adoring, then guilty, look on the face of his potential conquest. She regretted speaking out. She should've waited to see what happened.

'Leni,' Will said, straightening up and running a hand through his hair. 'Have you met Jenna?' It sounded like an office introduction.

'You're the new intern?' Leni didn't offer a handshake.

'I was just telling Jenna about our Andalusian highlights as she's going there soon.'

Leni registered his appeasing tone of voice and contrived casualness, used as a ploy to feign innocence. He lurched towards her and put a heavy hand on her shoulder.

'Really?' Leni backed away, shrugging him off.

'Excuse me.' Jenna's pretty features creased with anxiety. 'I'd better get back to the others.' Leni watched the younger woman's pert bottom wriggle from side to side in her tight body-con dress as she beat a hasty retreat to the ballroom.

'I'm sure an intern can Google or ask someone her own age,' she said, with loaded sarcasm, 'and Andalusia was our honeymoon.' Leni stressed the last word as she closed in on Will's reddened face. 'That was only eight years ago, and the highlights included each other, as I remember it.'

Leni turned on her heel and flounced into the toilet. Her fingers shook as she locked and leant against the cubicle door. She inhaled deeply while wracking her brains. Could this be another threat to their marriage? Why did he do it? He'd be taken for a fool in the office, trying to score at the company do. Refreshing her lipstick, she resolved to have it out with him tomorrow. He owed it to her to explain his recent moody and distant attitude. Something was wrong.

Returning to the table, Leni attempted to stay composed, chatting with her husband's earnest associate. She had to raise her voice as the lights dimmed and the music started up, stifling their conversation. Couples jumped up from other tables and flung themselves about on the dance floor to a cheesy 1980s pop track. The noise intensified as party poppers exploded streamers onto the tables, adding to the detritus. A reek of pungent aftershave assaulted her nostrils.

Will approached the table carrying bottles of wine in each hand and Leni calculated how much he might drink before their taxi arrived. Sharing a joke with a colleague, he smiled, and Leni knew she still fancied him, despite her worries about his behaviour. Apart from bolstering his ego, did these flirtations shore up his masculinity, or was it a subconscious punishment for the fact that they'd failed to get pregnant again?

'Who's for a top-up?' Will filled wine glasses nearby. He came around to Leni's side of the table, hovering with a bottle of red and a bottle of white. 'Can I give you something?'

Pouring mineral water into her glass before he could put wine in it, she looked up at him. 'A baby, please,' she whispered.

The taxi braked to a stop outside their house. The Chiswick residential road was quiet and the throbbing diesel engine sounded loud as Leni paid the driver and got out her house keys. In the frosty air, beneath a dark sky littered with stars, she shivered, keen for the evening to end.

Will slumped against the porch, hands thrust deep in pockets and his head drooping to one side. Leni flicked the light on and dropped the keys onto the console table. She took off her shoes and picked up the hem of her dress, to go upstairs.

Will staggered towards the kitchen. 'Fancy a nightcap?'

'Will, we've had a long evening.' Leni stopped on the second stair. 'Can we call it a night?' Not more alcohol. That would completely ruin the chance of sex. 'Come to bed. Please.'

'You're no fun these days,' he said, tearing at his bow tie. 'You used to love a liqueur after an evening out.' He grasped the kitchen door handle. 'I won't be long.'

She padded barefoot to the bedroom, hung up her dress, and slipped off her knickers. Wearing a silk and lace nightdress, she sat at the vintage dressing table, taking off her jewellery and brushing her hair. She spritzed Chanel onto her neck, hoping that Will would be upstairs by the time she'd finished in the bathroom. It wasn't often that Jake stayed over at a friends' house and they needed to make the most of it.

After dimming the lights, she got into bed. The pillows were plump and cool to her cheek and although she had every intention of waiting up for Will, within minutes Leni was fast asleep.

She woke with a headache and dry mouth. Morning light crept around the edges of the curtains. Will didn't move as she went for some water. Swallowing paracetamol tablets, she slid back into bed, settling against him in a spoon position. He stirred and draped his arm over her. His hand found her breast and she felt his erection. Drawing her nightie over her head she rolled onto him and kissed him. Their bodies entwined, Leni moaned with desire, but within minutes she felt him soften inside her. They switched position and she cupped her breasts towards him, her breathing becoming rapid as her pleasure increased. She felt close to orgasm, but with each thrust Will's enthusiasm seemed to diminish until they ground to a halt.

'Look, Leni, I'm just too tired.' Will withdrew. He lay on his back and rested his head in his hands, glowering at the ceiling.

'Don't worry,' she said, stroking his forehead. 'I don't mind.'

'Yeah, right. You don't mean that.' He folded his arms and turned to the window.

Leni swung her feet to the floor. 'We can try again tonight.' She went towards the bathroom. 'Jake'll be back, so we'll just have to be quiet.'

'Yeah, right,' Will muttered again, underneath his breath.

# 2

Leni and Will prepared to drive to Imogen's to collect Jake. 'Happy to do the return journey, if I drive down?' Leni asked, calculating that way Will wouldn't be able to have too much alcohol.

'As you like,' Will muttered, as he encouraged Monty into the dog crate. 'We won't stop for coffee.'

If you say so, Leni said to herself. 'Are we running that late?'

'If you hadn't spent ages on the phone with Kat, we might've had time.'

'We've got a delivery into the shop tomorrow.' Leni ignored his accusation as she buckled her seat belt. 'She's not in, so she wanted to brief me.'

'For half an hour?'

'For goodness' sake, Will. She's having Jake. There were things to sort out.' She shouldn't have to justify talking to her friend, and colleague, when it concerned arrangements for their son. 'The boys'll love playing on the Wii.'

'Is that really a stimulating activity for seven year olds?' He scowled.

'It's better than passively watching television,' she retorted.

They were silent for a moment. She tried a different approach. 'I'm off on Friday, so I'll get Jake's feet measured.'

'Are you telling me he's outgrown those shoes we got him recently?'

Was she somehow responsible for their son's growth spurt? 'He's a growing boy. I'll record his height and take a photograph against the sitting-room door.' She glanced past her husband to the lake on their left. 'Did your mum do that with you and Tom?'

'God. Can you see my mother doing that?' Will spat the words out, his mouth puckered like he'd swallowed something bitter. 'She put her heart and soul into Dad, Tom, and the farm. I was the after-thought.'

Leni rested her hand on his leg. 'I can't understand how a mother can favour one child over another. It won't be like that with me.'

She reflected on Will's parents' indifference to their younger son. They crowed about Tom's promotions, delighted in boasting how blessed they felt to be presented with four grandchildren by him. However hard he tried, Will couldn't live up to his exalted, industrious brother. She shouldn't be surprised that he was as emotionally dry as a desert.

'How are you fixed at work this week?'

'I've a few meetings lined up, but we're in a quiet period. I should be home at a reasonable time, if that's what you're asking?'

'What's got into you?' Leni withdrew her hand. 'You're always snapping at me these days. I can't say anything right.'

Will retrieved a bottle of water from the passenger well and took a long gulp, the sucking noise filling the void between them.

'I didn't tell you I was called in to see Dean before Christmas.' He wiped his hand across his mouth. 'I'm trying to team-build and keep stakeholders happy, and everyone wants something for nothing. Christ, I'm bending over backwards to keep it all sweet, then he lectured me on my expenses and threatened to limit my budget.'

'You should have told me. I'm sorry.'

Will threw the water bottle down. 'It doesn't help, you always pressurising me to perform, either.'

'What do you mean?' Leni's hands gripped the wheel.

'When did we last have sex for fun, because we fancied each other?' Will turned to face her. 'You act like some fertility guru, with all the food and hormone charts, telling me what to eat and monitoring my drink.' His voice rose. 'I'm fed up with it.'

She focussed on the car ahead to stop tears falling.

'I don't want to go down the IVF route, or for you to have another miscarriage.' Will spoke in a whisper. 'Shouldn't we just forget about another baby?'

She felt sick. His words rang true. Perhaps she was relentless about having another child? After Jake arrived they'd enjoyed sex whenever they felt like it, happy to get pregnant if it happened. She remembered nights when Jake was away and they could relax without fear of being caught. Will's foreplay had been so stimulating; he knew just how to keep her on the edge and hungry for him. Later, she'd wanted sex as often as possible, with minimum foreplay. She'd even texted him at the office, begging to meet during his lunch break because her ovulating conditions were perfect. The agony of losing a pregnancy, they couldn't go through that again. Maybe it was better to wait until they were happier together?

'Research shows how important it is to eat well, and drink less,' Leni said in a level voice. 'They've checked my ovaries.'

'Oh, great. So now you're blaming me.' Will flicked the heating switch off.

'I'm not saying that. Just stop drinking so much?' Leni's stomach churned, hangover and anxiety creating acid reflux in her throat. His silence unnerved her and she stole a glance at him. He glared straight ahead, his mouth set in a grim, tight line.

She switched on the radio. Sunday Morning Love Songs increased her desolation as she listened to dedications from loved-up couples. A track came on. One of their old favourites.

'Let's be friends,' Leni said, noticing the clouds lifting and a weak sun trying to lighten the late December sky. 'You love Mum's cooking, and Fran and Hugh are coming with the kids. Perhaps you and Hugh can take them out with the dogs after lunch, for a walk?'

'So you can have a moan about me to your family while we're gone?' Will said.

'Don't say that,' Leni groaned. 'Of course Fran's aware of our struggles, she's my sister. She's always been supportive. My family cares about our situation.'

'Is there anyone else you want to share it with?' Will grabbed his jumper from the back seat, shoved it over his head and thrust his arms into the sleeves. 'You may as well just shout it from the roof-tops that Will Parsons can't get it up any more.'

Monty whined.

'Please, Will. We're in this together – we can sort it.' If only, she thought. 'We're a team.'

Turning off the main road onto a small lane, Leni slowed as she noticed a patch of black ice ahead. The stark branches of an ancient oak tree stood sentry as she rounded the bend and Imogen's house came into view. The detached flint cottage, surrounded by a well-tended garden, was fronted by a sweep of gravel with parking for three cars.

'Let's enjoy today.' She switched off the ignition. This bickering wore her down.

Will got out of the car and marched up to the front door. Imogen came out and Leni watched incredulously as Will turned on the charming son-in-law act, asking after her mother's health and commenting on the journey, as if all was well with their world. She gathered her handbag and a bunch of pink roses from the back seat, then let Monty out of the boot.

'Hello darling.' Imogen embraced Leni. 'Good party last night? Jake'll be pleased to see you – he has some news.'

As he raced out of the sitting room, Jake bowled an imaginary cricket ball, then bounded across the Persian rug to clasp the dog in a tight hug.

'What a wonderful welcome for Monty,' Leni said, hugging Jake. 'Have you had fun with Granny?' She stroked his unruly brown curls.

'Look, Mum.' Jake jumped up and pulled out his bottom lip, showing a red gash where one of his milk teeth had fallen out and the tip of a white molar poked through. He rummaged in his pocket. 'My prize,' he said, holding up a shiny new coin. 'I got £2.'

'What a generous tooth fairy.' Leni smiled at her mother. How fast he was growing up.

'Come and see my Lego model, Dad.' Jake dragged Will to the sitting room.

'You look well, Mum.' Leni appraised her mother's lean frame and bobbed white hair. Dressed in slim black trousers, with a dark grey cashmere polo-neck and a long string of pearls around her neck, she reminded Leni of Audrey Hepburn in a 1950s black and white film.

There was a commotion outside. Rosie, Imogen's rough-haired dachshund, started yapping and racing round in circles.

'That'll be Fran,' said Imogen. 'Watch out for the galumphing hound.' She patted her hair and went to welcome the rest of her family.

Fran and Hugh, followed by their children, Luke and Cecily, were greeted with hugs and kisses while the excited dogs wound between the legs of the assembled group. After dumping bags and coats on hall chairs, they all piled into the steamed-up kitchen where Imogen issued instructions.

'Smart blazer, I like that.' Imogen touched Hugh's arm, clad in a heather-coloured tweed jacket.

'Thanks. I'm really pleased with it,' he said, smiling at Fran. 'A top Christmas present from my wife.'

'Would you be on drinks duty while I check the lunch?' Imogen turned to open the oven door. 'There's Prosecco in the fridge and orange juice in the door, for the children.'

Hugh popped a cork, poured glasses of bubbly and handed them around.

'Good to see you, old boy,' he said, clapping Will on the back. 'Golfing business keeping you busy?'

'Yes, it's pretty good at the moment.' Will proffered a bowl of green olives. 'How are your building works coming along?'

The two men went to the French doors overlooking the frost-laden garden, drawn into conversation about building materials and the efficiency of Hugh's workforce.

'Hey, you two. Let me see?' Cecily barged between Luke and Jake, who were intent on a Nintendo game.

'Luke, can I ask you to lay a fire for after lunch please?' Imogen interrupted their noisy talk. 'You did such a good job last time you were here. You've got fifteen minutes.'

Shuffling out of the kitchen, the children interrupted each another, swapping stories about their best Christmas presents.

When the food was ready, Imogen seated a child between the adults to encourage conversation and learn about table etiquette. Leni knew the routine. Her mother placed great importance on considerate behaviour in children, while her father, Robin, had also been a stickler for manners. Leni's memory from her childhood was that he'd lectured them all and presided over family meals with rather a Victorian, patriarchal attitude. She and Fran strived hard to measure up, but she enjoyed the more convivial atmosphere around the table, now that her father was no longer alive.

'This beef looks perfect,' Hugh said, carving thin slices of meat onto a large blue and white platter.

'The Aga's the secret.' Imogen donned gloves to pull a large tray of Yorkshire puddings from the oven. The children wriggled about in anticipation as the scent of the crispy puddings reached them.

'That beef went in last night. Long and slow is my preferred method,' she said. 'Other than fillet, of course. Robin always demanded that pink, and it's so ingrained that even though he's gone, I still cook it like that.' She sighed, and Fran gave her a quick hug.

Sitting down at the table laden with flowers, crystal glasses, and dishes of mustard and horseradish, Imogen shook her napkin onto her lap. She handed Jake his napkin and indicated that he should copy her. He did so with a great flourish. Dishes of vegetables were passed around and a large serving of floury roast potatoes diminished with each person. Fran offered the gravy to Jake.

'Leave some for others.' Will frowned as he watched Jake pour most of the contents of the jug onto his beef. Beside a heap of roast potatoes, Jake's vegetables appeared as a small adornment to his plate. They tucked into the food with relish, swapping stories of house renovations, school holidays and future plans.

'Hugh and I are walking the dogs after lunch,' said Will. 'Any of you lot want to come?' He pointed his knife at Luke. Leni noticed her mother grimace at the gesture.

'You said we were going out on the boat, Dad,' wailed Luke in accusing tone. 'Grandpa would've taken us.'

'That's not true, Luke. I said we might go if the weather's favourable, but it's far too cold, and it'll be dark soon.' Hugh's grave expression and measured tone of voice sounded solemn in the midst of the frivolity. 'I'm sorry, kids. Next visit, I promise.'

There were moans of dissent from Luke and Jake who tried pleading for a ride in the little motorboat their grandfather took them out in, before he became ill. Cecily seemed happy with the dog walking plan and got down from her seat to stand quietly beside Imogen.

'Granny, can I let the dogs out now?' She lisped, having lost her front tooth. She pulled at the napkin hanging from the collar of her green velvet dress.

'Best leave them in the utility room until we've finished or they'll be dribbling under our seats.' Imogen put her arm around her granddaughter. 'You've brought some rough clothes I hope? That party dress will get spoiled.'

Cecily returned to her seat and the minute she'd finished her apple crumble, jumped down from her chair to free the banished dogs. There was general commotion with adults clearing the table, as cousins gathered coats and hats, and pulled on wellingtons.

'Come on, Bracken.' Luke grabbed the dog's lead from the coat hook and rattled it. The labradoodle rushed straight past him and stood close to the counter where the remnants of the beef joint lay, almost within his reach, on the platter. The dog's nose twitched, sniffing the scent while his tail beat vigorously.

'See you when we see you.' Will slammed the utility door behind the walkers. A moment of silence fell over the three women left in the kitchen.

'Shall we relax in the sitting room and light the fire?' Imogen nipped off a withered leaf from a flowering plant on the windowsill.

'Oh, let's stay put,' Fran said. 'It's toasty in here. The boys can light it when they come back.' She loosened her trouser belt a notch. 'I can hardly move, I've eaten too much.'

'Peppermint or regular?' Leni asked, taking cups from the cupboard.

'Earl Grey, black and weak, please,' said Fran.

'Peppermint for me please, darling,' added Imogen, pulling a box of After Eight chocolate mints from the dresser drawer. 'My secret stash,' she smiled. 'I'll let the children have some on their return, I promise.'

'If there are any left when we've finished,' joked Fran. 'God, where's my willpower?'

The women sat nursing their tea. Imogen asked about Fran's house renovations and they were shown pictures on her mobile phone.

Fran changed the subject. 'What's up with Will? He wasn't his usual charming self.' She tucked a strand of hair behind one ear and fiddled with a large ring on her finger. 'Sorry, Leni,' she said, seeing her sister's downbeat expression. 'That was mean, but he does usually try to impress with his celebrity golfer stories.'

'That's to stop you asking personal questions,' Leni said, pulling her green cashmere cardigan close and taking a deep breath. 'Did you notice how he deflected the conversation away from talk of babies?'

Imogen put her hand over Leni's. 'Don't worry, darling. Keep being supportive. He admitted to me, in a quiet moment, that he's finding it stressful at the office, with the uncertainty of staff being laid off.'

'He's so secretive about where he is, and stays later in the office than he used to,' Leni said. 'I'm watchful of his every move, and his alcohol intake. It's not something I'm proud of.'

Fran leant her elbows on the table and rested her chin in both hands. 'I can't imagine he likes being policed.'

'Something's definitely up.' Leni nodded. 'Sorry, Mum, you'll say this is too much information, but our sex life has gone to pot. His appetite has totally diminished.'

Fran frowned. 'Stress can do that. Can he get checked out?'

'He won't hear of it. That'd mean admitting defeat.' Leni continued to stir her tea, searching for some answers. 'Money and baby talk totally stresses him these days.'

'Are you quite sure he wants another one?' Imogen raised her eyebrows as she stared at her younger daughter.

'Yes, I'm sure he does, Mum.' Leni banged the teaspoon down. 'What about what I want, or Jake wants?' She looked from her mother to her sister. 'I didn't envisage him growing up as an only child.'

'It's a blessing he has cousins,' Imogen said. 'He's popular at school and has his best friend Mikey to play with.'

'It's not the same though, is it?' Leni grimaced.

'You're getting anxious about it,' Fran said, draining her cup. 'That won't help either. My advice would be to concentrate on Jake and other things, like your trip to Dubai, you lucky thing. How long before you go?'

'Nine weeks.'

'Maybe if you try taking your mind off getting pregnant, it will happen. That was the case for a friend of mine,' Fran said.

'Will wants me to do another day at the shop as money's tight.' Leni pulled a chocolate mint from its paper case. She savoured the velvet texture. 'I know it's a luxury to have that spare day to get my hair cut, play tennis, or whatever, but I relish my four-day week.'

'I think Fran's right,' Imogen said. 'You need to be patient and loving, but if it doesn't happen this year, you'll need to consider your options together and decide what's best for all of you.'

'You're probably right,' Leni said, then quizzed Fran about her latest tapestry project to steer the talk away from her troubles.

Shortly after, noise from the family piling back into the house interrupted them. The children regaled them with stories of the dogs' antics, and what they'd seen and done, outside.

Trays of tea and biscuits were taken into the sitting room and the fire was lit. Half an hour later, Will looked at his watch.

'Time to go. School day tomorrow.'

Luke groaned and Jake whooped.

With noisy goodbyes and promises to keep in touch, one car was loaded with three passengers and a small dog, while the other car was laden with four passengers and a large dog. Imogen waved from the step before closing the door, relishing the thought of a nice bit of quiet in front of the fire.

# 3

Leni rested her hip against the worktop as she stirred vegetables in the sizzling wok. She mulled over the advice her mother and Fran had offered, but the seed of fear that she and Will were drifting further apart had already germinated.

The front door slammed and Will walked into the kitchen, dropping his keys on the Welsh dresser.

'What's cooking?' he said, slinging his leather satchel onto a chair.

'Stir-fry, ready in about five minutes.' Leni wondered why he didn't come over and kiss her. 'Then I'm taking Jake to Beavers.'

'Got any wine open?'

'It's Monday,' Leni said, irritation flooding her as she drizzled soy sauce over the vegetables. 'No alcohol night, remember?'

'Jeez, Leni, we can break the rules occasionally.' Will grabbed a bottle of burgundy from the fridge. 'I'm having one. I need it after today.'

'Didn't you have enough over the weekend?' she blurted out. 'It won't help your libido, either,' she muttered.

'Does it give you pleasure to kick a man when he's already down?' Will gulped his wine.

Leni bit her lip, cross with him for breaking their rule, and cross with herself for getting riled.

'I've had a hard day. I'm going for a shower.' Will drained his glass. 'Let's hope when I come down, you'll be in a better frame of mind.'

Didn't he realise how patronising that sounded? Of course she felt aggrieved, after catching him with the intern and his recent, secretive, behaviour. Leni knew she should draw him out, get him talking. Then she might get some answers.

She took the wok off the heat and bundled it, with shallow bowls, into the warming oven. Jake came in wearing a Scout scarf held in place with regulation woggle over a turquoise sweatshirt with proficiency badges down one sleeve.

'Alright, Jake?'

He peered through the glass of the stove. 'It's stir-fry,' she said.

'Yummy, my favourite.' He grinned. 'Can I have a banana milkshake?'

'Bring the milk over, then.' She adjusted his hitched-up sweatshirt as he went past. It had the freshly laundered smell she loved. It made her feel like an efficient mother and housekeeper.

'Those shoes'll need a polish before you go. How did they get so scuffed?'

'We played football in the yard at break. I did a really good tackle but Miss Brown told me off and said it was dangerous 'cos Mikey could've tripped or broken a leg.' Jake scraped a chair away from the table and sat down. 'I don't like break when Miss Brown takes it.'

'Before you get comfortable, could you feed Monty?' Leni said, as she whizzed ice, milk and banana together.

Jake opened the back door and before he could stop him, Monty rushed in, fur dripping and mud splashing from his paws. 'Oh, you're soaking!' He laughed.

'I expect he's craving your company, Jakey, he's been out there a while. You know how he gets under my feet when I'm cooking.' Now there's another job for me to do, she thought as she looked at the paw prints on the kitchen tiles.

Jake grabbed an old towel from the utility room and gave the dog a rub-down. He commanded Monty to sit, as he put handfuls of dried food into a dish and set it on the floor.

Leni made some custard to go with the lemon tart she'd bought on the way home. She then heaped steaming stir-fry onto each plate, inhaling fragrant spices and lemongrass. She went to the bottom of the stairs.

'Will, it's on the table,' she shouted. Surely he had to be out of the shower by now?

Leni and Jake were about to eat when Will came in.

'I had to take a call from Dubai.'

'Don't those guys ever stop working?' Leni asked.

Will shot her a withering look before retrieving the bottle from the fridge and topping up his glass. He held it aloft in Leni's direction.

'I'm on water tonight,' she said.

Will turned to Jake. 'What's happening in school this week?'

'We're going to the Natural History Museum.' Jake scooped a mouthful of noodles, leaving a smear of sauce on his chin. 'I'm going to look at dinosaur bones and take pictures of the fossils, so I can compare them to the ones at Granny's.'

'Good plan,' Leni said, 'and you can show her them when we're in Dubai.' She hoped that the more she talked about their impending trip, the better prepared he'd be for their absence.

'Are you going to miss my concert?' Jake's bottom lip stuck out.

'Wouldn't miss it for the world, buddy,' Will said, ruffling Jake's hair. 'We'll be back by then.'

'Daddy's away for five nights and I'll be gone for three.' Leni watched Jake lap up his father's affection. 'You can practise your hornet solo in front of Granny. She'll be your audience and sing along with the chorus bits.'

Jake made a face and raised his eyebrows. 'Granny can't sing with us.'

'Not at the concert, just for practice,' Leni said. 'You know she loves singing with her choir.'

Swallowing her last mouthful, she wondered how they compared with other families eating supper on a Monday night. Did other couples niggle as much as they did?

The first things Leni noticed when she got home were that Will hadn't bothered to load the dishwasher and the bottle of wine was almost empty.

'So, are you going to offer Jenna a permanent position?' She wiped down the work surface.

'She's bright and ambitious. She'll probably go overseas. The money's tempting in the Middle East.'

'You'll want to impress her, to keep her, then?' She searched his face for clues to his feelings.

'It's always the same: you find someone really talented, they stay a couple of years and then they take their enhanced experience to the competition.' Will sounded resigned as he tipped out the last of the wine.

'Other firms must have the same problem?' Leni clattered

dirty plates and cutlery into the dishwasher. She pinged on yellow rubber gloves and filled the wok with hot, soapy water.

'What do I know? I am Sales Director, not CEO or Chairman.' He drained his glass and plonked it beside the sink. 'It's depressing. Things are hard out there, Leni. You need to tighten your belt too.'

Will lectured her about budgeting. This was like being told off by the head teacher but she kept quiet, rinsing his glass.

'I do get it,' she glanced at the oversized railway clock, 'but can we leave it tonight? Jake's got a lift home and I'd like to look out my clothes for Dubai.'

'I'll sort the household finances by myself then.'

'Leave the file out and I'll take a look tomorrow before work.' God, what a drag, she thought, as she let down the lime-green plantation blinds shutting out the cold, black night. Was he making a mountain out of a molehill or was there justification to worry about their money? She'd light a Jo Malone candle and try to regain some equilibrium in the bath.

After a hot soak, Leni massaged lotion over her body. Dressed in leggings, a cashmere hooded top and velvet ballet pumps, she opened her wardrobe and ran a hand along the rail to identify clothes suitable for the heat. She chose sun dresses, light silk tops and a couple of capri-style trousers. She picked out a white Guess cardigan and two colourful pashminas for any evening, or air-conditioning, chills. So, which dress should she choose for the corporate dinner to go in Will's suitcase, in advance?

As Leni laid out shoes to match each ensemble she became excited about the trip and the opportunity to have a bit of fun in the sun. If she and Will could just get pregnant, things between them would improve, she was sure of it. Leni chose a pair of Tod's tan leather driving shoes for the off-road excursion, and for sightseeing and shopping she'd wear a pair of jewelled flats. She packed a pair of strappy heels into a soft fabric bag. Most of this could go in his suitcase, too.

After swinging open another wardrobe door, she rifled along her evening dresses, smiling as she recalled occasions when she'd worn them. Will had made friends with a number of wealthy undergrads at Oxford University and they'd had memorable evenings attending Glyndebourne and Covent Garden Opera, with one or other of them. How could she forget Josh McGregor, the flamboyant *bon viveur* from St John's College? His parents owned a stately home in Perthshire and they'd joined him for the annual Hunt Ball. She remembered shivering in a cold, draughty bedroom with an avocado bathroom suite down a gloomy corridor, hung with trophy stag heads and dark oil paintings of Josh's ancestors. She'd worn her favourite Vivienne Westwood red and green checked silk number in a nod to the Scottish location and he'd asked her what clan she came from. How she'd loved those carefree days, only themselves to please, regular hot sex, and confidence in their future together. Yet, even as she missed the frivolity of their lives back then, she wouldn't swap being Jake's mum for anything.

Her mind drifted off reminiscing about becoming a mother and then losing her father, both experiences creating such intense emotion. The first brought such joy and the second had been so wretched. Robin's diagnosis of prostate cancer had been a huge shock. He and Imogen had been planning their first cruise. Being of the stiff upper lip generation he hadn't visited the doctor to find out the cause of trouble with his waterworks. The diagnosis of late-stage cancer had completely rocked the family and it had only been a matter of months between diagnosis and death.

Flopping onto the bed, Leni felt an overwhelming sadness.

She missed the physical presence and emotional support of her father and was keenly aware that her relationship with Will was less fulfilling than in earlier years. She didn't want to become bitter because they couldn't have another child. She must count her blessings and cherish what they had. Sighing and stretching, Leni resolved to pull herself together and try harder to win Will's affection again. She had to.

Leni walked to work along Chiswick High Road, noticing empty shops which had recently gone out of business. Grubby, peeling billboard stickers announced property agents' particulars. Perhaps it would be sensible to meet with their financial adviser. She'd put away a small portion of her dad's inheritance. The rest of his estate was left to Imogen so she could stay in the seaside home they'd bought on his retirement. Leni silently prayed for her mother to remain in good health and, being a lively seventy-two-year-old, there was every chance of her finding a companion for walks or theatre trips but Leni didn't relish the idea of a stepfather. A new relationship might jeopardise her future inheritance.

She reproached herself for thinking selfishly as her reverie was shaken by a vocal fruit and veg seller. He deftly wrapped tomatoes in a paper bag for a customer. 'Best price on the High Street.'

The stall was piled high with plentiful, colourful produce and Leni stopped to buy grapes and a hand of bananas. She stashed the contents in her tote.

Reaching the shop, she cast an appraising eye over the window display. The boutique smelled clean and of new clothes. Taking out notes for Rachel, Leni stowed her bag and coat in the cupboard by the pint-sized kitchen at the back.

She ran through a list of jobs to be done then grasped a large box and manoeuvred it to the shop floor. She unwrapped new stock from polythene and hung them on a rail then she plugged in the steamer and got to work.

A young woman with a trendy hairstyle came in. Leni noted the expensive stone-colour trench coat, black patent boots and what appeared to be the latest Chloé shoulder bag slung across her body. The customer held up dresses to examine their cut and style.

'Are you happy to browse?' Leni took a long tunic of pewter metallic fabric and draped it on a padded hanger from a supply under the counter. 'Let me know if I can help with anything.'

'We're in the Caribbean for half-term so I'm looking for cocktail dresses for evenings at the resort.'

Leni showed the woman to the rail closest to the till where a range of colourful silk and jersey dresses were displayed.

'What size do you wear? I'd say you were an eight?' she said, pulling out a short, frilled, sleeveless dress in the appropriate size.

The woman picked out several items which Leni took to the fitting room. She pulled the thick swathe of green silk from behind a gilt tie-back, making a curtain across the cubicle. She checked the Louis XV chair was in place and that the full-length mirrors on three sides were dust-free, giving a good reflection of all angles.

'I've hung them in here,' Leni said, stepping aside for the customer. 'Let me know if you need to borrow a pair of shoes when trying things on.'

The woman bought a dress which Leni wrapped in tissue paper then put into one of the shop's signature red and white candy-striped bags, and tied the top with red ribbon. As the customer closed the door behind her, Leni's phone began to ring.

'Hi, it's me,' Kat said. 'How's business today?'

'Good, thanks, I've just sold one of the Pucci dresses.' Leni watched a group of Eastern tourists walk past the window, monitoring their GPS on a mobile phone. 'How are the boys?'

'All good. I took them to the park, and dragged them round Sainsbury's. I can pop over to the shop about 5pm? I'd like a quiet moment to talk about the stock, and Rachel, before your trip. Mum's coming over to mind Mikey and Jake.'

'She's a star. See you later, then.'

During the afternoon Leni made a few sales. As she finished cashing up, Kat came in, streaked blond hair tousled by the wind, one shoulder weighed down by a bulging bag and her free hand clamped to a mobile phone.

'I'll call you later.' After stabbing a button on the phone to end the conversation, Kat stuffed it into a pocket of her voluminous, acid-green coat. Tight blue jeans, ripped at both knees and customised with sewn-on patches below one hip pocket, encased her slim legs and a pair of decorative, vintage cowboy boots completed her hip look. 'Hi Leni, how's it going?'

They talked about the business then locked up. After making herbal tea and grabbing a stool from the kitchen, Kat sat beside Leni at the till counter. She logged on to her iPad.

'I'd like to show you a couple of new designers I've been following. They're hot,' Kat said in a breathy, animated voice. 'What do you think?'

Kat's face glowed with rapture as she scrolled through pages of high-end fashion.

'Totally cool,' Leni said. 'But what about the prices?'

They looked at profit margins, identifying whether their key customer base would buy from the costly range. Leni didn't want to put a dampener on her younger colleague's irrepressible enthusiasm. She ran through Rachel's list of responsibilities. As

Rachel had worked for Whistles and came with a reference from a retail friend of Kat's, Kat and Leni were both confident Rachel would handle customers with competence in Leni's absence.

'How's the internet dating going?'

'Dreadful.' Kat scowled. 'There's a wealth of dicks to choose from but a dearth of real men out there. I'm not going to bother for a while.'

'Listen, Will's school friend is coming over from Ireland to watch the International. He's called Connell, has a head of thick black hair and dreamy, blue eyes.' Leni swallowed her last mouthful of tea and took Kat's empty cup to the sink. 'He broke up with his partner a few months ago. I'll introduce you. I think you'd like him.'

'Oh yeah?' Kat looked doubtful. 'If he's so hot, why's he still single?' She went to activate the alarm.

'Just hasn't met the right woman.' Leni grabbed her bag and coat. 'I'd be glad that he's not hopped straight into another relationship. He's getting over the breakup.'

It was dark and cold outside, the pavement full of commuters rushing home to enjoy private interests, relationships, television and hobbies. The two women walked along Chiswick High Road, turning onto Marlborough Road towards Kat's terraced house.

Through the brightly lit window they saw Jake and Mikey playing a Wii game while Barbara read her *Woman's Weekly*. Kat rapped on the pane and both boys jumped up and elbowed each other out of the way to be the first to the front door.

# 4

It was Saturday. Leni, Will and Jake walked in Hyde Park and Jake played with his remote-control boat on the Serpentine.

'I'm looking forward to tonight's dinner party.' Leni reached for Will's hand as they ambled along, watching Monty rush from tree to tree, sniffing the urine-saturated roots. Groups of families, tourists and joggers jostled for space on the paths winding past shrub borders. 'It'll be a chance for us to have time together with Jake on a sleepover.'

'Me too.' Will squeezed Leni's hand. 'I'll make it up to you for being so withdrawn lately.'

She hugged his arm, feeling reassured by his admission, then called to Jake to bring his boat to the water's edge.

'Lunch time. Hard Rock, anyone?'

It was their favourite weekend restaurant where they could reminisce about much-loved bands from the 1990s and fill Jake's head with stories about rock stars. On the Tube home, Leni daydreamed about the day, with a warm feeling that they would make love tonight.

Getting ready to go out, she turned from side to side

appraising her outfit in the bedroom mirror. Smoothing her tight blue dress over her thighs, she added a slick of red to her lips. She pursed them together, pouting at her reflection and blew herself a kiss. This dress was a knock-out.

'It's not so cold tonight,' said Will, patting his cheeks with cologne as he emerged from the bathroom. 'We'll go by Tube and taxi it home.'

'Seriously? I've spent a fortune on this body-con dress and I really don't want to use the grubby underground.' Leni fastened a pretty Victorian diamond brooch she'd inherited from her granny onto the collar of her jacket. 'And these heels and no tights warrant a taxi.'

'I thought we'd made a pact at Christmas not to spend any money on new clothes?' Will fussed with his button-down collar.

'Come on, Will, is money all you think about these days?' Leni turned off the bedside lamp. 'Your firm's won a major contract in Oman and you're baulking at spending thirty quid?'

'It's being spent before I earn it these days. You've got to curb your shopping habit, Leni.'

It was as if Will had suddenly had a personality change, coming down on her like a ton of bricks. Where was the loving man she'd been with today? 'Excuse me, what about that new bike you bought? Did it have to be top of the range? I doubt it'll see the light of day before June.'

Will drew a cashmere scarf from the cupboard and banged the door shut.

'Listen, I need to keep up with the boys. You should see the bike Chris bought. I can't turn up on any old clapped-out nut-crusher when we ride together.'

Leni raised her eyebrows and shrugged. 'You have your toys and I'll have my clothes then. Fair's fair.' She chose a handbag from the collection in her wardrobe and turned away. Her hopes of an evening leading to sex were falling away as they bickered.

'How long will you be?' Will demanded. 'I don't want to be late for Adam.'

'I'm ready.' Leni dropped a Givenchy lipstick and a comb into her slim clutch bag and snapped it shut. 'Come on, Will, our boy's on a sleepover and we've had a great day. How about "*I'm loving the way you look tonight, Leni*", and hail a cab, like you always used to?'

'Plenty of cash to splash in those days,' he said, pressing two fingers between his eyebrows to ease tension. 'I don't like curbing our lifestyle, either. I'll think of something.' He squeezed her hand as they left the bedroom.

Crossing the polished wooden hall floor, she made a mental note to thank Vicky for her attention to detail, the next time she came to clean. She couldn't resist her habit of dabbing the soil to see if the plants had been watered, and she stroked a waxy leaf below the cloud of white orchids in a Chinese patterned bowl on the console.

The dinner party was fun. A young waitress regularly topped up the wine and between courses the men moved round two places, to talk to different guests. By the time pudding came, Leni felt fuzzy-headed, and conscious that her dress was tightening by the minute like a boa constrictor. She leant in towards Adam. He removed his jacket and slung it over his chair and, adjusting a shirtsleeve, revealed a TAG Heuer watch on his tanned wrist.

'You're looking exceedingly fit these days, Leni.' Adam's gaze was drawn like a magnet to her bosoms spilling forwards in the tight dress. 'Will's a lucky man. I hope he appreciates you. On a regular basis?'

Sleazy comment, she thought, but all flattery was welcome

when your husband barely noticed a new dress, or wanted sex when you did.

'I drove past him the other night coming out of The Distillers in Hammersmith,' Adam said. 'I thought it was you with him, but then I saw it was Kat. You two look similar from a distance.' He put his arm around her and squeezed hard. 'Both gorgeous.'

Leni sobered up and sat bolt upright, breaking away from his lecherous hug.

'Yes, people have said that in the past.' Leni tried to keep any emotion from her voice, asking in as casual a voice as she could summon, 'Which night was that, by the way?'

'What the hell? Call yourself a friend?' Leni rounded on Kat the minute she walked into Leni's kitchen on Sunday evening. 'I'd like an explanation.'

'Excuse me?' Kat recoiled at Leni's tone. 'You said you needed to talk. What's this all about?'

'Your drink with Will, on Friday night?'

'I can explain. I was going to tell you tomorrow, at the shop, face to face,' Kat said.

'Well, Adam told me at dinner last night. Will hasn't mentioned it, either.'

Kat retorted, eyes flashing, 'Why don't you ask him about it, then?'

'I wanted to hear your side of the story, before I tackle him.' After filling the kettle and plonking mugs on the counter, Leni slumped onto a padded stool at the island.

'Look, it was nothing. I went to meet a guy from Match. com at The Distillers. I got there early, bought a large glass of white and waited, but he never showed up. I was trying to finish my wine without necking it down, when Will came in with someone I didn't recognise. He spotted me and came over, making some derogatory remark about my drinking alone. I told him I was trying not to feel humiliated, but that's internet dating for you. You've got to get used to it.'

The kettle boiled, and Leni made tea and took biscuits from the pine food cupboard. What was she doing, arranging artisan ginger cookies? There was no need to be polite in this situation, but she'd loved this friend for years so she had a right to be heard.

Kat unwrapped her huge grey mohair scarf from around her neck, made a pillow of it, and sat down at a matching bar stool. 'He suggested I hang out with them until I'd finished my drink. He was teasing Sam about his wife having him on a short leash, only allowing him out for a quick drink. I thought he was showing off a bit, to be honest.'

Dunking her biscuit into her tea, she carried on. 'The place was rammed with an after-work crowd so we moved to a quieter corner, chatted for a while about this and that. Sam left and before I knew it, Will had ordered more wine.'

'Yes, he was supposed to be back by 7.30pm.' Leni scowled at the memory. 'He said he'd bumped into Sam and time ran away with them. I was in such a rush to get to yoga I didn't bother to ask questions.'

'I hadn't planned on staying for a second one but I already had the babysitter, and she wouldn't have appreciated me coming home early and getting paid for only an hour.' Kat repeatedly twisted a strand of blond hair around her finger. 'He asked me how I thought you were and about the baby situation, and everything. It seemed pretty casual.'

'There's a "but", isn't there?' Leni's shoulders tensed and her stomach knotted. What was coming next?

Kat leant an elbow on the counter and chewed her thumbnail.

'Will went to the Gents and I updated my Facebook status to say the bastard had stood me up. When he came back, we got onto the subject of my love-life and then he got a bit maudlin about life, and all that. He insisted we have one for the road and even though I protested I was really hungry, he wouldn't take no for an answer. I'm sorry, Leni, but he seemed so dejected, I thought I'd stay for one more and try to lift his mood.'

'He can be persuasive, I know.'

'He was quiet on the way back, then as I went to kiss him goodbye, he lurched into my face and tried to kiss me.'

'Bloody hell, Kat!' Leni shouted.

'Look, it was a drunken, thoughtless gesture and I'm sure he meant nothing by it. I totally brushed it off.' She was silent for a moment. 'I'm sorry.'

'I believe you.' Leni raked her hands through her hair. 'What am I going to do? There's definitely something wrong.'

'Have you had any other warning signals?'

'Just the usual. Staying late at the office, being cagey about his evening meetings, et cetera. I've always accepted his word for it.'

'You need to reach out to him. Don't interrogate him when he gets home, and put your sexy underwear on?'

'Ha, and I thought you were a feminist?'

'I am, but you've got to use your sexual power in this situation.'

'Why am I still obsessed about having another baby? I always thought I'd have more than one. I had the feeling that it'd bring us closer together. Maybe I haven't been as affectionate lately.' Leni shrugged. 'It's hard to stay positive when he's so moody.'

'Stay strong. You'll figure it out.' Kat drained her tea and stood to leave. 'Believe me, I'd never do anything to upset your marriage.'

Leni sighed. Of course she wouldn't. She passed Kat her coat and black fedora. 'I know.'

'I'll see you in the shop tomorrow.' Kat hugged Leni. 'Don't fight with him tonight. Sleep on it.'

'I won't but I'm going to make this trip to Dubai his last chance. If nothing's changed by the time we come back, I'm going to talk about separating.'

# 5

'Can I help with that?' The tall, dark-haired man stepped out from the window seat to stow Leni's carry-on bag in the cabin locker.

'Thanks. It's amazing how much you can pack into one of those.'

'Yes, so it seems.' He smiled, hefting the bag above his shoulder.

After shrugging off her pink cashmere coat and folding it, she laid it on top of the suitcase. She stowed her magazine away and retrieved a bottle of water from her handbag. Watching passengers fuss over their bags, and claiming preferred seats next to window or aisle, she imagined that some of them were excited and some anxious, as they set off on their journey.

After take-off, the plane levelled and she sensed an almost palpable relaxing of the cabin occupants. The man on the opposite side of the aisle plugged headphones into his laptop and the woman in front shook out a broadsheet newspaper.

'Have you been to Dubai before?' Leni turned to the man who'd helped with her case. She noticed how his blue, creased, linen shirt highlighted his deep blue eyes.

'Yes, a couple of times on business. What about you?'

'It's my first trip. My husband's firm has put in a golf course on the outskirts of the city.'

'That'll take some watering,' he teased, in a wry tone of voice. 'I'm Alex Taplow, by the way.'

'I'm Leni. Short for Leonora, the name my parents inflicted on me at birth.'

'It's lovely. A goddess or something?'

'It means light. Leonora was the heroine of Beethoven's opera *Fidelio*, which Mum and Dad saw when they were dating. I suppose it could have been worse, like Isis, although that translates as Egyptian Goddess of the Moon, which sounds really pretty.' Oh dear, was she blathering?

She reached up, shut off the air-con and drew her pashmina close. 'We'll be wining and dining the contractors then there's the obligatory team-bonding experience.'

'So, will you enjoy bungee-jumping?' Alex asked, eyebrows raised.

'It's a 4x4 off-roading trip.' Leni laughed. 'Fortunately we get twenty-four hours R & R afterwards for visiting the souks and the chance to do some serious shopping.' She shielded her eyes from the sun flooding in through the small window. 'It'll be fun, but any tips on other things to do would be welcome.'

'Shall I shut this?' Alex pulled the blind halfway down. 'I'd recommend the services of a guide. I know of one and he'll take you to places you want to visit, rather than someone who'll take you to each and every cousin's shop, to sell you something you don't want, or need.'

'That'd be great.'

She chatted easily with him as the refreshment trolley

trundled down the aisle. A flight attendant loaded with makeup and a high ponytail arrived at their row.

'Sauvignon Blanc, and some ice please.' Leni flipped down her tray.

'A bottle of Pilsner for me.' Alex accepted his drink and complimentary pretzels.

'Good health,' Leni said, pouring wine into her glass and raising it in Alex's direction.

'Cheers.'

'It's actually quite good.' Leni savoured the cool liquid slipping down her throat. 'What business are you in?'

'I deal in antiques and reclamation. I've a shop in Marlborough and a workshop for restoration and upholstery.'

So, he was creative. She noticed his large hands as he shook pretzels into his palm.

'I go to Dubai for Iranian carpets and Jordanian mosaics. My interest in Middle Eastern artefacts means I combine business with pleasure. Perfect.' He tipped them all into his mouth.

'I work in a boutique clothes shop,' Leni said. 'It's fine for now, but my dream is to run my own jewellery business. I've only done a short course so far, but I'm itching to see the intricate gold and silver work in the city.' She twisted her Theo Fennell wedding ring, surprised that she'd confided her dream to this stranger. A fleeting thought popped into her head about how a new baby might affect her goal, but she swatted it away, reasoning she'd start making pieces at home, while the child was still an infant.

'You should visit the silver mall, in that case,' he said.

'I've heard the mall's the most visited place on the planet, isn't that incredible?'

'Yep, my daughter would love it. She's fifteen, and can shop 'til she drops.'

'What's her name?'

'Chloe. That's "young green shoot", in Greek, and she fits the meaning perfectly.' He looked wistful. 'She's growing up so fast.'

Leni fiddled with her ring. How lovely to have a daughter. If she ever managed to conceive again, she'd like a girl next time.

'Have you got other children?' she asked.

'Jamie, he's thirteen and into sport and motor cars.' Alex smiled again, laughter lines crinkling around his eyes. 'How about you? Got any kids?'

'Just the one, Jake. He's seven, and currently being spoilt with his granny.'

'That's a great age. They soak up learning, don't they?'

It was Leni's turn to smile. 'Jake's OK academically, but football's all he's interested in. If he can't play, he spends every free minute on the Wii with his best friend.'

'Good for him.' Alex drank his lager. 'It's physical activity in a different form.'

Leni noted his relaxed approach to the games console. 'I do try to introduce him to other stuff. We've got so much going on in London but there's only so much time, isn't there?'

'He'll be learning useful skills on the field, like sharing, and team spirit. Jamie's always been passionate about sport whereas Chloe can take it, or leave it. Just different personalities.'

'My sister and I were the same. She was mad about ponies and I lived for ballet. Mum was driving us about every weekend to gymkhana or dance competitions.' Leni remembered the childhood competitive drive between herself and Fran, despite competing in separate activities. They both wanted the medals, and framed certificates on their bedroom walls. She was glad that sibling rivalry was a distant memory and felt a sudden rush of affection for her sister, who was so supportive to her.

'Jake'll be dashing about the beach with my mum's dog. Mum's a stickler for fresh air and loves swimming in the sea. He'll go in too. Hardly notices the cold, but probably not this visit. It is only March.' She laughed, and finished her last sip of wine. 'Do your kids like swimming?'

'Yes, they love the sea, too. We always took them on seaside holidays when they were young. I'd like to introduce some cultural interests, on city breaks, before they no longer want to holiday with their dad. I hope I haven't left it too late.'

Leni noticed he didn't say 'we' again. So, was he separated, divorced, or a widower?

They talked about cities which might fit the bill, handed back their empty bottles and glasses to cabin staff, then fell silent. Alex took out his newspaper and Leni read her book.

Before the plane made its descent, she squeezed into the lavatory to refresh her makeup. Examining the highlights of her recent cut and colour, under the artificial light of the tiny cubicle, she was startled to find herself speculating how she must appear to Alex. He'd been a very agreeable flight companion.

They landed and as the commotion of passengers gathering bags increased, Leni turned to Alex. 'It was great to meet you. Thanks for your tips.'

Alex shook her hand. 'Have a good time. I hope the city lives up to your expectations.' He fished in his wallet. 'Here's my card. If you find yourself in the Marlborough area, drop in.'

'Thanks, I will,' Leni said, reaching up for her things in the overhead locker.

'Let me get that for you.' Alex passed her coat over then carefully placed her suitcase in the aisle.

'Thanks.' Leni pocketed his card and pulled up the suitcase handle. 'I'm sure I won't need this.' She draped the coat over her arm. 'But it would just be my luck for it to be snowing when we get back to Heathrow. Goodbye.'

Leaving passport control behind, she walked through Arrivals and made a beeline for the taxi rank. That flight had gone so quickly, with someone fascinating to talk to.

Millions of city windows sparkled in the bright sun as the taxi delivered her to the immaculate entrance of The Grosvenor House Hotel. A porter whisked her suitcase away and ushered her to Reception where she signed in and logged on to the hotel Wi-Fi. Looking around the foyer, she sent Will a text.

> I've arrived, will pop to the room to freshen up. Where shall I meet you?

She gasped as she walked into their suite, taking in the sumptuous furnishings and being drawn immediately to the huge tinted windows, giving views of sky-scrapers to one side and the sparkle of the sea on the other. Large bowls of dusky pink roses sat on the hall and coffee tables, with a further display in the mirrored bathroom. Did the hotel put these flowers in every suite or had Will made a special request? How romantic. They were her favourite colour. She hung up her clothes and laid out her toiletries in the marble-clad bathroom. Her phone pinged. Will was waiting for her in the third-floor salon. After brushing her hair, touching up her lipstick and spritzing perfume onto her wrists, she went to the lift with a sense of anticipation. Why was she so excited? It had only been a few days since she'd seen him, but she felt a sense of hope that they could reignite their marriage here.

He was reading a paper, sitting in a silver velvet-covered armchair. He looked good in a Ralph Lauren polo shirt, jeans and suede brogues. Leni rushed over to him. His face lit up with a smile and he stood to embrace her.

'How was the journey? Tea, or are you ready for an aperitif?' He held an arm around her waist and looked intently into her eyes.

'Tea's probably best. The heat is incredible, isn't it?' Leni said, sitting down. 'You get a blast of it between air-conditioned building and taxi, and I should've expected it, but still it takes my breath away.'

'I've got used to it, being on-site and walking around the course. It's fabulous. I can't wait to show you.' Will ordered jasmine tea from the waiter. 'The team's done a great job, I must say.'

Will chatted about the golf course and what had been going on over the past few days, as Leni interjected with questions. She filled him in on Jake's activities and home life.

'How about a swim before we get ready for tonight's gathering?'

'That would be heavenly. It'll wake me up – my body could do with a good stretch after that journey.'

Leni slid into her new Agent Provocateur bikini, belted the thick, white towelling gown and slipped on a pair of Havaianas to go to the pool.

Will dived in and surfaced beside Leni, and gave her a kiss.

'Did you miss me?' She put her arms around him, treading water. 'Hope the company you've been keeping...' Her words were cut off by Will's mouth on hers. It felt so good.

'Some beautiful bronzed bods to admire, for sure, but apart from inspiring lustful thoughts about warm skin and sun cream application…' Will turned onto his back and floated lazily in the water.

'Well, I'm here now.' Leni splashed water at him and swam to the wide stone steps. 'Come on, let's have cocktails in our Jacuzzi bath?'

They dried off, took the lift to the thirty-second floor and dropped their costumes in the basin. As Leni bent down to activate the Jacuzzi, Will came up behind her and pushed himself against her bottom.

'Oohh, that's the sort of welcome I like.' Leni turned and held his smooth, naked body against hers.

'Did you say you fancied a cocktail?' Will hungrily kissed her, pushing his hips towards hers. 'Jacuzzi or bed?'

They fell on the bed, legs entwined, avidly exploring each other with their hands. Leni arched her back and, moaning with pleasure, took him inside her.

Afterwards, she curled alongside him, resting her head on his arm and stroking his chest. Happily satisfied, she decided to broach the baby subject.

'For my part, I'm happy to let nature take its course. If it's meant to be, I'll be over the moon to get pregnant again, but I don't want this issue tearing us apart.'

He kissed the top of her head. 'I'll admit I've been worried about the financial strain of another child, and anyway, I like the way we are. You, me and Jake, we're a good team.'

Leni's heart flooded with love. It seemed such a long time since he'd shared his inner feelings with her, and this honesty and openness reassured her.

'So, let's enjoy what we have,' Leni leant up on her elbow to look directly into his face, 'and if we do find ourselves with another baby on the way, promise you won't back-track, and will embrace its arrival and all that that entails?'

'I promise.' He kissed her on the mouth. 'And now Mrs Parsons, it's time to get our arses in gear and get downstairs.' He slid from the bed to take a shower.

'Do you know the seating plan?' Leni applied her lipstick with precision. 'I hope I'm not next to Graham – he forever talks shop which can be a bit wearing'.

'Why are these things so slippery?' Will didn't answer her question as he continued to fumble with his bow tie.

'Don't worry, darling,' she went over to him, 'I'll do my best if I sit beside him. Want a hand with that?'

She took the ends of the satin fabric and folded it into a neat bow. He brushed her cheek with his lips to avoid spoiling her bright-red mouth.

'You look good, Leni.' His arms encircled her waist. 'I'm sorry I've been such a prat these past months. I'll celebrate this success tonight but I've got to build on it. We must find new partnerships.'

'That's OK. I know you've been under pressure.' Leni put her hand over her diamanté brooch to stop it getting caught in his lapel. 'I've been preoccupied with Jake, the shop, and my jewellery course, rather than trying to understand your concerns.'

They stood at the glass window, admiring the huge, inky black sky and lights of the city. She loved this intimacy, and felt excited. There was no need to voice the words that minutes ago they might have created a new life.

Taking the lift to the third floor they emerged to find dinner guests gathered in groups. Will became engaged in conversation with his MD so Leni excused herself and went over to say hello to a colleague of Will's who she liked.

'So, how's the site?' Leni kissed Doug's cheek.

'Fabulous. When are you seeing it?'

'After the sand dunes thing. Looking forward to it.'

Doug's wife kissed Leni. 'Lovely to see you again. You're looking gorgeous.'

'Thank you, Sally. You too,' Leni said, smelling Sally's fragrant cheek. Over her shoulder Leni glimpsed waiters in long white tunics and trousers weaving between guests, holding trays of champagne glasses.

'Is it similar to the one you did in Abu Dhabi?'

'Well, it's comparable to many of our courses.' Doug sipped his drink. 'It's our *raison d'être* to know what golfers want.'

'Don't mess with a winning formula, right?' Sally added.

Another of Will's associates joined them and they made small talk. In Leni's peripheral vision something glinted, and at the same time she heard a deep, throaty laugh. A sleek young woman, with long straightened black hair, stood out from the crowd. She was wearing a designer tuxedo trouser suit; her single-buttoned jacket revealed an expanse of tanned cleavage, swathed in chains of gold.

'You've noticed Melanie then?' Sally held her glass in front of her mouth as she whispered to Leni. 'I hear they're all falling over her at the office. Well-connected in golfing circles, puts in long hours, and is bright and beautiful, to boot.'

'Bitch, I hate her already,' said Leni, and the two women collapsed into giggles.

Will suggested they find their table. Leni was relieved to find herself next to the firm's comms man, as he was more light-hearted and less intimidating than the MD, whose razor sharp intellect made her feel educationally inferior.

She must heed her own advice not to drink too much or risk

behaving in an inappropriate way. She remembered a Christmas party from her old Topshop days where she'd knocked back the booze and ended up sexy dancing with a junior. That had provided salacious gossip for days afterwards. It hadn't gone down well with Will. The memory was as fresh as if it were yesterday.

'Excuse me, this is my wife and this is our dance.' Will had stood between Leni and the slim-suited man with curls plastered with sweat to his forehead. Will glared at his back as the young man swaggered towards the bar.

'What do you think you're doing?' Leni twisted from Will's grasp as he propelled her by the arm from the dance floor. 'Barging in like that was embarrassing.'

'You're making a fool of yourself,' Will said under his breath. 'Let's get some coffee.'

'For God's sake, I'm just having a good time.' Leni tripped over her high heels, stumbling into Will's side. 'Where's the harm in that?'

Will hissed in her ear. 'You're acting like a juvenile at her first staff party, trying to score. He looked fresh out of university – bit on the young side, isn't he?'

'Bloody hell, I'll decide who I dance with.' She tugged at the hem of her mini skirt to cover her thighs. 'You're behaving like a dumb pack animal, the beefy male flexing his muscles to get the choice female.'

She slumped into a black leather tub chair in the lobby and flung off her red stiletto shoes.

He caught her hand and pulled her to the lift, then supported her as she staggered to their room. He poured instant coffee granules into the cups on the tray and tore off the fiddly lids from the pots of UHT milk.

'What about you?' she said. 'My behaviour is no worse than

that time you were wearing your ridiculous kilt, commando-style, and that receptionist girl put her mobile phone under it and "papped" your crown jewels. You had to chase her to the Ladies and wrestle the camera from her to delete that picture. Total humiliation.' Leni flung herself onto the bedspread of striped, static-inducing polyester.

'You think there's one rule for you and one rule for me?' she slurred, pointing a crimson fingernail at him. 'Sorry to disabuse you, sunshine, but it takes two to tango.'

Leni's unhappy recollection was suddenly broken by a waitress proffering a bread roll. She returned to the present, cross with herself for remembering negative times, when she'd felt so euphoric earlier. Old insecurities were rearing up again.

The meal had finished, speeches of thanks were given, and the guests gathered at the casino tables. Leni and Will played a few games of blackjack.

'Yes, c'mon.' Will's clenched fist punched the air when the roulette ball jumped into the numbered pocket he'd put his chips on. 'I feel a lucky streak coming on.'

'Brandy, as ordered.' Doug sidled up, swaying a little with arms outstretched, clutching two bulbous glasses. Will took the drink and Leni's heart sank. He looked well on the way to being plastered.

Sally came over. 'Had enough of the casino, Leni? Let's leave them to it.'

Leni waved at Will but he was engrossed in the next game. She hoped he'd come and find her.

The women talked about the dinner then moved on to family stuff. Leni felt comfortable with Sally. She shouldn't bad-mouth Will, but there couldn't be any harm in talking about children and pregnancy.

'I'm not getting any younger,' Leni said, watching Sally make a cynical face. 'I know women can have babies in their forties, but I didn't want too big a gap between number one and two.'

'What are you, mid-thirties?' Sally asked.

'I'm thirty-nine this year.'

'Oh, that's nothing to worry about.' Sally finished her coffee. 'You have time.'

They chatted about the passage of years and how busy life is with young children. 'It's been lovely catching up with you, but I must go to bed.' Sally stood up. 'Looking forward to our excursion tomorrow?'

'Fingers crossed I won't be the slowest driver or Jake'll be unhappy.'

Sally laid her hand on Leni's shoulder. 'Sleep well.'

The women parted company and Leni went to find Will. Putting her arm around him, she gave him a meaningful look. 'I'm going upstairs. See you soon?' Her lips lingered on his.

'Sure thing, babe. This winning streak may not last.'

# 6

When Leni walked into the dining room the next morning, the majority of the team were tucking into a full English breakfast. At the buffet table she helped herself to apple juice and a bowl of muesli, then glanced around to see where Will had chosen to sit. Dazzling sun flooded the room although it felt chilled with the air-conditioning on so high. She pulled her cardigan close with her free hand.

'Morning, Jim.' Leni sat next to the Finance Director and opposite Will. 'Looking forward to today?'

'Definitely, I quite fancy myself as an older version of Jenson Button,' he quipped.

'Much as I love driving, I've never done this sort of thing before,' Leni said, dipping her spoon into muesli with yoghurt and fresh apricots. 'I prefer a professional driver behind the wheel. I don't think I'm up to much after last night.'

'Hangover, is it?' Jim chuckled, and launched into a story about the previous company he'd worked for, in Cardiff, where they staged an unusual team-building experience in the Brecon Beacons. Each team of four included one non-sighted person and the challenge was to first build a raft, row it across a reservoir then cycle a cross-country course using two singles and one tandem bike. Team members took turns on the tandem and described the passing scenery to their blind passenger.

'It was a glorious day. The colours were so vibrant and it was very humbling, Leni, I can tell you.' Jim forked bacon and dripping egg into his mouth. He swallowed. 'Trying to describe the view while tumbling down the side of a mountain was pretty hair-raising. I am competitive but that time I realised I had someone else's safety to think about first.'

Leni shuddered and inwardly gave thanks for having all her senses intact.

'Now there's an idea. We should look into that for next year,' Will said. 'Coffee, Leni?'

He filled her cup and they discussed parts of Wales they knew. Leni enjoyed listening to Jim's lilting Welsh accent then sat up taller as she saw Melanie enter the dining room.

Sauntering over to their table, dressed in white linen trousers and an acid-yellow shirt, Melanie faced Will. 'What time are we leaving?' Her gold necklaces glinted in the sunlight and she flashed a charming smile around the guests at the table.

'Four cars will be at the front entrance at nine o'clock. It's going to be boiling out there so take a hat. We'll be given refreshments.'

'I plan on being in the winning team.' Melanie looked directly at Will then turned on her heel.

Leni watched the younger woman's captivating confidence and ability to turn heads as she strode across the room. She accepted that she, too, enjoyed admiring glances from others.

The cars took them into the desert. Leni was amazed by how quickly the city turned from being a modern developed metropolis to desert, with nothing but sand and dust as far as the eye could see. It wouldn't be her choice of place to live. After travelling for an hour towards the mountains they stopped at some high gates, then proceeded into the compound.

Refreshments were distributed as the instructor explained what the morning entailed and gave the requisite safety briefing. Leni felt a twinge of jealousy as Melanie manoeuvred herself to stand directly beside Will and get allocated to his group. As she looked around to see who she was being put with, she saw the women on the trip were evenly split between the five sand buggies. There was no need to be so possessive over Will.

They drove off in convoy along a track and then one by one each vehicle peeled off at a turning. Leni covered her nose and mouth with her scarf as dust enveloped them and terracotta-coloured sand sprayed from the back wheels. Passing rock formations which rose up between the dunes, they bounced and lurched from side to side, speeding across the terrain. It was like being on the biggest roller-coaster. Her stomach knotted as the car took off on an upward slope. She could see nothing but blue sky and as they accelerated it was as if they were going to take off. The flip side was coming down the other side of the dune. She screamed. Oh God, that was decidedly uncool, but it was out before she could stifle it. Feeling a flood of adrenaline she recovered herself once they were back on four wheels. Seeing the next hill looming into view she braced herself for the sensation of being hurled violently downwards. Her fingers turned white gripping the roll bar. The others seemed to be having the time of their lives, whooping with glee.

On the return journey Leni muttered a prayer of thanks for her safe delivery. What was it about having a child that made taking risks seem less fun than in the old days? It must be a maternal sense of self-preservation. Staying alive for Jake, being his mother, was more important than messing about with activities like this, just to keep up appearances. But she'd done it, and then she wondered how Will and Melanie's crew had got on.

Back at the hotel, some of the team went off for a swim while others met in the bar, taking a table close to the window. Melanie's windswept hair and flushed face made her look even more attractive, thought Leni. Will returned from the bar having ordered a round. They discussed the day's highlights.

'Thank goodness for Will. I thought we were going to flip the car over but he was so expert at handling it. He was awesome.' Melanie looked rapturous.

Will's face lit up with pride and Leni had a flicker of doubt again. Just because he'd been admired, that was no reason to suspect any treacherous behaviour on either side. After draining their drinks, the group went their separate ways for the remaining hours until supper.

The next morning, Will emerged from the shower with a bath sheet around his waist, towelling his wet hair. 'Want to go shopping after the site visit?' He tossed the towel onto a chair.

'I'd like that.' She put her arms around him. 'I love spending time with you, sexy man.'

They had breakfast and took a taxi to the golf course. The bright sun blinded them and an intense heat struck them as they got out of the air-conditioned car.

'We'll grab a buggy and I'll show you the best bits,' Will said, leading Leni to the Reception Desk and signing in. 'We won't stay out too long.'

Motoring around the course, Leni was struck by how

uniformly green it all was and how the lush planting and trees created an oasis of calm in the desert. They passed a lake where a spume of water jetted into the sky from a central fountain. They drove past the eighteenth and twenty-sixth holes where they saw greens-men fine-tuning the edges, then made their way back to the club house for a drink.

'It's magnificent. I'm so proud of you.' Leni raised her glass of champagne towards Will. 'The whole place exudes luxury and exclusivity.'

They finished their drinks and took a taxi to the vast underground mall where they made straight for the jewellery section. While window shopping from one luxury shop to the next, they stopped at a unit where something specific had caught Leni's eye.

'Would you like to try anything?' The sales assistant flicked a bunch of keys in readiness to open the security cabinets.

'I'd love to see that pendant.'

'Madam has exquisite taste.' He removed the velvet lined pad which held a long gold link chain and filigree ball pendant.

Will fastened it on Leni. She turned to the mirror and gently twirled the gold ball.

'It's beautiful. What do you think, Will?'

'I like it. It looks good on you.'

'But?' Leni said. 'You don't sound so sure?'

'Take a look at that cabinet? I saw some there that I think you may like,' he said.

Leni reluctantly removed the necklace and handed it to the salesman who returned it to its velvet bed. She wandered to the far side of the shop and peered over the glass, incredulous at the flamboyance and gaudiness of some pieces, and wondering which items he could've been talking about. As she drifted around the shop Leni concluded that although there were two or three other pretty necklaces, there was nothing else she wanted to look at.

Will came over. 'We should be getting back soon. Let's try one more shop.'

'We've only got an hour or so tomorrow, before going to the airport, haven't we?' She was disappointed that they might not find something. 'There's something about that pendant that speaks to me. It reminds me of the Theo Fennell one I had my eye on last Christmas, remember?' She followed him out of the shop.

'I do, but you earmarked our spare cash for getting the bathroom redecorated.' He gave a wry laugh. 'And you claimed to be happy with the Russell & Bromley boots I gave you?'

Leni linked her arm through his and hugged him. 'I know, I was happy. Good things come to those who wait, you said.'

Back at the hotel, Leni undressed. 'I'm getting a mineral water, want one?' She reached into the mini fridge.

'Sure,' he said, with his back turned.

She pulled out two bottles and poured the water into glasses.

'Come here and close your eyes,' he commanded.

She put their drinks down, stepped forwards and closed her eyes. There was silence and her heartbeat thudded in her ribcage.

'This is for you,' he said.

She opened her eyes as he put a black velvet box into her hands. Prising the lid up, she gasped. 'Oh my God, you bought it?' She traced a finger over the sparkling pendant. 'It's beautiful.'

He fastened it around her neck. 'Happy early birthday.'

They kissed and Leni went over to the mirror. Sunshine refracted from the gold filigree ball and she stroked the heavy chain.

'Thank you. I love it.' She laughed. 'I'll treasure it, always.'

'Well, we'd better get downstairs for our last dinner before heading home.'

Leni held her head high as she and Will walked into the restaurant. This was a good sign that everything was OK between them. A small nagging voice wormed its way into her head about affording such a gift, when he'd warned that they must watch their spending. Perhaps he had another project coming up that he hadn't yet mentioned, so he felt flush? Either way, she was sure he must still love her and she determined to be the perfect wife.

# 7

Will welcomed Kat at the front door. 'Ready for your first international?' He shrugged on his Barbour coat and tucked his university scarf inside as he zipped up.

'Yep, a real, live match. I grew up watching my dad shout at the telly whenever England were playing. Just don't want to show myself up, not knowing the finer points of the game.' She rearranged her hair below her cable knit hat with a big fur pompom.

'Aw, don't worry about that. Connell can fill you in on the rules of possession, stoppage and knock-ons.' He picked up his gloves and called out from the bottom of the stairs, 'Are you coming, Leni?'

'Almost there.' Leni buttoned up her Fair Isle gilet as she rushed downstairs. She kissed Kat and collected her coat and scarf from the rack. 'It's so cold after Dubai.'

'Alright, don't rub it in,' Kat said. 'Where are we meeting Connell?'

'We're linking up with the others at The Bunch of Grapes. It's tradition to have a pint there, en route,' Will said.

'Great.' Kat checked her reflection in the hall mirror. 'I hope he doesn't know this is a set-up?'

'What? He's only over for the game,' Will said, teasing her.

After putting her purse and mobile into her parka, Leni passed him the house keys. 'You hang onto them? No need to take two sets.'

They walked to Turnham Green. When the train pulled in, it was already crowded with match supporters. They filed in and the door closed.

'Bit different to being packed in with rush-hour commuters.' Will grabbed the overhead rail.

Keeping her knees soft to absorb the bumps as the Tube rattled along, Leni talked to Kat about Jake and Mike, who were excited to be spending the day at the Natural History Museum with Barbara. Kat posed with Leni for a selfie and forwarded it to Mike's phone.

Leni felt uncomfortably hot and was glad when it was their stop. They joined the throng on the escalators emerging into the fresh air at Twickenham. Walking towards the pub, Will read out statistics of the two opposing teams from his mobile and commented on specific players.

'Who else are we meeting?' Kat pulled her hat lower onto her neck and shielded her ears from the wind. 'Blimmin' cold, isn't it?'

Will spoke. 'Connell's from Dublin, but you already know that? He and I met on our first day at uni and we struck up conversation in the canteen queue. He's a really good bloke. I can totally rely on him, and he just cracks me up, he's so funny.'

A gust of wind blew Will's hair about. 'Luke and I met when we worked at IMG. We played squash together, and then Leni and I got to know his girlfriend, Jane. I was their best man.'

Leni cut in. 'Jane can't come today. Their youngest recently broke her arm.'

They reached the pub and Will pushed on the brass plate to hold the door open. 'Jeez, it's rammed, I should have known. You look about for Connell and Luke, and I'll come and find you. White wine?' he called out over his shoulder as he went to stand in line for the bar.

Leni and Kat jostled through the crowd and took over a high round table near the far window as it was being vacated. They hung their coats on hooks under the window ledge and scanned the room.

'So apart from a tall, dark and handsome one, what else should I look out for?'

Leni craned her head left and right. 'Luke's pretty bald. Well, he shaves what little hair he has left, and he'll probably be wearing a hat today.'

Will manoeuvred his way towards them. 'Here you go, girls,' he said as he extended large glasses in their direction.

Just as Leni had swallowed her first mouthful of crisp white wine she spotted Connell coming through the door, closely followed by Luke who was pushing a black beanie hat into his pocket.

'Over here!' Leni waved furiously, as Connell acknowledged them and made a mime gesture of getting beers in.

'Get one for me,' shouted Will, giving a thumbs-up signal.

Once gathered at the small table, introductions were made.

'Cheers.' Luke sucked at the tawny-coloured beer with large frothy head. 'Anyone eating in or shall we get burgers at the ground?'

'I'd prefer a pie and chips here. You don't know what's gone into those burgers from the vans. They look disgusting.' Leni's nose wrinkled in disgust.

'Good plan.' Kat surveyed the chalkboard displaying the menu of the day. 'I'll have the veggie option please.'

Will, Connell and Kat handed over cash and Luke went off to order, coming back with a numbered wooden spoon in a jar.

A moment later a large table became free and Luke pounced to secure it, followed by the others. Kat sat beside Connell. Luke returned to the bar to swap the spoon.

'So you're from Dublin? I've never been, but it's supposed to be a great city?' Kat sipped her wine and ran her fingers through her hair. 'I've a memory of being taken to the west coast as a kid and it rained the whole holiday and we had to kiss a stone for good luck. Now I know it's the Blarney Stone, but back then I thought my parents had totally lost the plot. Their squabbling didn't add any charm to the trip.'

'The West coast certainly gets all the weather, for sure.' Connell's Irish brogue was lilting as he talked about his home country.

'Ah, the Blarney Stone,' Luke added, 'you've got to be double-jointed to actually kiss its head, haven't you?'

They talked about Ireland and Jane's work in the NHS until their food arrived.

'So, what highlights of Dubai?' Connell asked Leni, breaking open the pastry on his steaming steak and kidney pie. She regaled them with the sand-dune experience and Will chipped in about the brilliance of the golf course.

When they reached their seats, the whole stadium crackled with anticipation. The crowd roared as the two teams came out of the tunnel onto the pitch. Supporters sang 'Jerusalem' at the tops of their voices. The referee blew his whistle and the next forty-five minutes passed in a haze of figures running at full tilt from end to end of the pitch, the rucks and line-outs explained to Kat as they happened.

When half-time came round Will stood up quickly. 'Beers all round?'

'Cider, please,' Leni said.

'Something soft for me.' Kat swiped strands of hair away from her face. 'Mum can't stay over, so if it's late I don't want her going on the bus, and I'll need to drive her home.'

'OK.' Leni tapped her friend's leg. 'You and Mike can pop over for a coffee in the morning and see Connell before he goes?' She leant forwards and repeated the idea to Connell.

'Great. I'd like that,' he said.

'Do you like him?' Leni whispered to her friend as Connell talked to Luke.

'Yes, what I've seen so far.' Kat covered her mouth with her striped mitten. 'I see what you mean about his hair and that accent makes me melt inside.'

The second half of the game raced along with England scoring to win the match. The roar of the fans' appreciation was deafening. Leni noticed Will had another pint in his hand as all the others finished their half-time drinks. Did he get an extra one in when he was at the bar?

A weak disc of sun lit the grey sky as the friends made their way back with the crowds to the station. Will, Leni and Luke walked up ahead, so Kat and Connell became engrossed in a conversation about bands.

'I saw Black Eyed Peas in concert last year,' Kat said. 'They were brilliant.'

'Really? I came over for that. It coincided with a CPD course I attended.' Connell's eyes shone at the memory. 'Wasn't it a brilliant gig?'

They chatted until the others slowed down and they were all ready to say goodbye. Luke made his way to the above-ground service. The others took the District Line.

'What are your plans tonight?' Connell asked Kat as they found two seats together.

'I'll pick up a pizza for Mum and Mikey. Cooking isn't one of my major skills. You'll probably have something exotic Leni rustled up this morning. She's a great cook.'

Will whispered to Leni. 'I may have to go into the office tomorrow.'

Leni recoiled from his beery breath. 'It's Sunday, and Connell's still with us?'

'He said he'd be gone by midday. He's fixed lunch with friends in town.'

'Oh, thanks.' She frowned. 'I planned to cook Sunday lunch.'

'Don't get in a state about it.' His mobile phone pinged. 'We can eat in the evening?' He scrolled his thumb over his phone, keeping it close.

'I wish you'd told me earlier. It would be good to have family time after being in Dubai.'

'Chill out. It's only a couple of hours.'

Her upbeat spirit deflated. Why did he have to spoil the atmosphere after a fun day? She linked arms with Kat to walk to her friend's house. The kids talked excitedly about their museum visit as Barbara quizzed Will and Connell about the game.

Once home, Leni sorted out supper while Jake went for a bath. Will poured drinks for them all, then he and Connell retreated to the sitting room. An hour later they sat down to roasted belly pork with puy lentils, and a potato and leek gratin. Leni dropped a couple of wine bottles into the recycling box and went to bed satisfied they were back on track. It had been a fun evening. It was a pity that Will had to go to the office on a Sunday, but on a positive note, she was glad Kat had met his old mate. They seemed to like each other.

The next morning Will made a couple of calls and confirmed he'd be out for two to three hours after breakfast.

'Catch you again soon, old buddy.' He grabbed his suede jacket and slapped Connell on the back.

'Don't work too hard.' Connell pumped Will's hand. 'Next year you must come over for the International at the new Dublin ground.'

'With the wife, or on my own?'

'The wife? Thanks.' Leni hoped he got her acerbic tone.

Will pecked Leni on the cheek. 'See you later.'

Connell left to pack his overnight bag. Kat and Mike arrived soon after, and they all sat in the sitting room until the boys got bored of the adult conversation and took off to Jake's bedroom, to play with his new Lego from Dubai.

Leni made her excuses to leave the room, to clear up the kitchen, so Kat and Connell could enjoy time alone. Even if it didn't develop into anything serious, she hoped they'd be friends.

Across town, Will listened to Nina Simone on the BMW's sound system as he cruised along Knightsbridge. He popped a mint into his mouth at Hyde Park Corner, and he felt his heart beat rapidly as he approached Albermarle Street. Lucky to find an on-street meter, he looked furtively left and right before entering Browns Hotel. Melanie sat reading *Vogue* on the banquette near the bar and he smoothed back his hair.

'Hi, I haven't got long.' He kissed her and sat down in one of the leather club chairs opposite her. 'Have you ordered anything?'

'No, I wanted to wait for you. Is it a bit late for coffee or too early for a gin cocktail?' She gave him an enigmatic smile. 'So, how long have you got?'

'Just a couple of hours. I told Leni I needed to look at plans, prior to tomorrow's meeting.' He licked his lips and caught the waiter's eye.

'Two negronis please.'

'How've you been, since Dubai?' She ran two slim fingers, nails expertly manicured, through her long hair to secure it behind one ear.

As her rings sparkled in the morning sun, he longed to stroke the pale flesh of her hand. His heart skipped a beat and his mouth felt dry. What was he playing at? Meeting her was madness, but his desire was so intense, he reasoned just one more time wouldn't hurt, would it?

'I feel like I'm taking two steps forward and one step back. Just as I think it's going to be OK, both personally and career-wise, someone or something comes along to put a spanner in the works.'

'Go on.' Melanie's lips brushed the glass as she sipped the amber liquid.

Will was intoxicated not only by the drink but by her assured femininity. He could contain her in his thoughts most of the time, but when she came close to him, like when they were rocking side by side in the sand buggy, or standing in the office lift together, he felt bewitched.

'Leni's more impatient with me these days and I'm chasing my tail with those fucking margins Dean's trying to squeeze out of me. It's ball-breaking.'

'I know just how to soothe that.' She drained her glass and

stood up, towering over him in her high heels. 'You settle up and I'll message you.'

He looked up at her quizzically then went to the bar as instructed. He reached into his inner pocket for his wallet and brought out some cash as his mobile phone beeped.

I'm in Room 38. Give me two minutes.

His hand trembled as he put his wallet and phone away. He went to the Gents and faced himself in the mirror. It's just a one-off, he thought. Surely I'm in Leni's good books since buying her that pendant? I deserve some fun and she wants me. Melanie wants *me*. He persuaded himself that he could do this without harming his marriage. He just wanted to feel alive again.

He felt aroused as he knocked on her door and as soon as it was closed they were all over each other, hands and tongues exploring. She pulled him towards the bed and they stood close, undressing each other, eyes devouring the shapes and contours of each other's bodies as they discarded their clothes. She moaned with desire as he kissed her and pulled her onto the bed.

Afterwards, they lay spent and tangled in damp sheets, their legs entwined.

'What do you see in me?' Will propped himself up on one arm to look at Melanie.

She laughed. 'I would have thought that was obvious during the last hour.'

'Yes, but you could have anyone you fancy. Why me?'

'Because you're hot, and I've always been attracted to the older man. It can't be a daddy replacement thing as I adore my daddy. He's always given me everything. Encouragement, adoration, and a big allowance!' She covered her breasts with the sheet and looked at her rose gold watch. 'I guess you'd better get going, much as I'd love you to stay?'

He ran a hand down her arm then went to shower. Standing under the forceful jet, he tried to quell guilty thoughts. If only Leni would back off. She constantly hounded him and made him feel inadequate. She'd caused him to stray. By the time he'd dried off, he felt almost righteous that this wasn't his fault.

He sat on the edge of the bed. 'Melanie, I really love this, but I can't offer you much.'

'I know that.' She stroked his bare back. 'Let's just see where this leads, and make no promises.'

'God, you're adorable. You'll haunt my dreams tonight.' He leant down to kiss her. 'Enough, or I'll jump back into bed with you.'

He considered his appearance in the full-length mirror.

'You look great,' she said. 'Leni doesn't know how lucky she is.'

'You're right.' He put his jacket on and squared his shoulders. 'Going to the office has never been so satisfying.'

It was Leni's day off and she considered how she might spend her free time, apart from housework and completing errands. Her pink cashmere coat had a stain, probably sustained on the return journey from Dubai, so she'd drop that to the dry cleaners, and she could use the time to browse for her mum's birthday present and perhaps find lamps for the spare room. She'd been meaning to replace the old ones for ages and Connell's recent visit reminded her that this job was still outstanding.

She delved into the coat pockets to check they were empty, and her fingers pulled out a business card. *Alex Taplow; Antiques, restoration and reclamation; Marlborough*, it read. A thought struck her and she looked at her watch. Why not go now? It could be fun.

It was mid-morning by the time she pulled into the Castle & Ball Hotel car park. In the Ladies she checked her makeup and hair. With the tip of a finger she smoothed a dab of concealer under her eyes and spritzed perfume behind her ears. While buying a mineral water at the bar she looked again at her phone for directions to the antique shop.

'Hello again.' Alex looked surprised as she walked in. Her heels clacked on the flag-stone floor. He shook her hand. 'How was Dubai? How did you get on?'

'It was wonderful. What a city.'

'Did you get a guide?' Alex asked.

'We didn't need one, in the end. It was a very full-on few days.'

'And how did you get on with the off-roading experience?'

'Apart from feeling terrified and wanting to throw up, I enjoyed it.' Leni laughed.

There was a pause as she looked about. She twiddled her rings.

'So, what brings you here?' he asked. 'Are you after something specific?'

'Lamps for my guest room.' Was that really the whole truth?

Alex indicated the interior of the shop. 'Have a wander. Ask if you want to know more about any pieces.'

'I will,' she said, hoping her cheeks weren't flushed as she looked into his piercing blue eyes. 'You've got a beautiful shop,' she added quickly, to hide her blushes.

Leni sauntered past an inlaid desk and an ancient oak sideboard with brass handles. The smell of polished furniture reminded her of her parents' house and she peeked at a price tag. Brushing her hand across a magnificent carved dining chair, with tapestry seat, she stopped by a French Empire period gilt lamp with deep aubergine silk shade. 'I love the bobble trim. This one might work.'

'I do have a pair of those,' Alex said. 'Are you after that particular period? I also have an early eighteenth-century reproduction lamp in classic design.'

'I'm not set upon any period, although the house is late Victorian. I just know the style I like, as soon as I see it.'

As she looked up at a sparkling chandelier hanging overhead and was dazzled by the reflection of some Art Deco mirrored wall lights, she realised that Alex's shop was high-end antiques and heard Will's voice in her head, remonstrating about over-spending. She was like a moth drawn to the flame. She couldn't help loving gorgeous things and these beautiful things were expensive.

'Before I got into fashion, I worked temporarily for a furnishing fabrics company. It gave me a love of this type of *passementerie*.' She trailed her fingers through the trim. 'I would tremble as I cut lengths of hugely expensive bullion fringe for clients, including the Sultan of Oman and Yemeni princes.'

'Yes, Middle Eastern wealth has a liking for this kind of thing.' Alex walked to the back of the shop. 'Come with me.'

My pleasure, she thought, following him to stand in front of two tall lamp-stands with dangling crystal tear drops. He looked pretty hot in those Levi's.

'Oh, those are stunning.' Leni stooped to inspect the dangling drops. 'In fact, if I buy them, I couldn't bear to put them in our guest room – I'd want to see them every day. How selfish of me.' A rush of mad excitement overtook her and she determined to have them. She gulped when she saw the price tag but heard herself speak in a confident tone. 'Sold.'

Alex wrapped each lamp in sheets of tissue before encasing them with bubble wrap.

'Have you got time for a coffee?' He activated the transaction with her credit card. 'It would be fun to trade Dubai stories.'

'I parked at the Castle & Ball. We could go there?' Was it a bit weird, going for a coffee with him?

Alex looked at his watch. 'I'll take a break now and shut up shop, briefly.' He pinned a compliment slip in the window:

*Closed until 1pm. Please call 07970 400126.*

He carried the lamps to her car. Leni handed him the rug kept in the boot for Monty, and she watched his hands secure the packages from view. She suppressed a flicker of lust as an image of this stranger's hands running through her hair popped into her head.

They took their coffees and sat by the window overlooking the High Street. Feeling awkward at first, Leni soon relaxed in Alex's laid-back company, and was chatting away about the silver souks and asking him what he'd bought on his trip.

She saw the clock over the bar. 'Goodness, I'd better fly.' She drained her coffee. 'I'm picking Jake and a friend up from school, and I don't know what the traffic will be like.'

'It was great to see you again.' He shook her hand. 'I hope you'll be happy with the lamps. Let me know if you want me to find other things for the house.'

'I will,' Leni said, getting her car keys out. 'Until the next time.'

'Safe journey.'

Driving east on the M4 Leni reflected on her decision to visit Alex. She enjoyed his company and was definitely on a bit of a high having bought the lamps. Perhaps she was reassuring herself that she still attracted other men? But she wouldn't tell Will. He probably wouldn't understand. Not that she really understood it, either, but she'd got a buzz from being reckless.

She wracked her brains as to what they'd eat for supper. Jake and his friend could have spaghetti, and there was bolognese sauce in the freezer. She'd stop at Chiswick M&S for some fish before collecting the boys. What time was Will due home, tonight? There'd be time to sneak the lamps into the spare room cupboard, for now, and fix something delicious, she thought, concentrating on the traffic approaching the outskirts of London.

# 8

Coming out of Bond Street Tube station, Will decided that he wasn't in the right frame of mind to stop at Selfridges before work. The pavements heaved with people clutching takeaway coffees and he overheard snippets of foreign conversations. Feeling calmer than when he'd left home, he still carried a sense of injustice about the row they'd had last night. Why couldn't Leni see his point of view? She had it easy, in his opinion. He brought in the lion's share of the family income and despite the useful injection of cash from her dad's will, it was time for her to contribute more. That shop won't last long in the current market, and they no longer had the funds to maintain their lifestyle now that a huge portion of his income was eaten up by the mortgage.

His balls were being busted at the office, but she didn't empathise about the extra hours he had to put in. And she was always reprimanding him for going out drinking with colleagues. To be fair, it wasn't always 'just business'. He'd had a couple of evenings with the delightful Melanie. He needed to allay Leni's suspicions so he could go on seeing his lover. As he remembered the last time Melanie's long black hair draped across his stomach, his belly flipped over with a quiver of lust.

He went through the revolving door into the foyer of his building, smiling at the pretty, blond concierge, who'd apparently told his secretary that she thought he was cute. God, it was flattering being found attractive at his age, when she could only be in her mid-twenties.

He stepped from the lift at the third floor. Marketing brochures lay on one end of the reception desk and on the other, a tall vase displayed orange gerberas and fresh green foliage. Photographs of golfing celebrities, and the firm's international courses, lined the wall. He flushed with pride and a sense of purpose. This was more like it. He was respected here; people listened to what he had to say. Will mouthed hello to the multi-tasking receptionist. She smiled at him as she answered a call via her earpiece and handed over some mail for the waiting bike courier.

The MD came towards him. 'Acquisition plans for the failing course,' Marcus said, handing Will a ring-binder. 'Let me have your thoughts later.'

'Will do,' Will said, before closing his office door and dropping the file on his desk. He pulled the blinds wide and hung up his suit jacket then sat down to study a report on a project he was supervising. His secretary tapped on the glass door.

'Morning, Will.' She placed a cup of strong coffee in front of him. 'Here are the press cuttings on Oman.'

'Thanks, Jan,' he said, stirring the coffee. He really should cut down on his caffeine but how to break the habit? The routine was ingrained, and he needed this first cup of the day to lessen the shaky feelings he'd had recently.

It was still bright when he finished work. He'd stop

for a drink before going home. He deserved it. He scrutinised a tray of silver charms in Selfridges' jewellery department. What would look good on that bracelet she had? Will reached for his credit card. Christ, he must stop buying these presents for Leni just because he had a guilty conscience. She didn't have a clue. He repeatedly spun the card in his fingers as the saleswoman wrapped the gift.

After pushing on the heavy glass door, Will stood on Oxford Street, tapping his jacket pocket, making sure he'd put his wallet back and the box was safely stowed. Traffic fumes clogged the air. Taxi brakes squealed and crowds drifted in all directions, like swarms of bees. Beads of sweat broke out on his forehead and he pulled at his tie, to stop the choking feeling.

His phone rang. He fumbled in his pocket for it.

'Hi Will.' Melanie's smooth voice purred in his ear. 'See you at Rowan's leaving do? We'll be in The Harrington – I'll save you a seat.'

'No, I'm not coming.' Will tried breathing more deeply but found he couldn't. His heart raced and panic enveloped him. Was he going to throw up?

'This has got to stop, Melanie.' A bead of sweat fell on his shoe. 'We've had fun, but I can't jeopardise my marriage any more.' He stumbled towards the crossing. 'I've got to go, sorry.' What the hell was happening to him? The pedestrians ahead appeared in double and a pain suffused his shoulder and left arm. As he plummeted forwards, he dropped his phone and a bright light dazzled his eyes.

'Don't push in,' the man beside him shouted, then watched in disbelief as Will's body crumpled onto the pavement, close to the wheels of an oncoming car.

'Clear the way, this bloke's fainted.' He dropped to the

pavement, grabbing the hand of the nearest pedestrian. 'Call for an ambulance, quick.'

Another bystander knelt down to see if he could help. 'Jesus, he's unconscious, he needs CPR,' he said, pumping Will's chest with force.

A group formed and morbid pedestrians stood motionless, watching the commotion. Within minutes sirens were heard and an ambulance pulled up sharply at the kerbside. Two paramedics leapt out and thanked the man for his CPR efforts. Lifting the inert body onto a stretcher and through the open doors of the vehicle, they continued to work on his heart as he was driven away from the scene.


The doorbell rang as Leni put a lid on the Le Creuset pot and turned the gas down. She wiped her hands on her apron. Surely Will hadn't forgotten his keys? How annoying. She'd only just finished reading to Jake and didn't want him woken up on a school night.

'Mrs Parsons?' A tall male police officer and a female police officer filled her vision. 'Is William Stuart Parsons your husband?'

'Yes. Why?' Leni looked left and right as if to find an explanation in the street. 'What's happened?'

'Can we come in, please?'

The officer removed his helmet and tucked it under one arm. Leni closed the door. The hall felt claustrophobic, suddenly.

'Go on through, first on your left.' Leni pulled at the strings and hung her apron over the newel post at the bottom of the stairs. The visitors stood in the middle of the room, their black uniforms creating a forbidding presence, looking incongruous beside the white sofas and bright kilim rug that they'd brought back from Turkey, last summer. Leni waved her hand indicating to sit down but they remained standing.

'We've grave news, Mrs Parsons. Your husband has suffered a heart attack and has been taken to University College Hospital.'

'Oh my God. No, you must've made some mistake?'

'I'm sorry to tell you that he was pronounced dead on arrival. The cause of death was recorded as a pulmonary embolism.'

Leni clapped her hands to her mouth. 'No, not Will.' She lurched backwards, falling onto the sofa. 'No, it's not Will. It can't be true. I don't believe you. He was fine this morning.'

'We need you to come and identify his body. I'm sorry.'

'What about Jake? He's upstairs.' A knife pierced her heart and she felt as if her lifeblood had drained away. 'What am I going to tell him?'

'Have you got someone who can come over?' The policewoman sat down beside her. 'Do you want us to stay with you while you tell your son?'

'No, no. I can't tell him. It'll break his heart.' Leni wailed, rocking back and forth.

Who could she ring? Her mum and Fran were too far away and Kat had Mikey to look after. There was no one, she had no one. She suddenly felt very alone.

The funeral cortège snaked along a rough tarmac lane, past a glade of ash trees and through an open five-bar gate. Leni looked from the window of the sleek, black car. It was impossible to grasp that the hearse in front carried Will's dead body. It was a perfect spring day and the beauty of the bright daffodils stabbed a pain in her gut.

Mourners congregated in an open-sided, green oak shelter,

which stood in a patch of coarse stones. She saw the faces of friends and Will's colleagues, but couldn't begin to imagine talking to them.

'It's beautiful, isn't it?' Leni clutched her mother's hand, repeatedly dabbing at the stream of tears with a sodden white handkerchief. The knife of pain in her belly was excruciating.

'Yes, darling, it is. He'd love it here.' Imogen leant over to see how Jake was managing. He looked pale and solemn and scuffed his black shoes together.

'It was right to let people wear casual clothes, wasn't it? He'd like everyone to be themselves. I couldn't wear anything other than black – it just wouldn't feel right.' Leni smoothed her skirt and put her arm around Jake. 'Daddy would be proud of you, being so brave.'

'You couldn't have done any more.' Imogen squeezed Leni's hand. 'The civil celebrant will guide us through it.'

'I don't know how I'll face his parents.' Leni's shoulders slumped.

'You must be strong for them, darling. It's a tragedy to bury your own child.'

'When do I play my cornet, Mummy?' Jake bit his fingernails and kicked the instrument case on the floor of the limousine.

'Halfway through. I'll let you know beforehand, don't worry,' Leni looked at his sad, pale face. 'If you change your mind, that's OK.'

'I won't change my mind. I'm doing the piece Daddy liked most.'

The car stopped and the funeral assistant opened the door. After inhaling deeply and gathering up her bag, Leni stepped from the car, head lowered, and reached back to help Imogen out. She clung hard to Jake's hand as they waited for the rest of the family to join them. The sun warmed her back and a scent of grass and foliage reached her nostrils. How could she get through this? The day was too beautiful. It was impossible to comprehend.

Will's parents stepped falteringly from the car behind, supported by Thomas and their other grandchildren. Leni and Imogen embraced them stiffly as Jake and his cousins stood awkwardly, staring at the ground. The celebrant came over and clasped Leni's hands, confirming small details about the service. Fran carried a garden trug filled with white roses which she offered to mourners. Leni saw some of Will's old university friends, but couldn't talk to them, just yet. She swallowed hard. Please God, don't let me be sick.

Walking a few yards over the grass they approached a large, open hole in the ground. Leni and Will's families formed a group beside it and other mourners gathered around. They all turned as the wicker coffin was carried towards the grave. Leni watched the solemn bearers, Tom, Hugh, Connell, Will's cousin and two old school friends, place the coffin on the temporary stand. The basket creaked as they gently laid it down. The service began with 'Bread of Heaven', one of Will's favourite hymns from school days. Leni tried to sing a few notes, but sadness overwhelmed her and her voice dried up. She clutched at Jake's hand as Imogen held her around the shoulder. Funeral-goers blew their noses loudly into handkerchiefs and there was lots of stifled sniffing.

In the middle of the service Jake played his cornet lullaby. It came out squeaky. Leni wept openly. There was clapping when he finished and he lifted his head with a shy smile.

Thick white straps were threaded under the coffin and each bearer held on tight as they lowered it into the hole. Leni's hair was caught by the wind as she stooped forwards to throw her rose into the grave.

'My son.' Karen let out an agonised wail as roses rained down onto the coffin and couples hugged, comforting one another in their grief.

'Beautiful,' Kat said, putting her arms around Leni. 'That was beautiful.' She snatched a spotty handkerchief from her pocket as tears coursed down her cheeks. 'Will would be so proud of you, dearest friend, and of Jake.'

'But he had so much more living to do.' Leni struggled to regain her composure and turned away. She watched Jake kneel down beside the grave.

'Goodbye, Daddy,' he said, leaning forwards. 'Bruno will keep you company.' He pulled a small stuffed bear from his pocket and dropped it onto the bed of roses. 'I don't want Daddy to be lonely.' Jake's voice croaked as he looked up.

'That's so kind of you, darling, and he'll be watched over by those guys,' Leni said, pointing to a pair of red kites circling overhead. 'We'll bring Monty here, and a rug, and you can sit and talk to Daddy.' She clasped him tight and struggled with her tears.

'Everyone's moving off now,' Fran said, guiding Leni by the elbow. Imogen held onto Hugh's arm and they all straggled back to the line of funeral cars ready to leave the field and make their way to the gastro pub a mile down the road.

As they reached the car, Leni put her arm around Jake. 'I'm so proud of you.' She squatted down and looked up at his face. 'You're the most wonderful boy in the world, and I love you very much.'

The grieving family and friends slipped into their cars and the long procession of vehicles wound its way, like a snail trail, through the country lanes to the wake.

# 9

Leni walked into Mr Grey's plush office, noticing a masculine smell in her solicitor's office.

'Please take a seat, Mrs Parsons.'

Leni sat on a leather chair, registering deep-pile carpets and oil paintings in heavy gilt frames. The large walnut desk between them added gravitas in the hushed atmosphere. Mr Grey reached for a sheaf of papers and put rimless glasses on to read the account.

'First of all, I'd like to offer my condolences for your loss.'

'Thank you.'

The solicitor leant forwards, clasping his fingers together and resting his wrists on the desk. 'This won't be easy for you. Wasn't there some family member or friend who could lend support through this difficult process and perhaps have come to this meeting?'

'Thank you.' Leni twisted her handkerchief round and round. 'My mother's staying with me to help with Jake, and I'm close to my sister and her husband, but neither of them were able to join me today.'

'Let me furnish you with some facts. You and William have

a joint mortgage which amounts to £490,000 and the estimated value of your property in today's market is £1.1 million. Will had investments in a pension, although he stopped paying into it. He cashed in a £20,000 ISA a couple of months ago.' Mr Grey looked up.

Leni rubbed the space between her nose and lip, an anxious habit. 'Why would he have done that? He didn't tell me.'

Mr Grey continued. 'There's a small life insurance policy so there'll be a pay-out on that. You may want to consider your major asset, your house, and whether it would be sensible to sell that to release capital, and purchase another property outright so you'll only need to fund running costs.'

Leni became aware that she must have been sitting there looking like a rabbit in the headlights. It was hard to take it all in.

'What is your current financial situation?' Mr Grey removed the cap to his Cross ink-pen to make notes on his pad. 'Have you any PPPs or ISAs, or private income? I need full disclosure to be able to advise you.'

'I work in an independent fashion shop, typically working four days per week. I was gifted £50,000 by our father when he passed away and the rest of my inheritance will be released on my mother's death. Most of that money went into making improvements to our house.'

Leni fought back nauseous bile coming up her throat. She wished she'd asked Hugh to come with her to be sure she grasped the figures properly. She glimpsed a future of being sole provider for herself and her son. She remembered happier, early years in their house, when they planned the side extension and created a garden, and she drew a blank about where she and Jake should go. Her current salary wouldn't be enough. She had a flash of anger towards Will for dying.

Her mind drifted away to a conversation she'd had with Will about private education and they'd argued their differences. He'd done well at the local comprehensive and gone to university. Although both she and Frances had achieved good grades at school, only Fran went to university to pursue her ambition to train as a surveyor. Having qualified, Fran worked her way into a partnership and earned a good salary, with job security. Wanting to earn money to fund her travel bug, Leni had gone straight out to work. A full-time position came up in the shop where she'd worked as a Saturday girl. How she'd loved that Interrailing holiday around Europe with a friend. She didn't regret it.

Returning to focus on where she was and what Mr Grey was saying, Leni realised, in a split second, that she should have trained in some profession. She'd been led by her giddiness of getting her hands on the latest fashions and showing off to her sister and friends. It seemed very shallow, now.

After the meeting, she drove to meet Fran, who'd been to a meeting nearby. Greeting each other in a tight hug, they ordered a sandwich and drink in the local café.

'I need a sugar hit,' Leni said, lifting a chocolate brownie onto her plate. 'I just don't know where to start.'

They sat in the far corner nursing their coffee.

'I don't think I can do this.' Leni's tears rolled down her face, unchecked.

'We'll support you,' Fran said, pulling out a load of paper tissues and handing them over to Leni. 'Mum says she'll stay with you to help with Jake, and I've got a week off soon if you're ready to make a start at looking at houses.'

'What a bloody mess.' Leni blew her nose hard into a tissue and, balling it up, slipped it into her pocket. 'And what about Jake? He needs his daddy.'

'You're his everything right now, so you'll just have to be both. You'll make sense of it, in time. One day at a time, and remember, Hugh and I are there for you, day or night.'

Leni burst into tears again and rushed off to the Ladies to splash cold water on her face and dab her eyes. There was little mascara left on her eyelashes; most of it had smudged down her cheeks. She loaded tissues with liquid soap until the black stains had gone and she felt able to return to the table.

Fran put an arm around her shoulder. 'You're in shock, still. You must be kind to yourself.'

Leni shivered and cupped her hands around her cup, trying to absorb warmth and comfort from the china.

'I keep thinking about the dreadful rows we've been having,' Leni said, stopping short. 'I'm still using the present tense.' She shook her head in disbelief. 'And the worst thing is, I'll never be able to say sorry to him.'

'Don't beat yourself up,' Fran said.

'The arguments were always about money. I didn't understand how worried he was. I don't even know the solicitor, and he knew more about Will's finances than I do.'

Leni's conversation repeated. It was one she'd been having since Will died, trying to accept his sudden death and its effect.

Fran walked with her to the car and they clung to one another.

'I love you.' Leni pressed her cheek against Fran's soft skin. She felt comforted by the familiar scent of coconut in her sister's freshly washed hair. 'Thanks for being there.'

'Are you sure you're OK to drive?'

'It's an easy run at this hour. I'll lie down before Mum brings Jake back from school.' As a breeze fluttered her jacket, Leni was incredulous that nature continued its circle of seasons whatever personal disasters the earthly residents were going through. 'I wonder how Jake coped today.'

'I'm sure it'll help him being with his mates at school,' Fran said. 'It's best for him to be in a routine and in his own home.'

'I expect Mum's been pottering, doing tidy-up jobs to keep herself busy.' Leni hugged Fran again. 'What would I do without you both?'

Driving home on automatic pilot, Leni was vaguely aware of other cars and people on the street but felt disconnected from it all. Millions of others must be suffering today, but each person's pain would feel unique. Flecks of blossom blew into the road and she experienced an aching spasm in her heart and felt detached from her body, which carried on as normal, while her mind was dazed. Memories, simultaneously crowding one upon another, had a misty quality to them as if they had happened to someone else. She was so tired.

After letting herself in at home and slipping off her boots, Leni went to find her mother. Imogen was ironing in the spare room, Classic FM playing on the radio and sun motes dancing in the atmosphere. Leni caught her unawares, noting her mother's downturned mouth making her face look forlorn.

'Hello darling.' Imogen put on a smile as she unplugged the iron and gave Leni a hug. 'How did it go?'

'Dreadful, it's worse than I thought.'

'Right, tea is called for.' Imogen folded the sheet she was ironing and put it on the pile. 'I baked a lemon drizzle that we can make a start on, before getting Jake.' She set mugs of tea and cake on the table and reassured her daughter of her support.

Leni explained her financial situation as best she could. 'It seems Will cashed in the ISAs without my knowledge. The life insurance will help with the mortgage. We'll move out of London to save money and get Jake into a good local school. I'll have to find a job with a decent salary. It is all so overwhelming.'

When they finished Imogen put everything in the dishwasher. 'Go and sit down. I'll go for Jake.'

'Thanks, Mum.'

Leni lay on the sofa with a soft grey throw over her legs, closed her eyes and took several deep breaths. Monty softly padded into the room and butted her hand for attention. She stroked his head for a few minutes before he made a few rotations and curled up beside the sofa. She must have slept for a while, then she heard the front door close and voices in the hall.

'In here,' she called, pulling herself upright. 'Hello Jake.' Leni patted the seat beside her and he slumped into it. He looked desolate as he levered off his school shoes.

'I'll get more tea and cake.' Imogen took his school bag and went to the kitchen.

'The boys wouldn't play with me. They were whispering behind their hands,' Jake said, kicking his foot against the sofa.

'Oh my darling boy, they don't mean to be unkind. It's just that they don't know what to say.' Leni hugged him.

'Are you going to die, Mummy?'

'Not for a very long time.' She squeezed him and kissed his head. 'You'll be a grown man before that happens. It's natural to feel sad about Daddy. You can talk to me any time. One day it won't feel quite so dreadful, and you'll be happy remembering him and all the fun times you had together.'

Imogen returned with a drink for Jake and cake. It seemed to break the mood as Jake said abruptly, 'When will I see my cousins again?'

Leni got the calendar up on her phone and showed Jake

how many weeks it would be until the next holiday when the two families would be together.

Life carried on slowly. Leni felt like she was living in a cloud of fog, her feet too leaden to do anything other than get to the local supermarket with her body going through the motions. She knew that she'd soon have to join the world that carried on around her. Maybe being busy and having work as a distraction she'd be able to live with her heartache for a few minutes at a time. At unexpected moments, grief caught her unawares and she'd find herself sobbing, then one day when she was standing at the school gates she realised she hadn't thought of Will for several hours, and knew it was a sign that she was gently mending.

Although he was quieter than before, Jake's bewildered face became less pitiful and the occasional bouts of tantrums, borne out of frustration and confusion, lessened. His friendship with Mike became less clingy and he started to play football again.

# 10

Leni parked in one of the three spaces at the back of Alex's shop. He'd locked the front entrance and was holding keys ready to shut the back door when she arrived.

He indicated the way to the restaurant, walking on the roadside of the pavement. Leni felt a gentle hand on her back guiding her to one side of a group of shoppers coming in the opposite direction, and again when they were obstructed by a pavement billboard.

'I hope you'll like this place. It does great mezze,' Alex said, holding open the restaurant door. Leni appreciated his manners.

'It looks lovely.' She felt a little light-headed. Was lunch with Alex such a good idea? She was slowly adjusting to being a single mum and didn't need to get tangled up in a new relationship, or jump into bed with a man just to prove that she was still alive and attractive.

A waiter ushered them to a corner table and she draped her napkin over her thighs as he poured water into their glasses and asked whether they'd like an aperitif.

'What would you prefer? Shall we share a half carafe of wine?' Alex asked.

'Perfect, whatever you recommend.' She still felt ambiguous when it came to decision-making. It had often been Will's choice about what they drank in a restaurant.

They ordered and Alex watched the waiter depart. 'I'm very sorry about your husband. How are you coping?'

Leni's eyes welled up. 'I'm up and down. Sometimes I feel strong and at other times I'm a complete mess. The dog running off in the park and not coming back, or a mechanical or electrical problem in the house, can reduce me to a total wreck. I am lucky to have my family. I don't know where I'd be without them. And Kat too.'

A tray of small dishes was delivered to the table and Alex waited until Leni spooned halloumi cheese and hummus onto her plate before spearing roasted red peppers with his fork onto his. They each took pieces of buttery pitta bread to mop up the sauces.

Leni mentioned the support she'd had from a close group of women while others had dropped off the radar, no longer inviting her out. 'It's amazing how quickly you find out who your true friends are. It's as if some people think death is a contagious disease, and others just don't know how to deal with the bereavement.'

'I experienced being dropped too,' Alex said. 'Some mutual friends felt they had to choose between me and Heather, my ex. Maybe it's easier in the long run, but you can't help feeling sorry for the loss of fun mates you had in the past.'

Noise in the restaurant grew louder as more people sat down to lunch. The waiter brought their mains and Leni leant forwards to inhale the aroma from her linguine.

'This smells delicious.'

A plate of steaming monkfish on a bed of glazed vegetables was placed in front of Alex.

'So how do you look after yourself? Are you keeping busy?'

'I love yoga and I go to the cinema. Jake and I hang out with Kat and Mikey. The boys have known each other since nursery.' Leni sat back and took a sip of wine, feeling the knot in her stomach relax as she savoured the cool liquid. 'I had thought I'd try playing the piano again, but my fingers aren't so good and my brain gets scrambled. I think it helps Jake having to practise his cornet if he sees me trying to master the keyboard. Do you play an instrument?'

Alex grinned. 'Guitar, enthusiastically, rather than anything else. I was in a band at uni and we had fun playing pub gigs and friends' parties. Now I strum for relaxation and to embarrass the kids.'

Leni found it easy to chat with him, liking his direct approach and how he listened to her answers without distraction. He leant forwards to replenish her drink and she clocked strands of grey in his thick dark hair. Sexy.

'At weekends I'm often in Lymington on the boat,' Alex said, gathering up his last mouthful. 'I'll pack the guitar, bottles of beer and my Nikon camera, then potter along the coast. Find a quiet bay and drop anchor for a picnic and swim.'

'Sounds wicked.'

'Maybe I could take you out on her this summer?' Alex said, wiping his mouth.

The waiter removed their plates and asked about desserts. They decided against having any, and ordered espressos.

'What's she called?' She was tempted but wasn't ready to commit to anything right now. 'Are we talking about a dinghy or yacht here?'

'It's an old Nicholson 32, called *Greta*. Sleeps four, although my children would dispute that, as they don't get their own cabin. It's great for ambling about, for a few days away. Heather didn't take to sailing, sadly.'

Leni logged that snippet of information but she didn't want details as to why Alex and Heather were divorced. It really wasn't her business. She liked him, he seemed kind, and moreover it felt good to appreciate lunch with someone other than her family or a friend, for a change.

Alex asked for the bill and Leni reached for her bag.

'My treat.' He smiled. 'It's a pleasure to see you.'

'Thank you. I enjoyed it.' She deliberated about insisting on paying her share but decided to let it go. She was in too much of a spin to analyse it further. 'Excuse me a minute.'

In the Ladies, Leni put her hands on either side of the basin, and talked to her reflection. 'Go on, admit it, you really like him.' She noticed her increased heartbeat. He hadn't mentioned another woman in his life. What skeletons might he have in his cupboard? She chastised herself for being this curious. After all, it was just lunch. She momentarily felt guilty as if she'd been unfaithful to Will. It was a strange mix of emotions.

They walked back to the shop and Leni's car. 'You've been so kind. That made me feel human again.' Leni kissed his cheek, smelling a lemon-scented aftershave.

'Not kind. It was good for me too. I need to raise my head from work at times.'

'My turn next, then?'

'OK, I'll hold you to that,' he said. 'Let me know when you're ready.'

She shut her car door and Alex gave a cheery wave as she drove off. Their conversation gave her plenty of food for thought but as she took the road to West Wittering she resolved not to tell her mum about the lunch as it may all yet come to nothing.

Imogen knelt on the padded kneeler, trimming off dead lavender stems. The sharp secateurs cut through the brittle stalks with ease and she inhaled the dregs of perfume from the plants.

'You're always in the garden, Granny.' Jake twisted lavender heads in the barrow beside them. 'I'm bored. When are we going to the beach?'

'Fifteen more minutes of tidy-up jobs.' Imogen crushed dead heads between her palms and breathed in the potency of the plants. 'Here, smell this.' She held out her hands for Jake to sniff. 'The sun will be higher so it'll be warmer for swimming. Afterwards we could visit Dolly's Tea Shop for a slice of cake and lemonade, or have something at home before Mummy arrives.'

She watched him wander off to find his football. His sun-freckled nose and floppy blond hair reminded her of Leni as a little girl and she wondered how Leni coped with Jake on her own. How they must miss Will. When she thought of her late son-in-law she felt a deep sadness, then a flash of gratitude that at least her Robin had reached old age, living a long and satisfying life. Will's death at forty-three wasted an unfinished life.

'Come and help me please, Jake, then we can go.'

She gathered the last strands and squashed them into the overflowing barrow. Jake grasped the handles and manoeuvred it to the compost heap. She helped him upend it to tip the contents out, and he then rested the barrow against the garden hut. He seemed happier when he was given a job to do. They stepped through the open French windows into the cool sitting room.

Jake weaved between the armchairs, passing a huge Chinese

bowl filled with potpourri, on the mahogany coffee table. He glanced at the portrait over the fireplace.

'Who's that man, Granny?' He hurled himself over the kilim-covered ottoman, landing with a parachute roll.

'He's my grandfather, so that makes him your great, great-grandfather and I'll tell you about him on our way to the beach. Now, you get your trunks, and bucket and net for the rock pools, while I get some supplies.'

Imogen went to make up a bottle of squash, then stowed biscuits, the newspaper and an old picnic rug into her old woven basket. Jake came at break-neck speed down the stairs, grabbing the mahogany handrail at the bottom to stop himself flying headlong into her. She clipped the lead onto Rosie's collar and locked the front door, and then they walked to a wooden garden gate, set in a high wall. Taking the path running beside the wall, they descended through woods carpeted with an abundance of scented wild garlic, before coming onto the village lane leading to the pebbly beach.

Imogen picked a spot then threw down the rug, anchoring it with the basket. The minute Rosie was released from the leash she trotted off to sniff at washed-up flotsam.

'We can leave everything here. Let's just take the bucket and net for the time being?'

They picked their way across rocks strewn with slippery green and brown seaweed, stooping to peer into pools and pointing out shrimp, anemones and molluscs. They watched the tide rustling over sea anemones and tightly clinging mussels. Jake poked at a barnacle until Imogen prised him away, reminding him that it was a living creature and should be left in peace.

Whistling for Rosie they set off along the beach, meeting couples and groups of people walking towards them, some with dogs. A cacophony of barking and rigorous sniffing of noses and bottoms ensued each time any dogs met. Crossing a small sandy stretch of beach, Jake rushed to the water's edge, tiptoed through the shallows and after a quick pause to make sure his granny was watching, took a great jump forwards into the foamy breakers.

'It's freezing, Granny.' He screamed with delight. 'You won't want to come in.'

She watched him take another big jump into deeper water. He tumbled about, shrieking with delight as waves broke over his back. His hair stuck up in clumps and water cascaded from his lithe, little body.

'Five more minutes then we'd better head back.' Imogen took her mobile phone from her cardigan pocket to video Jake playing in the water. 'I don't want you catching a chill before Mum arrives. Let's race back to the towel and I'll roll you up in the rug to get warm.'

As Jake was ruffled dry, he asked questions about how rock pools formed and how far away France was.

'Let's look up rock pools when we get home. I'm sure we can Google that.' She pulled his striped tee-shirt over his head then handed him his sweatshirt. 'The shortest distance of the Channel is twenty-one miles and I think the fastest hydrofoil to France takes less than an hour.' She gave him a biscuit and some squash.

Imogen slipped on her sandals. 'Now, where did Rosie get to?'

Jake burst out laughing. 'She's behind you, Granny.'

'So she is.' Imogen laughed and gathered up the beach things. 'You carry the rug then, and keep an eye on her until we get to the lane.' She slung the dog lead around her neck and checked her mobile.

'Dolly's Tea Shop next time. Mummy's messaged to say

she won't be long.' They chatted as they made their way back to the house where Imogen made coffee for herself and a mug of steaming hot chocolate for Jake.

'Whipped cream and marshmallows?' Imogen pulled a can of cold cream from the fridge. 'I don't really need to ask, do I?' She laughed, piling tiny white marshmallows on top and placing a long-handled teaspoon to the side. He spooned mouthfuls of froth eagerly. When he finished he swiped his hand across his face.

'Let's go upstairs and see what we can find out about rock pools in the books there. We can tell Mummy what we've learnt when she arrives.'

Jake trailed behind Imogen. He slumped onto the bottom stair and leant his head in his hands. 'I miss Daddy.'

Imogen stopped abruptly and made her way back downstairs to sit beside him.

'Of course you do, my darling. We all do.' She gathered him up in a big hug. 'It's quite normal to suddenly miss him and feel sad. He would be so proud of you, the way you are interested in everything and being so kind to people.'

Imogen kissed his cheek and nuzzled his neck. His skin was still cool from the sea and he had a salty smell about him. 'I've got a good idea. Shall we make a photo montage of Daddy?'

'What's a montage?'

'You gather pictures of him then cut them into shapes, and stick them onto card. We could frame it for your bedroom and that way, you'll see him every time you're in there. When you wake up or before you go to bed, you can have a little talk to him, as if he was still with us?'

'Yes, I want to do that.'

Imogen took Jake's hand and they went into her sitting room to hunt through photo albums and a box of loose pictures on the lowest bookcase shelf. They carried them upstairs to the small study bedroom where Imogen did her artwork and sewing.

Jake became absorbed cutting the photos and making a pile of them. Imogen found a piece of card and the glue stick and they started by laying out a design.

'This is good. You've chosen photos from lots of different times and places. Do you want to add in some of you when you were a baby? Those are in an album in my room, I think.'

'No, I like these ones. I don't remember being a baby.' Jake bit the side of his lip and tilted his head to one side. 'The ones of Mummy and Daddy and me make my tummy go all funny but I like this one.' It showed him with Will in a fake log careering down a water slide. 'That was Center Parcs, and we got soaking wet. It was brill.'

'Yes, that's great,' Imogen said. 'And remember, you can call me on the phone, day or night, to say how you're feeling. I'll come up and we can do some nice things together.' She hugged him tight and then pointed to the photo of him with a giraffe behind him with its tongue about to lick his hat through the fencing. 'You made a narrow escape there. You nearly got slobbered by giraffe goo.'

Leni pulled in at her mum's house, excited to be seeing Jake again. Yellow roses in full bloom crowded around the front door, and flowering shrubs gave off an intoxicating scent in the heat. She savoured this moment, where she was, knowing it as a place full of love and acceptance. After getting out of the car and letting Monty out, she stretched her arms in big circles. Slinging her overnight bag across her shoulder, she reached for her cardigan and a large pot of fresh basil, wedged in by her walking boots.

'Hello?' Leni walked into the cool hallway. Beside the front door a tall wicker basket held umbrellas, tennis racquets and two gnarled walking sticks her father had used in his later years. Those took her back. He was such an enthusiastic walker.

Dropping her bag and putting the herbs on the hall table, she called again. 'Anyone home?'

'We're upstairs, darling,' Imogen's high-pitched voice replied, 'in the sewing room.'

Monty scampered up the stairs, meeting Rosie on the landing, and the two dogs circled each other, their tails wagging furiously. Leni walked to the room that she and Fran had shared as children. She loved seeing family photographs displayed on an oak chest and familiar paintings on the wall.

Jake and Imogen were sitting on the floor, surrounded by a sea of old photographs.

'Mummy.' Jake jumped up and hugged her.

'We've had a wonderful time, haven't we, Jake?' Imogen rose stiffly to embrace Leni. 'He's swum in the sea, found all kinds of treasures, and now we're making a photo collage.'

'Come and see what I made.' He pulled at Leni's hand.

'You have been busy. That's a beautiful picture.'

Imogen removed her glasses; they dangled from a gold chain. 'Shall we have tea? Mummy's had a long journey and we can put this in a frame after the glue's dried.'

At the bottom of the stairs the women turned left to the kitchen as Jake disappeared right into the sitting room. 'Just want to get what I found.'

Imogen set about making tea. 'Builder's or herbal?'

'Builder's, please.' Leni sat at the scrubbed pine table, petting the dogs, who'd followed them into the room.

Jake rushed in brandishing a faded photograph album and turned to the second page.

'I've found ones of you and Auntie Fran, when you were little. Look at this.' His voice was high-pitched with excitement.

He thrust the album towards Leni. A muted colour picture showed Fran and her, sitting with Imogen in an ornate basket, on top of a huge elephant.

'How old were you then?' He wriggled from Leni's grasp. 'Can I ride on an elephant, Mummy?'

'That was in Jaipur when Grandpa was overseeing an engineering job.' Imogen leant in to examine the photograph. 'We were so lucky having that time there with you. The Maharajah would invite us for sumptuous meals and we'd be entertained by singers and exotic belly dancers. I was presented with a beautiful sari. The women showed me how to wear one. It's pretty simple once you knew what to do, but there was so much fabric, it seemed complicated at first.'

'I wish I remembered more of it.' Leni reached down to pick up a few scattered photographs. 'Here's lovely Raj.'

'Who's Raj?' Jake sat back on his heels.

'Our wonderful cook and gardener.' Imogen looked wistful. 'He was a gentle soul. Nothing was too much trouble for the Memsahib, which is what we married women were called by the Indian people.'

'Did you have to go to school?' Jake bombarded Leni with questions. 'How often did you ride an elephant?'

Imogen laughed. 'There are plenty of stories, Jake, but first, shall we have some of those flapjacks we made yesterday?' Imogen offered her hand to pull her grandson to his feet. 'This boy's been a wonderful help. As well as cooking, he put all the deadheads onto the bonfire pile. He can come and stay any time.'

'What do you like doing best at Granny's?' Leni asked.

'Going in the sea and looking for creatures.' He crammed

flapjack into his mouth. 'I like it better than London, but I wish Mikey was here.'

'Well, Mummy says you can spend some of your summer holiday here,' Imogen said, 'and perhaps Kat might let Mikey come for a few days too?'

'Wicked.' Jake jumped up. 'I'm going to show him that crab I found this morning.'

'Hey, rinse it in clean water first, please,' Leni said to Jake's departing back. 'Otherwise the car will stink.'

Imogen stirred honey into her lemon tea and pushed the plate of flapjacks towards Leni.

'He seems happy. Did he talk about Will at all?' Leni took a bite, examining the oats and seeded slab.

'Just once. When I said goodnight last night he asked where dead people go? I reminded him about when Sooty died and how we buried him in a favourite blanket, under the tree where he'd been happiest, trying to catch birds. We both had a cry then, but I think he felt better for it.'

They heard Jake filling his bucket from the outside tap. Scent from the cut roses wafted across the room.

'Now, Leni, while he's busy – what plans have you made about the house?' Imogen sipped her tea.

'I've got an estate agent coming to do a valuation and a meeting with our financial adviser to work out the best options re the mortgage and investments. I'm thinking of Pewsey or Upavon, where I could probably find something decent for around £300,000.'

'Do you want me to come with you? Shouldn't you rent first to see if you like it?'

'I'll have another think, but I've pretty much decided it's the best option. It's a fresh start for us.'

Imogen got up and pulled items from the fridge. 'Supper around 7.30pm OK?'

It was quiet, both women lost in their own thoughts. Imogen rinsed four shiny red tomatoes under running water, patted them dry and sliced them finely into a bowl. 'What time are you off tomorrow?'

'We'll be away early. Jake's getting a haircut and we need to buy some stuff.' Leni sighed. 'He's growing so fast.'

'Yes, he is. He's a lovely boy.' Imogen ground black pepper and sprinkled a pinch of sugar over the tomatoes and put the dish on the table. 'He's got some confidence back, but I worry about the effect of a move so soon after Will's death.'

'I know, I've been thinking about that. There are advantages. The cost of living will be better, we'll be closer to Fran and the cousins, and he can do more physical stuff, like climbing trees and building dens. I want him to enjoy the sort of childhood you and Dad gave us. London's a struggle.'

Imogen rubbed Leni's back. 'I know, but he'll miss his pal, Mike. That's another loss.'

'Yes, that's been worrying me too. I've suggested to Kat that Mikey comes to stay with us during holidays and she can have Jake from time to time. I hope he'll settle once I get him into Scouts and perhaps another club where he'll make new friends.' Leni cleared the tea things off the table. She didn't want to dwell on any negative aspects. 'I'll take the dogs out, or do you want a hand with anything?'

'No, I'm only doing salmon, new potatoes and salad. Then I'll take the paper into the conservatory. Jake's a darling, he doesn't need much entertainment from me, but, oh my, I do get quite tired these days.'

Leni kissed her mother's soft, powdered cheek, whistled to

Rosie and Monty, and called out to Jake to see if he wanted to come.

'I don't want a walk – I've already been with Granny. I've got to sort these.' Jake was arranging his collection of seashells and pebbles, placing the dead crabs on top of the piles.

'OK, I won't be long.' Leni smiled to see him so happily absorbed in his task.

Leni's thoughts flitted about. She agonised over money, doing mental arithmetic working out how much they'd need to buy a house and what amount they could live on. She considered her work situation and what she'd do for a living. Would there be enough from the house sale for a buy-to-let property, as an investment and regular income? If she and Alex started seeing each other, would a relationship make life complicated?

House martins flitted overhead and she reined the dogs in when a car came speeding towards her. People drove too fast on these lanes. Opening a metal gate, she un-clipped the leads and they followed a thin badger track across the field. Walking calmed her and as she finished the circuit, getting closer to the house, she stopped to enjoy being bathed in beautiful, summer evening light.

After supper, Leni took Jake upstairs and he clambered onto his bed for a bedtime story. She snuggled up as close as she could, and stroked his floppy, freshly washed hair. She wouldn't mention moving out of London just yet. He seemed so content, and it could upset him.

'Sleep tight.' She kissed him, left the door ajar and went to brew peppermint tea.

Joining Imogen in the conservatory, she sat down. 'He's settled and so happy. Thank you for everything, Mum.'

'All I want is for my family to be happy.'

Leni blew on the hot drink. 'My girlfriends want to treat me to a holiday. Isn't that lovely? Something to look forward to?'

'That's very thoughtful.' Imogen drew a hand through her silver hair. 'Have you made plans for Jake, or do you want me to have him here?'

'Oh Mum, that would be fabulous. It probably wouldn't be for the whole week. Kat can have him for a couple of nights. I've said I'll have Mike later in the year or when she really wants a break.'

'Well, let me know when you've got a date in mind. It may work for me to take him over to Fran's for a night. It's so nice for the cousins to play together and it'll be good for Jake.'

Leni drained her cup. 'Would you mind if I turn in now? I'm exhausted from thinking everything over so much.' She leant over to kiss Imogen's cheek.

'Goodnight, darling.' Imogen put a hand on Leni's arm. 'Try not to worry. Jake will come round to the idea of moving. Perhaps you could get him a kitten to look after, to have something depending on him? My advice is to get him into the local drama group as soon as possible, so he meets other children and makes friends.'

# 11

It was Saturday and Leni dropped Jake to football before putting the finishing touches to the house, getting it ready for a valuation. She opened the front door to welcome the Foxton's estate agent, hoping he was going to be an improvement on the first negotiator she'd tried. That man had barely concealed a sneer during his appraisal and his hair, teased to within an inch of its life, flashy outsized watch, and pointed shoes didn't help her warm towards him.

'Yes, well, it's clearly a family house. New occupants will certainly need to make improvements and put their own mark on it,' he'd said.

Who did these jumped-up wide-boys think they were? His shiny suit, swaggering manner and derisory tone left her with little confidence. She was glad to see the back of him before instructing the next local business.

An impeccably dressed man, a hint of grey at his temples, thrust his hand towards her. He carried a slim iPad.

'Mrs Parsons? I'm Nick Callaghan, pleased to meet you.' He had a dry palm and manicured fingernails.

'Come in. The house will get a deep clean before photographs can be taken,' Leni apologised. 'The vacuum only picks up so many dog hairs.'

'It's a delightful entrance – the front looks very pretty.' Nick stepped across the threshold looking left and right, taking in the initial effect of the hallway and stairs. 'You needn't worry, Mrs Parsons. We're used to seeing properties in every state.'

Leni tried to see her home through a stranger's eyes. Damn it, she'd missed some black scuff marks on the skirting boards and a faint trail of fingerprints up the stairwell.

'Boys can be so physical when they play,' she said, biting one side of her lip, 'they let off steam ragging about on the carpet, like a batch of over-enthusiastic puppies.'

'It's the same in my house. I've got two boys.' The agent smiled at Leni.

'How old are yours?'

'Fifteen and fourteen, and very competitive with one another, so they're a handful.'

'I've got a seven-year-old but his friends are often round, so it's bedlam at times.' Leni grasped the polished brass handle of the sitting-room door. 'Shall I show you the house or do you prefer to wander around alone?'

'Do show me, please.' He made a note of something on his pad. 'I'll take photos as I go as an aide-memoire for writing the brochure copy. When's a good time for the professional pictures to be taken?'

'The steam clean is being done on Tuesday and I'm around first thing on Wednesday if that works for you? Do you need me to be here?'

'It's not essential if you're happy for our guy to come in while you're out. You can drop a set of keys into the office, if you go ahead and instruct us.' He glanced at the ceiling, making a note of the original coving and ceiling rose.

Ushering him further into the room, Leni smelled expensive aftershave and noted, with approval, his crisp, ironed shirt and tailored suit. This man ticked the boxes regarding her sartorial standards.

'How long have you been here?' He measured the room using an app on his mobile phone.

'Eight years, just married and pregnant with our son. It's a wonderful family home, easy for the park and Chiswick High Road shops, then you've got the M4 and M3 on the doorstep.' Leni remembered happy occasions pushing Jake around the park in his Bugaboo stroller, enjoying Sunday brunch as a family and pointing out wildlife as they ambled beside the Thames at Chiswick Mall. She sighed. It would be a wrench to leave all this behind but she must look forwards now, no going back. She returned to the present. 'It's an easy ride into the city from Turnham Green Tube.'

He made a few more notes and within the hour had completed his visit.

'That's great, thank you.' He passed Leni his business card. 'I'll email the valuation and our terms.' They shook hands. 'This house will sell quickly.'

As she opened the front door, she heard the engines of an aeroplane making its descent into Heathrow, and felt the light wind that ruffled the leaves of the tree overhead.

'Thanks for coming.' She must trim the box spirals standing sentry on either side of the front door and remove the weeds poking through the paving slabs by the black, wrought-iron gate.

She made tea and sat in the area to the side of the kitchen.

She and Will had laughingly called it a conservatory, but in reality she'd been disappointed because it was just a fifteen-square-metre glass box tacked onto the side of the house. She'd tried to encapsulate a conservatory feel by furnishing it with wicker chairs, fern motif cushions and large potted plants, but it was a cold spot lodged between their house and the neighbour's wall. It was only good for sitting in on a sunny day. She wondered if new owners would replace it with a proper conservatory, or fit under-floor heating, to make it more useful throughout the year.

Lying back against a cushion, Leni let her mind wander. She remembered the conversation she'd had with Will about the cost of a conservatory as if it were yesterday. The clarity of the memory was piercing. She could hear his voice reasoning that the cost of putting on the extension would be a good investment, not least a place for Jake's toys. Will detested toys in the sitting room and held the view that there should be a 'clutter free room', like his mother and father's 'parlour' at the farm, where family congregated on high days and holidays, and the furnishings were kept spotless in case 'important' visitors came. Really, what an old-fashioned view.

Within minutes, her mobile buzzed. It was 3pm and she gulped the last inch of lukewarm tea. Brilliant. It was a text from Alex asking if she'd still like to go out that night and whether she had any preferences for what they might do.

'*Yes, still good for me,*' she typed, trying to think of something witty in reply. She'd like to see the Royal Opera House live screening of *Madam Butterfly*, but wasn't sure if that was his thing. '*Happy to let you choose!*'

> Right, I've a plan. I'll pick you up at 6.30pm,
> and dress for a cool breeze.

She tried to interpret the sartorial clue but she didn't like surprises.

'*Something outdoors? Active or sedentary?*' She had to ask; she wanted to look right for their date.

> Dinner cruise on a barge and a nightcap
> sound OK?

Although she'd lived in London for eight years, Leni had never been on a river cruise as Will had deemed it totally uncool and too touristy, but now she thought it might be amusing and it was certainly different to what she used to do. She replied '*Looking forward to it*', then called her friend.

'Hi Rachel, you still alright to have Jake after footie, and stay overnight? Alex has just firmed up our date.'

'Ooh, sounds promising. Got your best undies ready?'

'Hey, cheeky, no smutty insinuation, thank you.' Leni was glad she wasn't on FaceTime speaking to Rachel as she felt her face flush. 'Slowly does it. I'm not exactly experienced at this dating game, you know.'

'Well, you had a smile on your face when you told me about him. It's a good opportunity for you to get to know each other better.' There was a pause as Rachel held the phone away and called out, 'Jake, your mum's on the phone.'

'I'll come for him around ten o'clock?'

'Yes, that should be fine. They'll have scoffed cereal and be glued to cartoons on the telly, no doubt. We're off to Ed's parents for lunch so you can have a coffee and fill me in on how it went.'

'Hi Mum.' Jake's young voice sounded upbeat and breathy. 'We're making a Lego super-digger, and we're going to watch *Superman III.*'

'That sounds fun.' Leni was flooded with gratitude for her

friend's support and happiness hearing her boy sound so cheerful. 'I'll pick you up tomorrow morning, but call me any time if you want to – I'll have my mobile phone with me the whole time.'

'OK, bye Mum.' Jake handed the phone back to Rachel.

Leni had a shower then picked out clothes for her date. After changing from a linen print dress and cardigan into an azure blue shift with leggings, she finally settled on a pair of white jeans, a colourful silk top and block heels. Looking at her three leather jackets, Leni selected the blue, Karen Millen, biker-style one with zips and fringing on the cuff. It was a warm June day but it could get cold later on, being on the water and walking through the city.

She spritzed perfume in a wide arc and stepped into the mist as the doorbell rang. She almost tripped at the bedroom door, feeling nervous about seeing Alex again.

Standing on the step with one hand in his pocket, Alex beamed at her as she opened the door. He looked distinctly rugged and healthy. They kissed on both cheeks. Leni indicated for him to go into the kitchen and as he walked along the hall, she cast a lascivious look at his buttocks and long legs, which were clad in slim, dark denim jeans worn with a lightweight jacket and checked shirt. Excitement and nerves knotted in the pit of her stomach.

'Would you like a drink here before we go out or are we on a tight schedule?' she said.

'The barge departs at 7.30pm from Regent's Canal. We can get a Tube or taxi?'

'I'm happy to take the Tube, if there's time.' She looked at the clock. 'Where are you staying?'

'One of those Airbnb places in Maida Vale. It's pretty convenient.'

'Yes, my friend Rachel rents a room out on that. It's OK if you don't mind strangers in your house.'

'I thought I'd try it,' he said. 'I like new experiences, and it makes a change from a hotel.'

Leni liked his self-confidence; he sounded like someone who knows his own mind. She draped a print scarf around her neck. 'Had we better go? Don't want to be left high and dry when the ship sails, so to speak.' She collected her handbag, activated the burglar alarm and locked the door behind them.

They chatted about their music tastes on the way to the station.

'Do you like jazz?' Alex asked.

'I enjoy trad, but am not an aficionado of modern. I prefer rhythm and blues, and anything with a sax in it.' She tried not to listen to the sound of her heels clacking on the pavement as she adjusted her stride to keep pace with him. 'What bands are you into?'

'The Killers, White Stripes, Franz Ferdinand, Kaiser Chiefs.' He turned his head towards her. 'How about you?'

'Pretty much everything. My favourite's Bruce Springsteen. We saw him in Hyde Park a couple of years ago. He was awesome.'

At Turnham Green she flashed her Oyster card then Alex tapped his debit card on the barrier and they descended onto the outdoor platform. A dusty wind blew some paper rubbish about. Sitting together and rocking with the motion of the train, she studied the map, too inhibited to talk in the silence of the carriage.

Back on the street a gaggle of trendy youngsters surged towards them and Alex took her hand in his. It was warm and dry, and she thought how comforting and intimate this little gesture could be. She liked it. They made their way beside the brown, turgid water to the canal boat and after handing over their tickets, Alex chose a table close to the front.

'What would you like to drink?'

'I'd love a gin and tonic,' Leni said, shrugging off her leather jacket and lodging her small bag under one thigh.

'Good choice.' He signalled to the waiter.

'What are your top films?' Leni asked.

He rested an elbow on the table and sat casually to one side before answering.

Sipping her ice-cold drink as she listened to his reasons for his choices, she absent-mindedly picked out the lime with the straw, biting off the flesh before dropping the peel back into the glass. 'Oops, I forget where I am sometimes. I just love fresh lime!' She wiped her fingers on her napkin.

Alex grinned. 'When in Rome, as they say.' He chewed his lime, his face pinched from its sharpness.

Leni gasped and dived into her bag for her phone.

'Is everything alright?' Alex asked.

'Sorry. I need to check on Jake. He hasn't stayed overnight with any of his friends since his father died.' She looked at her mobile. 'No message. I'll take it that no news is good news.'

'How's he coping?' Alex leant forwards so he didn't have to talk loudly.

'He seems OK most of the time then has sudden flashes of anger or overwhelming sadness. He sometimes wets the bed. Mum's great, and his best friend, Mikey, cheers him up. They've known each other since they were tiny, when I started working with Kat in the shop.'

A waiter came to take their food order.

'Red or white wine?' Alex asked.

She didn't dither over this decision. 'Sauvignon Blanc,

please. I'm very fond of the New Zealand ones. Rather too fond, my girlfriends might say.'

After they'd ordered they talked about the merits of working for someone else or being self-employed.

'I love sourcing pieces for clients' houses but I get a real sense of satisfaction working with wood, and restoring pieces of furniture that already have history,' he said, pausing as he twirled his wine glass in his fingers. 'I enjoy how I spend my time, whether that's being creative doing restoration, or being inquisitive trying to find that special item of provenance for someone.' He took a sip of wine and smiled. 'I guess you could say that I love my job.'

Was that it? Was that why his marriage failed? He was so caught up in his work he forgot to notice Heather and the kids? She wanted to know more. Perhaps there was a weird character trait she'd yet to learn about. She momentarily wondered if tonight was too soon to ask, but decided to dive in.

'What went wrong for you and your wife? If you don't mind my asking? Tell me to back off if you'd rather not talk about it.' He didn't appear to be an uncaring person.

'No, that's alright, although it'll be the potted version, or you'll be bored rigid.' Alex stopped talking as their food arrived. 'I wasn't her type, supposedly. She thought I was, at the beginning. I've always worked with my hands. The beauty in old furniture and the heritage of antiquities talk to me.' He paused to eat a mouthful of Cornish hake and pearl barley risotto. 'Her idea of fun didn't involve sailing along the south coast or delving into *brocante* shops when we visited France. To be fair, she suffered from bouts of depression, and I was probably not very sympathetic as I didn't understand it. She became dissatisfied, and little by little, the love we had was eroded by her scorn and put-downs in front of friends and, worse, the children. It was soul destroying.'

Leni thought about this. Was it a case of differing interests and expectations, or was Heather justified in her feelings? Not that Leni would find out; she was only hearing one side of the story.

'That is sad,' she said. 'I know about trying to measure up. My father set the bar quite high and the worst thing was when he was disappointed. Chips away at the self-esteem, doesn't it?'

Alex nodded in agreement. 'I think Heather thought she was marrying into landed gentry and that she'd want for nothing. I remember saying to her in the early stages of our relationship that my family was asset rich, cash poor.' A rueful smile played across his face. 'She'd want new stuff and we'd argue when I didn't agree to get rid of things, when I felt they still had life in them. Now, I see that I could have compromised more.'

'That's a sentiment echoed by millions of couples after they've got into difficulties,' Leni said, savouring her flounder with seaweed and brown shrimps. 'This is delicious, by the way.'

The barge eased through a narrow bridge then made a tight arc to change direction and head back. Its table lights twinkled in the glass roof reflection as streetlights glowed from the side of the canal. Their plates were cleared and Alex poured the last of the wine into their glasses.

He spoke in a measured tone. 'Any discord and I would disappear into my workshop. I'd reason to myself that the long hours I put in were to build the restoration side of the business, but I realise I didn't read the warning signs. When I took the Marlborough premises on, there was even less time for us as a couple. Then she started seeing Bob. He had a nine-to-five job in sales.'

'You thought you were doing the right thing at the time.' Leni reflected that she hadn't dealt very well with her own problems. 'It's always about communication, isn't it? Dealing with small niggles before resentment builds up and blame starts to rear its ugly head.'

The waiter hovered nearby. 'Any desserts for you?'

'Not for me, but don't let that stop you having one,' Leni said. She looked around at another couple of diners who appeared to be having a whale of a time, telling raucous stories, and laughing loudly.

'The baked custard with rhubarb and pistachios sounds too good to miss. Bring two spoons please,' he said to the waiter. 'You may change your mind when you see it.'

Alex straightened up and took a deep breath. 'I'm simplifying things, of course. The marriage broke down in incremental steps. I played my part by behaving like an ostrich, with my head in the sand, being insensitive to her mental state.'

There was a silent moment as he appeared to reflect on this fact.

'I understand that,' Leni said. 'I ignored the signs that Will was unhappy. It's likely that my constant pressure to have a baby drove him into the arms of another woman, who made no such demands on him.' She sighed. 'I figured out about his affair after he died. I'd been kidding myself that it was just a flirtation.' The recollection of that deceit pained her. 'But it's easy in hindsight to imagine doing things differently, if you had your time again.'

The pudding arrived and Leni changed the subject. Their date was turning into a confessional. 'Where do you like to sail?'

Alex recounted anecdotes of eccentric characters he'd met during sailing trips. Smile lines creased around his eyes and the frown lines on his forehead disappeared.

'Perhaps you could come out for a sail in a few weeks' time? You could bring Jake too, if you think he'd enjoy it?'

'That sounds great – he'd love it.' Even as she spoke, she wondered about how quickly they seemed to be moving, with another date in the diary. She'd have to think about the consequences of introducing a new man to Jake and how that might affect him. It was an exciting thought though, and whatever else happened between them, it would be a stimulating experience.

The barge had docked at the jetty and, after disembarking, they walked towards Notting Hill. He took her hand.

'I like that,' she said.

They chose an intimate bar off Portobello Road for a nightcap.

'I want to get this,' Leni said, after they'd ordered at the bar.

Wedged on a squashy leather sofa, Alex gently probed Leni to tell more of her story. She found she was relaxed enough to open up about Will, and his demons, as she called them, and it was cathartic admitting to her feelings, but as she reminisced, the pain of his death and the sadness they'd endured erupted. Her eyes spilled over with tears and she fumbled in her bag for a tissue.

'I realise I shut him out with my anger. I was still desperate for another baby and just hoped our problems would go away if I got pregnant.' She blew her nose. 'It's not easy to accept your own failings, is it?'

'I'm sorry. It's still raw for you. Would you like me to get you home?'

'I'm alright now.' She swiped a tear from her cheek. 'Thanks for listening.'

'I'm happy to listen, any time.' Alex took her hand between his and looked into her eyes. 'I want to be your friend.'

'Well, I'll try not to cry next time.'

'I'm OK with it.' He let go of her hand. 'Let's find you a cab.'

Leni gathered her jacket, scarf and bag, and they left the bar. While they were standing close together on the dusty pavement she wanted to kiss him, but didn't want to be the one to initiate it. They'd become more formal with each other out in the open.

'Let me know about the sailing. Or we can do something else? When the time's right for you.'

'I will – that'd be lovely.' She wound the silk scarf around her neck. This was a perfect opportunity for intimacy but his words about being her friend held her back from asking him home. Was friendship his way of saying he didn't want to get involved? Did she want to? 'I'd best get a taxi.'

A black cab came towards them and Alex flagged it down. Leni stood on tiptoe to kiss him lightly on the mouth. 'Thanks again.'

''Til the next time, then,' he said, and closed the door behind her.

As the taxi pulled away, Leni turned around and watched him stride off into the dark night. An opportunity for intimacy had just been lost, but with doubts in her mind, she reckoned she just didn't feel ready for that next step.

Lying in bed later, she examined her feelings. Alex seemed genuine and their rapport was increasing, but was it too soon to get involved in a relationship? It felt disloyal towards the memory of Will and she shouldn't complicate her life, let alone Jake's, at this stage. There was work, the holiday with her friends coming up, and the house to get on the market, and surely that was plenty enough to consider right now?

# 12

The cabin crew opened the exit doors and people jostled to retrieve suitcases and bags from overhead lockers. After some commotion, Leni and her four friends lugged their cases in single file to the front of the plane. Standing at the top of the metal staircase, enveloped by intense heat, she drew a deep breath, taking in the oily smell of hot tarmac and scent of native shrubs. This holiday in Ibiza could be heaven or hell, she thought. Where would she go if she felt like howling? Then again, she could forget the constant anxiety she felt about everything, with the loving support of her friends.

'Remember that trip to Barcelona when Alison left her panama in the taxi?' Grace said, making the others giggle as they reminisced about mishaps on earlier holidays they'd shared. 'We spent hours trying to get it back, then you went and bought an identical one in the hotel shop.'

'Yeah, well, you can't have too many hats,' Alison retorted. 'What about you, with that bloke in Agadir trying to sell you a leather jacket? He kept on and on, and you ended up buying two. He saw you coming.' They all laughed at the memory and filed towards the border control. Grace stood beside Leni.

'Got my passport and my euros, now I just need a sexy Spaniard to make this a holiday to remember.'

'You're incorrigible,' Leni said, pulling her passport from her leather tote bag. 'Essential features: hairy, brown eyes, olive skin and a heavily accented voice and you'll swear he's the one for you? Lucky we've got separate rooms so I won't hear the seduction.'

'I'm excited just thinking about the possibilities.' Grace smiled and squeezed Leni's arm. 'It's got to be more fun than internet dating and don't forget, you might meet someone.'

'Don't be crazy. I'm nowhere near ready.' She wasn't going to mention meeting Alex just yet until she felt more sure of her feelings towards him. It was three weeks since they'd had dinner and although they'd exchanged texts and spoken on the phone once, she wanted to keep some distance between them. She'd concentrate on putting the house on the market and preparing Jake for a new school. So much responsibility weighed heavily on her shoulders.

They shuffled forwards, inspecting adverts of products and services on wall posters. It was only a short flight yet it felt unlike the UK, Leni mused, from the flooring to the smell in the airport.

'I think I'm smitten already.' Grace nodded her head in the direction of the passport booth. 'He's definitely my type.'

'Too good-looking to be sitting there, checking credentials all day.' Leni gently propelled Grace ahead. 'Go on then, knock him dead.' She watched her friend blush as she stepped up to the window.

Then it was Leni's turn. '*Hola senor, como estas?*' She flashed a wide smile for the officer. She thought his return smile implied an acknowledgement of his good looks, as if being on the receiving end of flattering glances all day was his due.

'Is the weather going to be good this week?' she asked, in her best schoolgirl Spanish.

'Of course,' he replied in English, with a nonchalant shrug of the shoulders. 'Enjoy your stay.'

The five friends spilled into the arrivals hall dragging trolley suitcases and getting their bearings on where to find transport. Alison and Rachel led the group out to the taxi rank.

'Gosh, you forget how much hotter it is than England.' Claire swiped her brow then replaced the wide-brimmed straw hat on her head.

'Lovely, isn't it?' Rachel turned to the others. 'Right, we'll need two taxis and I'll pay them both as I've got the kitty money.'

The drivers piled the luggage into two boots and they were on their way. Leaning her head out of the open window, Leni took advantage of the breeze and admired the profuse pink-blossomed shrubs that lined the division of the dual-carriageway. Was that oleander? She shifted about to stop her back sticking to the leatherette seat.

They drew up to the hotel, checked in and agreed to meet by the pool after they'd unpacked.

Relaxing on sun loungers, with cups of coffee on the small table between them, Leni and Claire watched Grace sashay towards them, clad in a bikini and brightly coloured wrap around her hips. She swung a beach bag in one hand and clutched a tall glass of pale yellow liquid in the other.

'Pina colada for me,' she said, mocking them for their coffee choice. 'My holiday has officially begun.' She pulled up a lounger to join them.

'Have you been to Spain much, Leni?' Claire adjusted her ample bosoms inside her bikini and leant back on the lounger.

'Yes, I love the country. Donkey's years ago, before it was

121

fashionable to buy a property abroad, my parents bought a villa in Nerja, to the east of Malaga. It was a small fishing village and they'd go there for weeks at a time and Fran and I would join them there from boarding school.'

'Lucky you. My family holidays were spent in a rain-sodden caravan in some bleak corner of the UK, with parents bickering.'

'Oh, lovely,' Grace said in ironic tone.

'How dreadful, I'm sorry, Claire.' Leni grimaced at the vision and drained her coffee. 'My only regret is that I didn't use the time to get better at Spanish. I was a self-conscious teenager and asking for stuff in a shop was excruciating. I'd clam up and let Mum do the talking. She got pretty fluent coming over for years and using those language cassette tapes.'

The women debated what activities they might do in Ibiza. Leni relaxed in the heat, enjoying the company of good friends.

Her mind drifted off and she remembered one holiday, aged about sixteen, when she'd had a crush on the waiter at the restaurant her family often went to. She'd flirted with him every visit but when they met on the beach one day and he'd asked her out, she'd taken fright and turned him down. In hindsight, she realised she just wanted to test her power of attraction, within the safety of her family being nearby. She remembered an artist she'd enjoyed a romance with, the summer before she met Will. Tears pricked her eyes. She felt hot.

'You alright, Len?' Grace looked across. 'Something upset you?'

'Just memories.' Leni wiped tears away with her beach towel. 'I'm a muddle of emotions these days. Just as I think I've come to terms with Will's death and look forward to relishing things, like this holiday, it hits me and I still can't believe he's dead.'

'You're doing well.' Grace went to sit on the edge of Leni's lounger and gave her friend a hug. 'Cut yourself some slack. It's going to take time.'

'Yes, just enjoy the holiday,' Claire added. 'Read, eat, drink and relax, and allow others to take care of you.'

'You're all so good to me – where would I be without my friends?'

'You'd do the same for us,' Claire said. 'So, want to try the yoga class later?'

'Who's up for windsurfing? I saw lessons advertised on the noticeboard.' Grace jumped to her feet, fixing her sarong around her white tummy. 'And more importantly, who wants another pina colada, as I'm off to the bar?'

'I might give it a try. It'll take my mind off everything,' Leni said.


'Let go of the boom and allow the sail to drop to the water!' Nathan shouted in a loud Australian accent from the powerboat. She did as instructed, jumping off the sleek windsurf board into the cool water. Nathan reached over the edge, grabbed the end of the sail and made it secure.

'We'll drag it to shore. Hop on,' he said, holding out a hand to help Leni on board. God, this was going to look ungainly, she thought, hoicking one leg over the side and allowing herself to be pulled in. Bouncing up and down as the boat cut through the water, they reached the jetty and Nathan tied a rope from the front to a metal ring on the floating pontoon. He dropped into the shallow water and hauled the windsurf board and sail onto the sand.

'You did great,' he said, a wide grin across his weather-beaten, tanned face. 'How do you feel?'

'A big improvement on yesterday's lesson,' Leni said, peeling her hired wetsuit down to her waist and momentarily wondering how her body looked. 'I got a better feel of the wind and felt more confident.'

Leni's exposed skin started drying in the hot sun. Following him into the surf shop to book another lesson, she couldn't keep her eyes off the muscles rippling in his back and the tattoo of a snake on his shoulder. Nathan logged on to the computer to view his schedule.

'My arms feel stronger but I wouldn't like the wind to be any gustier than it was,' Leni said, the smell of canvas and rubber wetsuits assailing her nose. 'Can I buy you a coffee or something?'

'Yeah, coffee would be great, thanks.' Nathan booked her in for the following day.

They walked along the seafront to a café with chairs and tables set up outside on wooden decking. She bought cappuccinos and apricot pastries, and they chatted about windsurfing, Nathan advising her on improving techniques that would create less tension in her body by harnessing the wind. He checked his watch, stuffed the last mouthful of pastry into his mouth and drained his coffee.

'Got another session, so I'd better go. Thanks for the coffee. I'll see you tomorrow.'

'Looking forward to it,' she said, remaining seated. She felt like she'd jumped a small hurdle, following her own plans and enjoying conversation with a man who knew nothing of her background. She had fun watching men and women on the beach, playing volleyball, some swimming, and all seemingly practising their flirting skills. A pair of bronzed bodies lay motionless, lapping up the sun, on bright beach-towels, surrounded by paraphernalia of books and magazines. Others sought shade under striped parasols. She inhaled the scent of dry, fragrant leaves as cicadas buzzed in nearby scrub bushes.

Leni slung her beach bag over one shoulder and walked two blocks from the seashore back to the hotel. Passing the fruit and vegetable shop, and pharmacy, she made occasional eye contact and nodded to a few people as they passed by. She bounded up the smooth marble steps, swung open the glass front door and waited at the reception desk.

'*Buenas tardes, senorita*, did you have a good day?' Sebastian greeted Leni with a cheerful smile. 'How did the lesson go?'

At check-in four days ago, the Spanish clerk had pointed out a notice challenging guests to a windsurf competition at the end of the week.

'*Buena, gracias*,' Leni said. 'I've improved, but I won't be in your competition this year, or for some while yet. That's for the experts, not beginners like me.'

'Perhaps you will come back next year and take part.' Sebastian's smile revealed perfect white teeth as he handed over her room key. 'Enjoy your evening.'

She relished the thought of a soothing bath and rubbing arnica cream into her arm where she'd knocked it falling off the board. Still, she thought, she hadn't tumbled off quite so many times today. Leni locked the bedroom door, dropped her kaftan on the bed and bikini in the washbasin and ran a bath.

'I shall enjoy a few glasses of wine tonight,' she talked to her reflection in the mirror. She brushed her hands down each arm and across her stomach and thighs. 'I've worked hard for it.'

After washing her hair and enjoying a long soak, Leni smoothed moisturiser into her face and body lotion over her limbs. Using the full-length mirror inside a cupboard, she appraised her body, twisting around left and right to get a good angle to see her buttocks and admire how tanned she'd got in just a few days of sunshine. Pulling back the thick cotton bedspread she slipped, naked, between the crisp, densely threaded, white sheets. Sun shone through the gauzy curtains and she closed her eyes, daydreaming about the handsome, bleached-blond windsurf tutor. The sensual fantasy fuelled a rising desire as she stroked her hand across her breasts, over her stomach and between her legs. In a state of exquisite arousal Leni stimulated herself to a shuddering climax. Soothed by the orgasm, she drifted off to sleep with a moment's pleasant thought that she'd rest before cocktail hour and her next adventure.

'What did Nathan say?' Rachel propped her sunglasses on her head as Leni joined her to sit on the low marble wall near the pool.

'He can spare some time at 5pm after he finishes teaching,' Leni said.

'Are you going to go?' Rachel's expression was incredulous.

'Yeah, why not?' Leni admired the bountiful red bougain-villea climbing up the wall beside them. 'You know who I'm with. Send out the search parties if I don't show up by dinner?'

Rachel was cynical. 'Do you feel you know him well enough? He's very young.'

'Oh Rachel, I just want a bit of fun. It's been a hell of a few months. Nothing will happen.' Leni raised both palms towards the sky and shrugged. She didn't need to feel guilty; she wasn't a married woman any more. 'I'll go to the end of the bay with him, get a few photographs and then I'll be back.'

'You don't know if he's any good with a passenger. These guys ride motorbikes like they're at a rodeo, weaving and dodging through traffic at speed.'

'I haven't had that buzz for years,' Leni said. 'Fran and

I had mopeds when we were teenagers. I loved my Honda 50cc, freedom at my fingertips.'

'Please be careful.' Rachel stood up. 'I'm going to shower and rest on my bed. I've had too much sun today.'

They used the back steps to go into the hotel. 'It'll be fine. He's a nice guy.'

A group of men, sitting in the cool reception area, were engrossed in a game of cards, drinking espressos with chasers to the side.

Leni pressed the lift button. 'I may not tell the others? They'll only lecture me and advise me not to go.'

'I don't want to lie, so what do I say if they ask me where you are?'

'That I've gone into town to look at the shops?'

Rachel grumbled as they got into the lift, 'Seems a bit reckless to me.'

'Thanks.' Leni hugged her friend. 'I'll tell them when I see you all at dinner.'

Later that afternoon she met Nathan at the Surf School. He was wearing a pair of worn-out shorts, and the hairs on his muscular brown legs glistened in the sun. His face lit up as she approached.

'So you decided to come then?' Nathan scooped up his sweatshirt and keys.

She loved his accent. His body was hot, too, which was an incentive. 'Of course, I can't wait to see further afield. We've kind of done the beaches and bars in this neck of the woods.'

He locked up and they went around the back of the building. Leni put on the helmet he held out, slung her shoulder bag across her body and straddled the bike behind him. She hoped she looked as cool as she imagined.

'Hold onto me. The cove's about fifteen minutes away?' He revved the engine. 'Any problems, just tap my shoulder.'

He drove up the sandy track that led to the main road out of town and turned right. As they sped along the coast, Leni looked at azure waves rippling in the sun, watched palm trees and shops whizz by until they reached the open road and left the town behind them. This is heavenly, she thought, feeling vibrant and adventurous. Scrubland and crops of craggy rock filled the space between the road and the sea. Passing through a small village, Leni urgently clutched Nathan's waist as he swerved to avoid a mangy dog that ran out into the road. 'Missed him,' he yelled, laughing. An old man, hunched to one side with arthritis, shook his fist at them. Groups of locals were sitting on plastic chairs in their front yards, drinking and hands gesticulating furiously as they talked.

Passing through a dense clump of trees and twisting round two sharp bends, they travelled up an incline for a few hundred metres. A sign announced a scenic look-out point and Nathan slowed down to turn right. The tarmac road ended in a small car park and Nathan drove across it slowly to find a small, rough track used by cyclists and walkers. He stopped in a gap in the scrub, cut the engine and pulled off his helmet. Leni climbed off and, after removing her helmet, looked all around. She relished the smell of fragrant bushes and dusty red soil, and took a deep breath. There was a warm on-shore wind and although it was still bright, the ultramarine blue of the sky was fading.

'There's a great viewpoint over here,' Nathan called over his shoulder as he strode towards the cliff edge.

Leni tiptoed carefully through the scrub, banishing thoughts that she'd probably been a bit reckless, driving off with a stranger, but he hardly seemed a dangerous bloke.

'Any snakes on this island?' she asked, glancing left and right.

'Don't you worry, it'd be sticking to the undergrowth and if you get bit, I'll suck out the poison. Seen it done at home.'

'Thanks, that's reassuring.' Leni reached the promontory where Nathan was standing, taking in the view. 'Not.'

She saw bay upon bay of glittering sea and sandy beaches backed by woodland. The villages they'd driven through looked like dolls' houses in the distance.

'Wow. This is brilliant.' She set up her small tripod and fixed the camera to the top to take a few preliminary shots.

'I'll just get the beers.' Nathan walked away. Really? She hadn't expected him to do that. Beers and motorbikes, was that a good idea?

After taking a selection of shots Leni went to sit beside Nathan who was relaxing on a rock on the headland. He flipped the lid off a bottle of beer and held it out towards her.

'Got what you wanted?'

'Thanks, it's fabulous to see other aspects of the coastline. It's very beautiful.'

Leni drank from the bottle and asked Nathan about his life on the island.

'I won't stay here forever.' He twisted his leather wristbands. 'My girlfriend's on at me to settle down but I've got itchy feet and there are other places I'd like to live. It's a dilemma.'

'How old is she?'

'Ava's thirty-two and ready for kids.'

'I can understand her concern. If she waits until you're ready, there may be fertility issues. I should know.' Leni turned her head away.

'Oh?'

Leni told him a little about Will and their lost baby. She bit her lip. 'I won't say any more or I'll cry, and it's been such a lovely day, and you've been so nice.'

'Come here.' Nathan pulled her into a warm hug and stroked her back. 'I thought there was something about you. When you weren't windsurfing or talking about your mates, I saw a pained look in your eyes.'

'We weren't always happy but I miss the physical and emotional connection,' Leni said, realising as she said it how much she liked his bare, strong arms around her. 'Being able to share your thoughts and laughter with someone.'

Nathan gently drew her head around, and kissed her mouth.

'You're beautiful – do you know that? I'm ace about people and I liked you the first time we met.'

Leni stared into his eyes. Her heart skipped a beat and a flicker of excitement wove its way down her body.

'I'm probably ten years older than you.'

He stroked her arm and rested his hand on hers. 'It's simple chemistry. Your smell and your soul drew me to you. I wanna kiss you.' He drew her into his arms, his hard chest pressed close.

She forgot about the awkward position they were in, and the rock digging into her thigh, as she gave herself to this kiss. It encompassed her and she was oblivious to her surroundings. It was like dropping onto a warm feather bed, being enveloped and supported, and she let go of her inhibitions. Minutes passed before she broke away.

'I haven't kissed like that for years.' She sighed. 'Just need a reality check that this is me, right here, right now?' She felt exposed, as if she'd bared something of herself in her passionate enjoyment of the embrace.

'Live for today, that's my motto,' Nathan said, finishing his beer in one swig. 'Take your happiness where you find it. You're a long time dead, as you've seen with your husband.'

Leni caught her breath. 'What about responsibilities? Can you go through life being hedonistic? Isn't that a bit selfish?'

'Hey, lighten up. You're allowed a bit of fun, you know.'

'What about Ava?'

'She's cool. She doesn't try to own me.'

'You must meet lots of women. Temptation is beguiling, I get that.'

'Look, Ava's a free spirit, and anyway, our relationship is solid.'

'I'm sorry, it's none of my business. I was cheated on, so my views are probably different.' Leni felt chastened. It would be easy to slip her clothes off and enjoy sex with this dishevelled young bloke who was offering himself on a plate.

She checked her watch. 'I'd better get back.'

'Want to meet up later?' he asked, stroking her arm.

'Where's Ava?' She clocked that she even considered his suggestion.

'She's visiting her family in Sweden.'

'It's not the sort of thing I do.'

'Live a little, Leni.' He kissed her again then walked towards the bike.

Leni followed him, heart fluttering, mouth dry. He was hot and she hadn't had sex for so long. It was tempting. She put her arms around him as he started the motor.

'I've got to pick up something from the apartment on our way back, OK?'

'Right.'

Driving along the coast road, the motor throbbing between

her legs, Leni drifted into a reverie. The beer had relaxed her. That kiss was intoxicating. She felt high and happy. He pulled up at a block of flats with metal balcony rails facing the sea.

'Come up. I won't be long,' he said, unlocking the door. 'I've got to drop a spare batten to a mate.'

Leni stepped into a cool dark hallway and followed him into the living room. At the door, a woven basket overflowed with deck shoes, windsurf boots and trainers, and in the main room, a tatty armchair and old sofa were strewn with throws in a myriad of designs, and potted plants filled the balcony with colour. She sat down tentatively as Nathan rummaged across a desk, scattering documents as he went. Her heart was beating hard.

'Book-keeping isn't my strong point. Gotta do some paperwork soon.' He grinned, holding a white box aloft. 'Found it.'

Leni stood up. Nathan dropped the slim package on the sofa and put his arms around her.

'What's the hurry?' he said.

Leni kissed him hungrily. She wanted him and gave up all pretence of any scruples. Her fingers roved across his head, neck and back as Nathan cupped her bottom in his hands, pulling her hips closer. His erection pushed into her and, tearing off each other's clothes, they stumbled onto the sofa. It was hard and fast sex, both fervent participants.

Lying for a while, limbs entwined, Leni listened to their breath slowing.

'That was so good.' She kissed him gently as she extricated herself. 'Where's the bathroom?'

'Down the hall, on the right.'

She leant against the locked bathroom door. What the hell

was that all about? She'd behaved like a bitch on heat. She cleaned herself with paper. So what? It felt amazing; it was a natural urge that had overtaken her sanity.

In the bedroom she dressed quickly, glancing at Nathan. Her appreciative gaze ran from his blond, rumpled hair, across his relaxed, naked frame to his tanned feet and toes. Oh God, she'd just had sex with this gorgeous man.

'Hey, you.' He woke, and smiled at her. 'That was fun. No regrets?'

'None, and you've reignited my libido, so thank you.' She kissed him. 'I feel 100% alive.'

'I guess you want to get back?'

'Please. I've got about fifteen minutes before my friends will be suspicious, wondering where I've got to.'

'Give me a minute.' With no apparent self-consciousness, he got up and went to the bathroom, reappearing in fresh shorts and tee-shirt.

As they sped towards the hotel on the bike, a frightening image of pregnancy buzzed in her mind. She'd been irresponsible, not asking if he'd had a condom. Just because she couldn't get pregnant with Will, she shouldn't have presumed she was totally sterile. Shit.

'Bye Leni. You'll be right,' he said, in Australian slang, dropping her off at the hotel gates. 'You gotta warm aura. And a nice arse, too,' he added, threading her helmet over his wrist.

'Thanks.' She felt sick with worry.

'Keep up the windsurfing,' he shouted, as the bike roared into the road.

She walked up the drive. Was her behaviour so bad? Shouldn't she feel guilty about Ava? Strangely, she didn't. You only get one life, she repeated Nathan's creed. Live for today.

All the same, she'd have to get a morning-after pill when she got home.

Quickly showering and slipping into a dress, Leni got to the bar just as Grace announced they were ready to go into the restaurant. Rachel raised her eyebrows and gave her friend a thumbs-up signal.

'How'd it go?' Rachel asked. 'Tell me everything, later?'

'It was all fine – nothing to report. I took loads of pictures and stayed safe on the bike.' She wasn't going to mention sex with Nathan. She wouldn't be judged by Rachel, or anyone. It was exciting, casual sex, nothing more, nothing less, and the only thing she felt bad about was not using protection. OK, she did feel a little grubby about it. She'd better get checked out.

With much chatter and laughter about their holiday, the group of women ate dinner then opted for cocktails in town, enjoying the frivolous mood of their last night together.

On the plane home Grace sat beside Leni. 'So, what's the latest about your move to the country?'

'I like the look of Pewsey and Fran would be less than half an hour away. The school there has a good reputation.' She didn't have to do much inner wrangling; it sounded like a good plan as she voiced it out loud.

'When would you leave London?'

'I guess by the time everything goes through, it'll be around Christmas. Hard to think of the cold and snow right now, isn't it?'

'So Jake wouldn't be in his new school at the start of the school year.' Grace looked concerned. 'Does that worry you?'

'Yes, just about everything worries me,' Leni sighed, 'but I reckon it's the best solution. Besides, he can always start in the January term.'

'How's Kat taking it?'

'She's wonderful. She's been supportive. I've given notice and, fortunately, Rachel wants more days, so I expect Kat will find another assistant for Saturdays and cover days.'

The two women continued to talk about their families, work, and hopes for the future, and soon they were back at Heathrow. After noisy and emotional hugs, and promises to share photographs, they dispersed across the city.

# 13

'What are you particularly looking for?' The young estate agent indicated the mahogany chair on the far side of his desk. 'I'll register you, then you'll be on the system for email alerts whenever something suitable comes in.'

Leni had been thinking about the answer to this question as she drove from Chiswick to the market town of Pewsey. She'd passed King Alfred's statue and taken a space in the Co-op car park, making a mental note to pick up a few groceries in return for using its two-hour free parking.

'Where are you living now? Are you new to Pewsey?' he continued, adjusting the computer monitor to face him. 'Ms, Mrs?' His fingers hovered above the keyboard as he looked up.

Why did the property industry often attract salespeople with a pushy way of asking personal questions? It was none of this whipper-snapper's business.

'I'm moving to be near my elderly mother,' she lied, watching him stab in this information along with her email address, phone number and current house situation.

He pulled glossy brochures from the filing cabinet and

flicking through them like a pack of cards, Leni discounted several.

'I'd like a period property and it must have a garden.'

'I can probably get you in to see one or two today.' He scrolled his finger over the mouse. 'Swan Road would be tomorrow, if you're still in the area, or we can fix another date if you prefer?'

'I've only got today, so I'll look at these and get in touch if there are any I'd like to see inside.'

Dropping the brochures into her much-loved Mulberry handbag, Leni said goodbye, carefully closed the glass door and walked back to her car. Many of the High Street facades were adorned with hanging baskets filled with tumbling flowers, and the town looked pretty in the warm late summer sunshine. An attractive woman of a similar age to Leni was being pulled along by a juvenile black Labrador and as they passed each other on the pavement, the animal lurched forwards to sniff at Leni's feet.

'He's got a thing about shoes, I'm sorry.' The woman looked mortified. 'I hope he'll grow out of it.'

'It's alright, I love dogs.' Leni stroked his big head. 'He can probably smell Monty, my terrier. Enjoy your walk.'

She fantasised about the woman becoming a new friend, dog owners being an approachable bunch on the whole, and that they would walk their dogs together.

After buying the local paper, bottled water, a sandwich and a bag of apples, she sat in the car working out a route to the properties she wanted to drive past. Setting the satnav, Leni made her way to the outskirts of town with mounting anticipation.

The cottage was red-brick, Victorian and semi-detached. Parking beyond it and strolling back along the pavement, she lingered as she drew level with its waist-high flint wall, glancing about to see if anyone was watching her. The garden was well tended and thank God previous owners hadn't put in uPVC window frames, she thought. A gravel path of pale stones led to the front step where a large pot of pink geraniums, variegated ivy and abundant blue lobelia stood sentry beside the door. 'Forsythia Cottage' was etched in the sandstone arch above it. Leni scribbled a big star in the corner of the particulars. She definitely wanted to view this one, and soon.

Further along the lane, she studied the other houses. What would it be like living here? she wondered. In London, she knew her neighbours on one side while the occupants on the other changed so frequently, she was barely on nodding terms, let alone knowing their names. She'd need to explore local amenities and find a junior football club for Jake. It was all very well using Google, but there was nothing like walking around, sitting in a café and talking to local people, to get a better feel for the place.

Leni drove to two more properties, stopping briefly at each and making a note of her first impressions. Confident that her gut-reaction was a powerful tool, she phoned the agency to make an appointment to view two of the three houses.

A girl answered. 'Bear with, I'll check the diary.' She put Leni on hold. 'Right, Sean can do 4pm at Forsythia Cottage and 4.45pm at the other property as it's near. Got the directions?'

'Thank you, yes. I'll meet him there at 4pm.' Enthusiasm at the prospect of country living was tempered by fear that it would be a complete contrast to her previous decade. She felt a surge of empowerment as she reflected that Will was no longer able to dominate her and she'd make this decision alone.

It was 12.30pm. She'd drive around the area, find a park or quiet field to eat her sandwich then have coffee in a pub. It was likely she'd get some low-down on the town and its inhabitants from a local resident propping up the bar.

At five to four Leni parked, applied a slick of lipstick and ran a brush through her hair. Fortunately, Sean wasn't the obsequious agent she'd met this morning and he gave her a cheery wave and smile as she approached the gate.

'Nice to meet you. Isn't it a beautiful day?' He selected the front door key. 'The garden is at its best, this time of year.'

Leni glanced around, inhaling the smell from the cottage garden flowers bursting with colour against the boundary wall. A waft from the Albertine rose climbing over the porch made her feel extraordinarily happy, as she remembered her childhood home. Her mother was a genius with roses and that smell took her right back.

They walked through the cool hall and Sean opened a door into a small, light-filled sitting room. There was an open grate and shelves lining both sides of the chimney. The current owners had stripped the place of family photographs and personal ornaments, leaving the bare bones of the room, with just an artfully placed bowl and set of fine Victorian crystal glasses on the shelves. The room was furnished with an off-white sofa, two blue and white striped armchairs and a blue, yellow and white patterned rug. Two pine coffee tables on either side of the sofa picked up the pine in the window shutters. It was lovely.

'It's so light and airy, despite being small,' Leni said.

'Yes, it gets the sun in here in the morning and the back gets it in the evening, I understand. Shall we go through?' He ushered her into the dining room.

'It's a lot darker in here.' Leni didn't like the feel of this room so much, which only had natural light from a tiny window in the side wall and what was coming through the open door into the kitchen.

'You could probably open it up a little. It's old, but it's not graded.'

'Let's see the kitchen, so I can understand the layout better.'

Leni liked the simple kitchen. Blue gingham curtains, placed at half window height, picked up the pale blue painted units and the white of the appliances and Belfast sink. It reminded her of a holiday home, uncluttered and undemanding. She opened cabinet doors and peered into the eye-level oven.

'It's charming.' She peered over the curtains to see the view. 'I think you're right: a section of this interior wall could be removed to make the middle room lighter. I used to love a separate dining room, but I don't think I'm going to need it and a larger kitchen-diner would be more useful.'

'Would you like to see the garden now or go upstairs?'

'Bedrooms first, please.' She peeped through the window of the stable back door as she followed him. 'The garden looks delightful from here.'

Two double bedrooms and a single one occupied the first floor. The bathroom was mainly white with blue towels hanging over an old pine, freestanding, rail. They were all modest rooms. She would enjoy creating a more sophisticated decorative scheme in the house but could live with the plain *décor* until ready to embellish with a new colour palette.

'What about the owners? Have they found somewhere else?'

'It's a young couple. They've got a little girl and a baby on the way. They're currently staying with his parents in the Midlands and as he's got a new job starting in Manchester, they're looking for a smooth sale.'

So that's why the *décor* was simple and unadventurous. The

young couple hadn't yet found their style, or perhaps they'd been advised to paint everything white so as not to put off potential purchasers with bright or outlandish colours.

'It's smaller than my house in London, but it has a similar charm and I'm always attracted to period property. I like to imagine the people who've lived here in the past.'

'London prices are still holding so your sale should be relatively quick?'

'All being well, with no broken chains in the process.'

They returned to the kitchen and Sean unlocked the back door. A grey metal table and chairs were positioned on a small stone patio which led to a lawn, walled on either side. Densely planted borders lined both sides and a display of forsythia drew Leni's eye towards the bottom of the garden. A tree, heavily laden with juicy-looking apples, gave dappled shade to the wooden bench underneath its branches. She walked to it and sat down, facing the back of the cottage, and the adjoining house. What sort of neighbours would they make? She had a good feeling. It would be incredible to settle on the first house she viewed, but somehow it felt very welcoming and 'spoke' to her.

They visited the next property, which Leni liked less, but she kept any negative comments to herself. She didn't want the agent to know how much she wanted Forsythia Cottage as he'd expect her to offer the asking price on it. There were negotiations to be made and it was a delicate dance for vendor and purchaser, to both feel they got a good deal.

Sean shook her hand. 'Let me know your thoughts and if there's anything else you want to know, please don't hesitate to call.'

'Thank you.' Leni got her car keys out and walked along the pavement. She made a few notes on the particulars and called her mum as she sat in the car.

'Hi Mum. I've seen a darling cottage which I think will work very well.'

'That was quick? You only saw two today?' Imogen's voice sounded full of doubt.

'I know. I'll look at others, but I've a really good feeling about Forsythia Cottage. I'd like you and Fran to see it, if possible, and I'll bring Jake too, the next time I come?'

They settled on the following Saturday and Leni texted Fran to see if she could join them. She then dialled the agent to make the appointment. Fingers crossed, Chiswick would be snapped up quickly, she thought, as she listened to the ring tone. Just before they answered, she clicked off. It would look too keen to book a second viewing straight away. She could make an offer, to show that she was serious, tomorrow or later in the week. It was exciting, but nerve-wracking at the same time. Maybe she should talk to Hugh as he was switched on about money, and, being in the surveying business, would give her sound advice.

She dialled Kat's number and put the mobile onto loudspeaker.

'Just setting off from Pewsey.' She plugged in her seat belt. 'Should be with you in an hour and a half.'

'No problem. Jake and Mike are fine, and I'll give them some pasta.'

'You're a star.' Leni started the car and looked in her mirrors for traffic. 'I'm still having Mikey this weekend? Let's sort details when I get to you.'

'Great, I look forward to hearing all about it.' Kat rang off.

Leni made a mental list of what needed doing to prepare for a sale. Most of her furniture would work at Forsythia Cottage but she'd sell or donate some items. She'd be able to move two double beds and Jake's single bed directly into the cottage, although being smaller rooms, wardrobes and storage may be an issue. She imagined where she could put a chest of drawers and started to envisage how each room could look, with furnishings in them. Most of the curtains in Chiswick had been made to measure but she'd take several pairs with her as she was so attached to them. Would they be a sad reminder of her life with Will? Would they be a comfort to Jake to ease him into living in a new house? It may be better to buy new curtains, and not have the bother of getting the present ones cut down and remodelled.

Leni had barely noticed the journey as she pulled into Kat's road. Her major task would be to get Jake on board with the move. She'd do anything to make him happy and dreaded adding to any insecurity since his dad's death. It wasn't going to be easy.

Kat welcomed her into the house and they drank wine while the boys finished a game. Leni told her about the house and they deliberated about the advantages of moving from London and the effect it may have on both their sons.

'I hope the boys will continue to be friends,' said Kat.

'Of course.' Leni grabbed her friend's hand. 'Our friendship is important, too.'

'It sounds like you've fallen in love with the cottage.'

'I have. It'll suit us. It's in a terrace, close to the shops, park and the school.'

Kat twiddled a strand of hair in her fingers. 'Can you meet the head teacher and have a look around?'

'Yep, I got hold of an admin woman who was in school before term starts and we've got an appointment.'

'That's great.' Kat finished her wine. 'I'll feel happier that you're not jumping feet first into the unknown.'

Leni drained her glass. 'I know it looks like I've made these decisions quickly, but I'm ready. To start over. I can be myself,

Jake's mum, and be responsible for us both. I let Will treat me like an accessory to his success. This has been a wake-up call for me.'

'And I suppose the proximity of that hot antiques guy's got nothing to do with it?'

'Touché,' Leni said, getting up and hugging Kat, then calling to Jake. 'Time to go.'

'When's Mikey coming over?'

'Remember, you're going to the sports club, then Mikey's with us at the weekend?'

The boys jostled each other playfully as they went to the front door.

When they got home and Jake was ready to go to sleep, Leni sat on his bed, tucking his duvet close.

'Looking forward to seeing some of your other friends at the club?'

'Yes, but why isn't Mikey coming too?'

'He's seeing his dad, and stepmum.' Leni stroked his hair from his forehead, noticing Jake's wistful look as she mentioned the dad word. 'They want to see him, too.'

She read him a story then kissed him goodnight. She worried about his dependency on Mike's friendship. Talk about moving and going to see a new school and house would have to wait; he had enough to cope with right now. The idea of getting him a kitten was a good one.

Leni fixed up for Jake to meet Alex in three weeks' time. He'd take them on a sailing trip to Cowes. She hoped they'd like each other; it would be a deal breaker for the new relationship.

# 14

'Pull the fenders up now, Jake,' Alex called out from the cockpit.

Alex manoeuvred the yacht with precision from its mooring and they headed into the estuary. The wind caught at Leni's hair. She shivered, excited about being with Alex again, and partly with nerves about how Jake would get along with him. She watched her son inch along the deck, one hand holding the ropes to two round white fenders, while sliding the other along the cabin rail. He stepped into the cockpit to stow them in a locker then climbed onto the banquette cushions to stand close to Alex, at the helm.

'Watch out ahead, and keep your eyes peeled for windsurfers and dinghy sailors,' said Alex. 'Remember, if something's on the right it's called starboard, and anything to the left of the boat is port-side?'

'Aye aye, Captain.' Jake saluted.

Leni could see that Alex was at ease. He'd promised to take them sailing when the forecast was fine, and she was thankful they'd made it, as she was itching for them to meet. The sun shone, refracting light on the rippling water; the harbour was as picturesque as a postcard scene.

'Ready to hoist the mainsail, Leni? Want some help from the Skipper's Mate?' Alex gestured towards Jake.

Recalling some of the instructions she'd been given earlier, she was still nervous about which order to do things and whether she could break something, in doing so.

'What do I do with the straps once the sail goes up? I may need a hand.'

After untying the straps holding the sail to the boom, she pulled on the rope at the bottom of the mast to pull the sail up. She tipped backwards and forwards trying to keep her balance. The huge white sail unfurled, with the noise of flapping nylon getting louder as it went up the mast. When it was taut, Leni tied off the rope in a figure of eight. Alex reached her side, made a few adjustments, and gave her arm a squeeze.

'Great job. That's perfect.'

'Oh my God,' she cried out. 'Is Jake in charge of this boat?'

'He's holding the helm steady and doing really well – you can relax.' Alex took a large stride and swung into the cockpit to take over. 'Thanks, mate.'

'That was brilliant.' Jake's face shone with pride. 'Did you see me, Mum? I was in charge.'

'Incredible, Jake.' She laughed, thinking that she must stop worrying about his every move or she'd be a frazzled wreck. She hugged him and kissed his head.

The boat progressed towards open water. Alex switched off the motor and the juddering sensation ceased. In its place was the sound of water lapping against the fibreglass hull, and the vibration of the wind in the taut sail. Steep wooded hills replaced the jumble of houses of the town, and dark trees bent inland from decades of wind. She spotted a few sheep on far hills.

'This is how I like it, so peaceful.' Alex turned to her. 'Would you like a turn on the helm?' He grinned and offered his hand for her to stand beside him.

She could barely see over the high teak shelf, and was intrigued by the array of instruments before her: a pair of binoculars, some pencils, and a beanie hat rested on the non-slip mat, beside a rolling compass set in a brass stand. She planted her feet wide as instructed and Alex encouraged her with calm instructions.

'Keep your eye on the tip of the headland and keep it at around two o'clock or twenty-five degrees to the starboard prow, like this,' said Alex. He momentarily took control to demonstrate.

She adjusted the steering according to the waves and wind to keep a straight position. The mental concentration was exhausting.

'Now you're in charge.' Jake let out a loud whoop of joy.

As they voyaged into the Solent, the rolling motion of the boat began to feel normal. As she observed the blue of the sea and contrasting green countryside, she wondered how long it would take to learn to sail a vessel like this, and she admired Alex's skill. She gazed at his strong, tanned legs with well-defined calf muscles, and yearned for physical intimacy with him, imagining her legs wrapped around his thighs.

She blushed as she caught him smiling at her. 'Isn't this brilliant, Jake?' She cast off her erotic fantasy. 'Is it as good as you thought it would be?'

'It's awesome.' Jake used his favourite new word.

Leni took a cushion and sat down leaning against the mast, stretching out her legs and trying to quash horny thoughts of Alex. She relished the warm autumn sun and lulling motion of the boat. What a delightful way to spend the day. After a while her quiet reverie was broken by Alex's voice.

'Better run though the mooring process before we arrive in Cowes.' He explained how to take the sail down, secure it to the boom and get the fenders ready, but not tie them until they knew which side they'd moor up. He demonstrated, once again, how to tie a clove half-hitch that Jake continued to practise.

Leni noticed her anxiety returning. How was Alex going to park this thing? It seemed impossible with so many other boats, and obstacles, in every direction. Small craft dodged away from larger boats and Leni turned to the source of some shouting. Orders were barked out, military style, by a rotund, red-faced sailor, in charge of an inflatable dinghy with outboard motor. In it were sitting a tight-lipped woman, and two surly children, who looked as if they would rather be anywhere else than on the water with their embarrassing, dictatorial father.

Alex appeared unflappable, using the motor in forward and reverse to bring the boat alongside the jetty. He jumped down onto the floating pontoon.

'Pass me the line please, Jake.'

Alex secured it to a metal cleat and repeated the process at the other end, before returning to the cockpit to turn off the engine and make the boat secure.

Leni gathered her denim jacket and bag.

'I'm ravenous. It must be the sea air.' She watched Alex unclip the metal lines between the struts to create an opening, and toss the adjoining rope ladder over. 'OK, Jake?'

He got up from peering into the forward hatch and scampered over.

Clambering over the side, Leni was glad she'd chosen to wear her striped Breton tee-shirt and new pink leather deck shoes, which looked the part, even if she was such a novice sailor. She held out a hand for Jake.

'Watch out, I'm going to jump.' He leapt from the deck to the pontoon.

'Who's for mussels and chips?' The platform juddered up and down as Alex stepped onto it.

'Yuk, not me.' Jake looked disgusted. 'I'll have the chips.'

Alex led them through the streets until they reached the restaurant he recommended. 'Warm enough to sit outside?'

They found a table overlooking the water. A waiter in a long black apron handed them menus, and a carafe of iced water and glasses from his tray.

'Can I get you something to drink?' he asked, looking like a university student on his summer break, with a deeply tanned face and tousled blond hair.

Alex ordered a bottle of Sauvignon Blanc and a Coke, and they enjoyed the warm sun as they talked about the morning's sail. While choosing from the menu they overheard snippets of other diners' conversations and a nearby group of men were swapping anecdotes, appearing to outdo each other with raucous tales. Leni noticed a uniform in these sailing fraternities, all red chinos, deck shoes and rugby or Breton tops.

'Thank you for a wonderful time, Alex. Apart from one dreadful weekend on a canal boat that I'd rather forget, my seafaring experience has been limited to the cross-Channel hydrofoil. Pootling about with my sister and our dad in his day boat doesn't really count, as we were mainly trying to catch fish on a reservoir. Worlds apart from today's sailing, which was heavenly.'

'You seem to have a good constitution, not feeling nauseous.' Alex smiled at Leni. 'What did you enjoy, Jake?'

'Doing the fenders and I liked the spray on my face when I sat at the front and some waves came over the top.'

'What a tonic, eh, Jake?' Leni raised her glass and they clinked them all together.

Jake beamed with delight, his curly hair wild and unruly, and the freckles on his face and arms appearing to have multiplied by their thousands during the morning. 'Brilliant. I want to be a sailor when I grow up.'

'Well, here's to enjoying more trips together,' Alex said.

That's encouraging, Leni thought. He wants to do this again. Jake was clearly won over, and she must admit, she'd be more than happy to spend time with Alex in future.

The waiter arrived with their food. A number of seagulls circled overhead and swept close to the table, landing on the nearby wall. Used to London pigeons, Leni was surprised to see how large an adult gull was, in such close proximity.

'Keep an eye on your chips, Jake,' Alex said.

'Shoo. Go away.' Jake flapped his arm and the birds hopped a few steps back while keeping a beady eye on potential scraps from the other tables.

The day was going well. Leni liked the way Alex included Jake in every conversation and asked his opinion on subjects ranging from his best-ever ice-cream flavour to the greatest holidays he'd had.

Jake talked unselfconsciously about the time Will had taken him camping in Cornwall and the fun he had with cousins during the school breaks.

'What about you?' Leni asked Alex. 'Favourite beaches? Best places for catching fish from the boat?'

'I catch as much seaweed as mackerel in the Solent, I'm afraid.'

They ate, drank and laughed their way through lunch. Walking back to the marina, they stopped and Leni bought them all an ice-cream.

It was cloudy as they sailed back. Leni donned her puffer body-warmer and a spotted scarf to keep her hair from waving across her face. Although Jake moaned that he didn't feel cold, he consented to wear his hoody. Alex pulled a fraying wool jumper over his head.

'Guess this one's seen better days.' He laughed, poking his finger through a hole. 'Must go shopping one of these days.'

'It suits you, I like it.' Leni surprised herself, remembering how in the past, she'd be down to the nearest charity shop casting off Will's worn-out clothes.

They returned to the marina and Alex secured the boat in its berth.

'A cup of tea before you hit the road?'

'Lovely, thanks,' Leni said, removing her scarf and running a hand through her hair. A mirror would be useful now; she must look so dishevelled.

'I think I can even find some hot chocolate in the stores.' He fixed the swinging hob into its static position and put the kettle on. Although he was a big man he moved nimbly about the cabin.

'Cool,' Jake said, grinning with delight.

'And I can supply the biscuits.' Leni retrieved a packet of oat biscuits from her bag and held them aloft. 'Ta dah.'

Soon, the little cabin was steaming and Jake jumped up as soon as he finished his drink.

'Can I go and look at the other boats now?'

'Just be careful.' As she popped her head out of the cabin, she shielded her eyes from late afternoon sun which had burst forth on their return. She watched him onto the pontoon. 'Don't go far.'

Alex took her in his arms for a lingering kiss. Leni loved being enclosed in his warm and reassuring embrace, and melted into his strong frame. She felt a spasm of longing.

After a few minutes, she reluctantly pulled away. 'I could spend hours kissing you, but I can't relax with Jake roaming loose by the water.'

'Right,' he said, stroking her hair. 'When can I see you again?'

'Very soon. There's nothing I'd like better.'

After gathering her things together, she stepped down behind Alex onto the pontoon and spotted Jake on the neighbouring jetty.

'Time to go now,' she called out.

'Coming.' Jake raced along the swaying jetty.

'Slow down, Jake, best not to run,' Alex cautioned.

'Got everything?' Leni said aloud as she checked she had the car keys.

'Will you come again?' Alex shook hands with Jake.

'Yes, please. It was really cool.' Jake looked windswept and happy.

'It was really cool,' Alex repeated the sentiment as he hugged Leni. 'Talk soon.'

He walked them to their car and waved them off.

The evening sun had dissipated into a pale sky, the sunset brief and hazy. Looking in the rear-view mirror she watched Jake doze off, his head lolling to one side. She'd be ready for her bed too; she was so tired from the fun and adrenaline rush of the day. What Alex had said and done during the day replayed in her mind and she scrutinised her feelings towards him. They were growing hotter.

Leni opened the front door to find Kat dressed in an oversized, mohair, striped jumper and a pair of baggy boyfriend jeans. Blond hair escaped in wisps from the messy pile on her head. Somehow the effect made her look even more petite. She clutched a bottle of white wine.

Leni accepted the proffered bottle. 'I see you mean business.'

'I want every last detail.' Kat followed Leni into the kitchen and sat on a high stool at the island unit.

'So, tell all. I want to be the first to hear.' Kat hooked her feet on the metal bar and rested her elbows on the granite. 'How was Alex? Was he the perfect sailor? Did Jake enjoy it?'

An onslaught of questions came as Leni shook crisps into a wooden bowl and decanted green olives into a glazed dish with silver-rim. They were so cheap, she'd bought a load of them in different colours on holiday in Marrakech, years ago. How life has changed since then, she thought, sitting on the opposite bar stool for a gossip with her mate.

'It was wonderful, better than I could have imagined,' she said. 'Of course, the weather helped. The sea sparkled, the sky was blue, and Jake took to the whole thing like a duck to the proverbial.'

Leni popped an olive in her mouth and sucked her fingers clean of the oily residue and went to the Welsh dresser for napkins.

'How was Jake about you and Alex?' Kat swallowed a large swig of wine and took a handful of crisps. 'What were the sleeping arrangements? Did you have to field any embarrassing questions?'

Leni looked at her friend, brimming with anticipation, eating crisps, drinking wine and talking, all at the same time. She dodged the second question.

'It was all brilliant. Lymington looked pretty, but we only passed through on the way to the marina. We had a quick coffee, he gave us a safety briefing and explained where we were going, then we learnt how to tie the fenders on and raise the mainsail.'

'What are fenders?' Kat looked puzzled.

'Sausage-shaped white buoys to secure along the side of the boat,' Leni said. 'They stop the boat getting damaged at a pontoon. That's a floating walkway, before you ask, and there's a special way of tying ropes, which are called sheets, for some reason. Jake knew how to tie a few knots from Beavers and I got the hang quite well, so I didn't embarrass myself. We had to practise the knots before we set off so we wouldn't lose any overboard.'

Leni got cashew nuts from the cupboard and brought the wine over to replenish their glasses. 'My bottom's gone numb from sitting on these stools. Shall we sit on comfy chairs next door?' She moved their glasses and snacks onto a cerise pink, wooden tray.

Glancing at her mobile phone on the window ledge she saw that there were no messages. She could relax. Jake was in bed and she'd check on him a bit later, and Alex wouldn't ring without sending a text first. She liked his consideration.

'How do you keep this place so clean?' Kat kicked off her shoes and tucked her feet under her thighs on the oatmeal sofa. 'My house is such a mess.' She sighed, looking at the Jo Malone candles on the mantelpiece, pots filled with profusions of white orchids, and photos of Will and Jake in polished silver frames. Monty nonchalantly licked a paw as he lay in his tweed bed.

'I really admire how you've coped,' Kat continued. 'Death and moving house are two of the three most critical events people have to face in life.'

'You know I'm a bit OCD.' Leni laughed then became serious. 'Jake's my priority, helping him get through all this. That's kept me going and then, of course, meeting Alex. I've been lucky.'

'You deserve it,' Kat said, fidgeting with her hair. 'So, guess what my news is?'

'Spit it out.'

'Connell's been in touch again.'

'What?'

'He wants me to visit him, in Dublin. What do you think?'

'That's brilliant – you should go. I'd have Mikey when Rachel covers at the shop.'

'What about your house being on the market? Would that be awkward for viewings?'

'I'd have a crazy, whizz-round in the boys' bedroom squirting a copious amount of air freshener in there.' Leni laughed. 'Anyway, prospective buyers are after a family house, aren't they?'

'It always looks gorgeous to me.'

'I'd take the boys for an outing. I've been told it won't take long to sell and I'm keen to move, so I'm open to offers.'

'Do you have to rush things?' Kat's brow creased. 'You'll need all the money you can get for it, as the next bit of your life is insecure. You can't live on savings for too long.'

'You're right, but I feel so much more optimistic.' Leni refilled their glasses, bubbles of happiness welling up inside her as she thought about the future, her new home with Jake and her life, with Alex in it. 'Anyway, going back to Connell—'

'No, hang on a mo, you still haven't answered my question.' Kat scrunched her hair into a messy bun, securing it with a colourful band. 'Did you and Alex sleep together?'

'We didn't end up staying on board. It was just a day sail. Jake and I went back to Mum's for the night.' Leni's cheeks flushed. 'Not that I didn't think about it.' She laughed. 'I'll fix up another date when Jake's with his cousins. In a few weeks' time. I expect it'll be a lot colder, probably need my thermals.'

'Ha!' Kat guffawed. 'That sounds romantic, bobbing up and down on the briny, squeezed into a tight cabin. I can't get over how you've changed, Leni. It used to be all five star and haute cuisine, and you wouldn't be seen dead roughing it.'

'Well, there's something refreshing about that, not having to appear flawless and have the perfect life. It'd become a bit of an act for me and Will, keeping up with the Joneses, and having all the latest things, in order to fit in.'

'I know what you mean. It's self-perpetuating. Being a single parent and not having a trust fund, I've never had to compete like that.'

'Kat, you're the most socially conscious person I know. You put me to shame when I think of all that material stuff we coveted.'

'Is Connell like Will, do you think? Is he concerned about how others view him? He seems to be his own man.'

'He's self-assured, and quite opinionated, but you'll never have a dull conversation with him. Connell can talk about anything, to anyone, at any time.'

'Well, I could listen to his Irish accent all day,' Kat said, draining her glass and slipping her Keds back on. 'I've had such disasters with men on the internet. It's so much nicer to have a personal introduction. I automatically feel I can trust that he is what he says he is.'

'I'm really pleased for you.' Leni smiled. 'Do you reckon men talk about women as much as we do?'

'No, but it's time I went. My neighbour's daughter is with Mikey and I promised I wouldn't be late.'

'I feel a bit sad,' Leni said. 'I'm going to miss all our chats.'

'Hey, now.' Kat hugged her friend. 'I'll be down to stay so often, you'll be sick of the sight of me.'

Leni closed the door behind Kat and returned to the kitchen to make a cheese omelette. After watching the news, she cleared up and let Monty out for a few minutes. After checking on Jake as she passed his room, she got ready for bed. Finding it challenging to calm her stimulated thoughts, she jotted down a list of notes, turned the radio dial to quiet classical music, and read her book until her eyelids started drooping. Tomorrow was another day and would take her closer to a new life.

September was busy. Leni took Imogen to see Forsythia Cottage and put an offer in. Four couples were keen to buy the Chiswick house and within weeks there was a bidding war between two of them. Demand's outstripping supply, said the agent, making sure he negotiated the best deal possible, with an eye to the percentage he'd get from the sale.

One Friday, when she wasn't working, Leni took Jake out of school to meet Mrs Grayling, head teacher of Pewsey Primary School. First they were escorted into a cookery class to watch children making a batch of cheese scones. They were then introduced to the geography teacher. Jake was astonished to see a live parrot in a cage.

'My class are drawing maps of South America and we're learning about the animals that live in rainforests.' He ushered Jake forwards. 'Do you want to meet our pet parakeet?'

Jake blushed, seeing the children looking at him, and took a step closer to the bright green bird.

'Hello.'

'Hello,' the bird mimicked and skittered excitedly from side to side on his perch. 'Got any seeds? Got any seeds?'

The teacher tossed a few sunflower seeds into the cage. 'His ancestors come from Brazil and we're studying the food these birds like and what type of habitat they live in. Do you like birds?'

'We have hundreds in Kensington Park. They make lots of noise and my mum says people don't like them being there. I like dogs. We have a dog called Monty.'

'What food does he like best?'

'He loves biscuits and does a little rollover before wolfing down his dinner.'

The children laughed and Jake looked pleased. They said goodbye, looked into the dining room and, lastly, visited the vegetable plot outside.

'The children love to grow things that they can eat in the canteen.' Mrs Grayling bent down, examining the leaves on the potato plants. 'Which vegetables do you like, Jake?'

'I like most things, especially spinach. It makes you strong.'

'That's right.' She stood up. 'Well, it was lovely to meet you both and I hope we'll see you here, soon.'

Leni and Jake said goodbye and went to the car, parked outside the perimeter metal railings.

'What did you think of it?' Leni checked her rear-view mirror as she drove away. 'They looked like they were having fun, didn't they?'

'I didn't like their sweatshirts, but I liked the tyre and log activity thingy. I think I will grow some vegetables.'

That sounded promising. She asked what club or activities he'd like to do in Pewsey.

'I want to do football first, then sailing, and I'd like a BMX bike, for tricks.'

'Football, of course, and we can think about a bike. What about having a kitten when we live in the country? Would you like that?'

'Yes, I want a cat.' He bounced up and down in his seat. 'Can it sleep on my bed?'

'A cat needs its own bed but they often choose a warm spot where they're most comfortable. You'd need to take care of it and be careful introducing it to Monty. His nose might be a bit out of joint?'

'What does that mean?'

'Well, he may feel like we don't love him as much any more, getting a new pet.'

'I love him to pieces and I can love two animals, Mummy.'

'Yes, darling, we can love lots of people, and things, at one time.' Leni patted his knee, feeling positive about getting a cat and, more importantly, that the school looked welcoming and Jake seemed happy with it. Fingers crossed, the house sale and cottage purchase would go smoothly. There were so many threads to pull together to make it all work. Just one slip in the process and the whole chain would fall apart.

They were silent, lost in their own thoughts, as the miles flew by.

'How much longer?' Jake asked. 'Shall we play I spy?'

# 15

Leni had been up for two hours when the removal van pulled up at 8am. As soon as any of her neighbours' cars had departed she'd been out with orange cones to secure the space for it. She watched her breath in the frosty atmosphere. Thank God it was dry. Two heavily built men jumped out from the cab and made a recce of the rooms, asking Leni about access at the other end and noting any extra heavy, or fragile, items. Boxes were stacked high in the sitting room. It was strange how her home had become just the shell of a building. She felt quite detached. Perhaps the packing-up process and sorting of accumulated stuff from a marriage had leached her emotions as each object was regarded, saved or discarded. She'd felt pangs of sadness going through photograph albums, then euphoric, wrapping up an abhorrent *objet d'art* that Will had inherited from an aunt. What a joy that had been, to box it up for the charity shop.

'The house contents are straightforward, then there are a few pots and tools to come from the garden,' she said, pulling her sleeves up and pushing her hair off her face. She must look a state. Exhaustion was kept at bay with adrenaline.

Jake wandered into the kitchen, sleepy and blinking.

'Hi Jake. This is Pete and Craig. They're going to load up the lorry starting from upstairs. Be careful not to let Monty in. I've shut him in the garden.'

'Won't he be cold?' Jake peered out from the back door window to see the dog nosing in the bushes.

'It won't be for long, and he's got a fur coat, remember?'

'Where's the cereal gone?' Jake asked, no longer appearing concerned about the dog.

'Beside the cool bag. Everything we need is in there, so keep an eye on it.' Leni pulled out a jar of coffee and turned to the men. 'Do you want a hot drink before starting?'

'No, we'll have the van loaded within a couple of hours. We'll have it then, with our sarnies.'

She led them upstairs, showing them the furniture, lamps and boxes in each room. In the guest room she stopped. 'Those green sacks in the corner, with labels on, are for my car. I'll move them in a minute.' She felt guilty that she hadn't got them to the charity shop before it closed yesterday, but would nip them in shortly, as she set off. She reckoned she'd still be ahead of the van, which would be going at a more sedate pace.

After standing at the door of Jake's room, looking at it for one last time, she gathered her energy to strip his bed, stuffing his duvet and pillow into a blue Ikea bag. He came in as she was stowing his reading lamp between the padded contents.

'If you go brush your teeth and run the flannel over your face, I can pack the last few things in here. It'll mean you're all set at the other end and we won't have to look through hundreds of boxes to find your overnight stuff for your room.'

Jake looked troubled. 'What if I don't like it there, Mummy?'

She knelt down and held his arms. 'I hope you'll like it,

darling. It'll take a bit of adjustment but you've already shown how brave you are, without Daddy. We'll look after one another.

'It's OK to be nervous about new things.' She helped him on with his tee-shirt. 'You'll be closer to your cousins and once we've settled in we'll buy that kitten.'

'I'm going to call him Billy.'

'We'd better make sure we get a boy then.' She laughed and stood up. Loud voices and hefty footfall could be heard on the stairs as her mobile pinged. It was a message from Kat.

> Best of luck today, girl. Ring when you can,
> to say you're OK.

What a dear friend Kat had become over four years. She fantasised about how lovely it would be if Kat and Connell got together; she'd be so happy for her. She pinged a thumbs-up emoji in reply.

'Can you help load some bags into the car with me please, Jake?'

They stowed the overnight bags in the boot and put the green sacks on the back seat. Jake played with his Nintendo, sitting on the car rug in an empty sitting room, as Leni moved the last few herb pots from the garden to the front path. Despite the coldness of the house with no heating on, she was sweating profusely by the time she finished running a damp cloth across all the windowsills and skirting boards.

She checked her watch and put the kettle on. 'I'm making tea now, if you'd like one?' she called to the men, swiping a hand across her forehead.

Pete and Craig accepted tea and ginger biscuits, which they bolted down in minutes.

'Thanks.' Pete put his empty mug down on the counter.

'Last few items now, Mrs Parsons. We should be good to go at 11am.'

'Great. I'll whizz round with the vacuum in the rooms you've cleared.'

When everything was finished, she asked Jake to put Monty in his crate and wait in the car. She did a final inspection of the rooms. 'Goodbye, home. We've had great joy and sadness, here.'

After waving off the removal men, Leni and Jake dropped the bags to the charity shop then drove to the estate agents to deposit the house keys. There was a nerve-wracking few minutes while they waited to hear that the money had gone through and the sale had completed. She telephoned the Pewsey agents to confirm the Forsythia Cottage completion was still on target for 1pm, and with some trepidation that it would all go smoothly, they set off for the M4.

In the new house, they emptied boxes, made up beds and stowed crockery away. Later, they walked with Monty to the chip shop. They flopped down on the sofa and ate the hot chips straight from the paper, Monty sitting at Jake's feet in the hope of catching a morsel. Leni gathered up the greasy papers, stuffed them into the kitchen bin and washed her hands. Unable to locate a towel, she wiped her fingers on a clean tea-towel.

'Take yourself off for a bath and I'll be up in a minute.'

She looked out of the window, glass of red wine to hand, and dialled Kat's number.

'We've arrived. And I'm shattered.'

'Have you got the heating working and hot water on? What's it like?'

'It's cosy but we are in chaos. Boxes seem to have multiplied and there are pictures to hang and books to shelve, that sort of thing. It'll take days.'

'Don't worry, it's only five days to Christmas,' Kat joked. 'Seriously, take your time. It's not a race to get it all as you want it. Is Jake OK?'

'A bit overwhelmed, I'd say.'

'Is your mum coming?'

'Not sure when, yet. We've got Christmas and Boxing Day at Fran's, then Jake's at Mum's for a couple of nights. How are you doing?'

'We've been busy with end-of-term stuff and Christmas, like you, and we had a manic Saturday at the shop. Quite a few blokes came in and most of the handbags have sold.'

'No wonder. You have a great eye for what people want.'

'Thanks.' Kat put on a posh voice. 'Well, it's exclusive, one-of-a-kind, isn't it?'

'Like you are.'

Kat laughed. 'We'll be down for February half-term. Is that still alright?'

'That feels aeons away, but it'll soon come round. If I get cravings, I'll call you to wallow in London memories. But I'd better go now, Jake's in the bath. Give Mikey a kiss from me.'

'Will do, love. Goodbye.'

Leni drained her glass and gave it a cursory rinse under the tap. Smiling at this newly found, carefree attitude to her standards, she went upstairs.

'I found the bubble bath.' Jake was covered head to toe in soap suds, his face beaming from a halo of bubbles.

'So I see. Can you rinse off now? I think we both need to get to bed.' She pulled a towel from the hooks. 'Shall we go Christmas shopping for the cousins tomorrow?'

'Awesome. Will we get a tree, too?'

'As long as you help me find the decorations.'

'Deal.' Jake stepped out of the bath, water dripping all over the floor. Leni wrapped him up in the towel and rubbed his back, arms and legs vigorously. She handed him his pyjamas. 'Brush your teeth and I'll be in to say goodnight shortly.'

Leni went to her bedroom and pulled the curtains shut. It seemed so much colder in the country. The light outside was different to what she was used to, and she listened for noise of traffic and people. She resolved to check the loft insulation and, shivering, she took her wash-bag, nightie and slippers from her overnight bag and left them in the bathroom. The hot water had better be plentiful so she could top up Jake's bath. A quick dip was all she had energy for tonight.

The next day, they went into town to buy groceries and contributions for Fran's Christmas Day lunch. On the way home they stopped at the large garden centre to buy a small Norwegian spruce tree and new fairy lights. Searching among unpacked boxes, she found the bag of decorations and they dressed the tree with garlands, baubles and seasonal figurines. It looked rather basic compared to the flamboyant display she used to make in Chiswick, but she was too tired to care. Who's going to see it, anyway? She hid Jake's new skateboard in her bedroom cupboard.

They spent the next couple of days exploring and getting the house straight. When she was ready to drop, Leni suggested a trip to the cinema for the latest *Ice Age* film. Anything for a quiet couple of hours, no decisions to make, and a chance to recoup her energy in a darkened space.

On Christmas Eve, when Jake slept, she stuffed a comic, chocolate coins, and a box of Lego into his stocking. She delighted in this annual ritual as she tiptoed into his room to leave it on his bed. Her heart filled with love, watching his chest gently rise and fall, eyelashes lying soft on his cheek. My beautiful child, my lifeblood. Taking a mug of herbal tea to her bed, she read a novel for a few minutes before switching off the light. Tomorrow would be a busy day, and despite loving spending time with her family, she felt exhausted from the move, and doubted she had any reserves for witty conversation.

The next morning, Jake dashed into her room. 'Hey, Mum? This is the Battletron spaceship I wanted.' He clutched the Lego.

'So your letter to Father Christmas arrived?' Leni rubbed sleep from her eyes and clocked that it was 6.30am. 'Jump into bed and keep warm.'

He climbed into her bed and they looked at the instructions on the box.

'Best make it on the kitchen table. Some pieces might get lost in here,' she said, enjoying a brief hug before he clambered out of the bed and rushed off. 'Get your slippers and dressing gown on. I'll be down in a second.'

Leni thrust her arms into her cashmere dressing gown, slipped a pair of leg warmers on and sank her chilly feet into her Ugg short boots. Heavenly. She must get to grips with the timer on the heating system. It shouldn't be complicated to set it. They ate porridge, and between mouthfuls of toast with honey, Jake fiddled with the Lego to complete the model.

'Happy Christmas, Monty.' Leni held out a new squeaky toy. The dog sniffed it and whisked it away for closer inspection.

'How's it going?' she asked.

'Nearly finished. Can I take it to show Luke and Cecily?'

'Of course. Just remember to bring it home so you can play with it.'

Leni cleared the breakfast things and went to shower. After dressing and fixing her hair, she dialled Alex's number, feeling like a nervous teenager.

'Happy Christmas.'

'Happy Christmas, Leni, and to Jake, too. Are you getting on OK? Feeling a bit more like home?'

She told him about the house and asked him about work. 'Are you still on for doing something on 28th?'

'Looking forward to it,' he said, a smile in his voice.

'Me too, as long as everything's OK with Mum.' She watched a neighbour load bags into his Audi and when his wife came out, wearing a pale sheepskin coat, they both got into the car and drove away. 'When are you seeing the children?'

'I'm picking them up this afternoon and I've got to get them back for the panto in Swindon on 27th. Then they'll stay at my parents' for a few nights from New Year's Day.'

'It's great that they still enjoy panto.'

'Chloe goes under duress, but I think she quite enjoys it.'

'I'm in West Wittering for New Year, then we'll get geared up for new school and new job. Help!'

'Anything on the horizon?'

'I've approached a jewellers and am meeting a gallery owner on the 29th. There might not be any openings at either and I guess it may take weeks. In the meantime, I'll get Jake settled and hopefully meet some of the mums at his school.' She tried not to sound anxious, but what if there weren't any local job opportunities? She'd have to cast her net further afield and be prepared to commute. Work needed to fit in with school hours, although Jake could attend the after-school club, but that was another cost to consider, and depended on how much she'd be earning, for it to work.

'It's lovely to hear your voice again,' Alex said. 'I've really missed you.'

'And yours, too.' Leni's heart soared at his admission. 'Let's speak on 27th to firm up plans.'

She went downstairs, wrapped the chestnut stuffing she'd made in greaseproof paper and foil, and put the presents into a brown leather holdall she'd given Will for Christmas a few years previously. She had mixed emotions. Happy, having spoken to Alex, but at the same time, unhappy, for Jake's first Christmas without his father. It seemed like a lifetime ago since Will died. She wasn't upset not to be spending time with her in-laws over the holidays but she'd have to take Jake to see them at some point soon. He should keep up with both sets of cousins, really, but it didn't help that they tried to lord it over Jake with their horse-riding prowess, chess skills, and frequent ski holidays. Or maybe that was just Will's take on things, and some of his hurt and inferiority complex had rubbed off on her. She would ask Jake if he wanted to go or just wait for an invitation from Thomas. Let sleeping dogs lie and all that.

'Ready, Jake?' she called out, slinging a coat over her arm and picking up the dog lead. 'There you are, Monty.' She stroked his head and slipped him a dog biscuit. 'Christmas, here we come.'

After locking the front door, Leni glanced up and down the road. It was so quiet. Where was everyone? All indoors, prepping veg like crazy, knocking back their favourite tipple? Whatever her neighbours were doing, she was certain they'd be gearing up for the roller-coaster ride that this special time of year brings to so many families.

She was pleasantly surprised at the lack of traffic on their journey to Lower Chute. After thirty minutes they pulled into Fran and Hugh's driveway, and another noisy family celebration got underway. During the days and nights they spent together, there was much eating, drinking, laughing and reminiscing. The children took delight in their new toys and they played boisterous rounds of charades and board games in front of the fire. They walked the dogs in frost-laden fields and visited the Hawk Conservancy Trust to learn about birds of prey. After breakfast on 27th December, Leni said goodbye.

'Have fun with the cousins,' she said, hugging Jake tight.

'Are you taking Monty?'

'Yes, it's not fair to ask Fran to have him, as well as you.' She laughed. 'I'll bring him to Granny's, so you'll see him in a couple of days.' It was great that his apparent concern was to see the dog again, rather than needing her.

'I'm going to meet a gallery owner to talk about a possible job.' There was no need to mention that she'd be seeing Alex, too. 'Be good.'

Pot, kettle, and black, came to mind as she said it.

# 16

Monty started yapping at the sound of the doorbell. Leni glanced into the sitting room on her way to the front door. Candles reflected sparkly light in the over-mantel mirror and the fire in the log-burner crackled. It looked so pretty and the burner was brilliant, sending out masses of heat into the room. Her heart pounded as she opened the door.

Wrapped up in a green Barbour and a woollen scarf, Alex beamed and said hello. He had an overnight bag slung over his shoulder, a bottle bag over one wrist and a large, gift-wrapped box balanced in both hands. His rugged good looks captivating her once again.

'Hi Alex, come in,' Leni said, watching her puffs of breath in the frosty air, and her excitement increasing as she gazed at him. 'Shall I take that?' What on earth could this be?

'How was your Christmas at Fran's?' he said, shrugging off his coat and scarf, and hanging them on the rack. 'Did you have a good time?' Dropping his bag, he went to stroke the dog. Monty responded with enthusiasm, wagging his tail and rolling over for a tummy rub.

'Lots of fun. Exhausting, too, with so many of us all together,' she said, leaving the box on the coffee table and pulling an expensive-looking bottle of Malbec from its casing. 'My favourite, thank you. I've made some mulled wine or would you prefer whisky, or beer?'

'Mulled wine sounds perfect. Can I wish you a Happy Christmas, first?' He enveloped her in a close hug and kissed her tenderly.

She stroked his back as he ran his hand over her hair. His body felt strong and muscular, and a flicker of anticipation whipped through her, a visceral reaction to his smell and rugged manliness.

'Mmm, and a very Happy Christmas to you, too.' Did her mouth taste of the wine she'd sampled minutes ago?

'It's been too long since that sailing trip to Cowes. I'm sorry we couldn't find another day to go out since then.'

'Me too. These past months have been incredibly full-on with the move.' She kicked herself for letting so much time elapse, when he brought such promise of pleasure.

'Perhaps you could come again in the spring?'

'I'd love to.' That's a good sign; he's thinking ahead.

He smiled. 'I'd almost forgotten how gorgeous you are.'

'Flattery will get you everywhere.' She smiled, not minding his naïve chat-up line. 'How was your Christmas?'

'It was fine.'

That sounded hesitant. She'd been so beside herself with excitement about tonight, just the two of them together, that she decided not to press him for details. There would be time later if he wanted to expand on it.

'Make yourself at home by the fire – I won't be a moment.' Leni went to the kitchen and brought in a tray of nibbles and wine. They sat close together on the sofa and swapped stories.

Alex scooped dip onto a carrot baton. 'Aren't you going to open your present?'

Leni pulled the ribbon from the box and lifted the lid revealing an antique, oval, copper bucket lying in white tissue paper.

'It's beautiful.' She held the handle and turned it to see all sides. What was it for?

'It would've been used for cooking or carrying things in the early nineteenth century, but I think it'd make an attractive planter? It's the same period as the house.'

'Yes, it's striking,' she said, picturing it filled with waxy, yellow daffodils on a window ledge. 'Thank you.'

She passed him a small parcel, embarrassment flooding her. 'I've only got you a little something, I'm afraid. For the boat.'

He pulled two blue and white striped porcelain mugs from bubble wrap. 'I like the anchor and compass details. We'll use them when you next come aboard.'

They looked so measly compared to his thoughtful present. She'd have to do better next time. Would they still be seeing each other next Christmas?

'Want to come and see the kitchen?' Leni collected the debris and carried the tray out. 'Are you hungry?'

He peered closely at a couple of pictures on his way through the hall. 'These are pretty,' he said, stopping in front of two watercolours depicting Indian palaces.

'Mum gave them to me when Dad died. They lived close by.' She imagined that he probably had a good knowledge of art and wondered what he made of her pieces. 'I love them.'

'What an experience, spending time in India. You'll have to tell me more.'

'Wish I could remember more,' she said, filling a glass carafe with water.

'This is a nice kitchen. I like its simplicity.' He wandered over to the pin board of photos and leaflets, and then examined one of her vintage vases. 'Can I help?'

'No need, just a few minutes for this,' she said, pouring boiling water onto couscous. She wanted to appear unflappable. 'It's a tagine. I hope you haven't got any allergies?' She put the tagine dish on a metal rack and pulled a bowl of yoghurt and cut limes from the fridge.

'No. I eat almost everything, although I've never been presented with sheep eyes or animal brains.'

'No kidding.' Leni remembered the Malbec. 'Shall we have your wine?'

'If you're happy to have it now?' Alex went to collect it from the sitting room.

They sat down to eat and talked about the popularity of celebrity chefs. She asked him if he liked to cook.

'I'm good at a few staples, curry and a roast, that kind of thing, but it's not much fun cooking for one.' Alex squeezed lime over his food. 'Did you eat in all the fashionable restaurants when you lived in London?'

'In the early days, yes,' Leni drank some wine, watching him savour a mouthful of her signature dish, 'but when Will got more senior, he attended so many work functions, he didn't always want to go out on other evenings. We stopped appreciating everything that London had to offer.'

'Expensive, too?'

'Yes, and Will got more fretful about money. I didn't know why—' She stopped abruptly.

Alex spoke softly. 'It must have been difficult.'

'It was hard for Jake. He had a close relationship with his dad. It was tough when Will became withdrawn and less present. Jake thought he'd done something wrong.'

'Does he understand now, about what was going on?'

'I told him that Will was under a lot of pressure at work and how sad we were not being able to have another baby. I reassured him of our love and said we were trying to work things out. He can ask questions when he's older, if he needs to make sense of it.'

'You're a marvellous mother to Jake. He's a lovely little boy.'

'Thank you.' She jumped up with the empty plates to hide her blushing cheeks. 'It's tough being a single parent. Fran and Mum have been amazing.'

'I guess fractured families are the norm these days.'

Leni loaded the dishwasher. 'Did you hope to find someone else after your breakup?' May as well ask. She'd shared something of herself, after all.

'I enjoyed some dates but didn't go looking for a serious relationship. My work and the children became my focus. In time, I realised I enjoyed my own company, could make my own plans, but there was an empty place in my heart. I put a sticking plaster on the wound.'

He hesitated, but Leni didn't rush to fill the silence. She admired him for sharing this poignant revelation.

'The pain over the divorce, well, I didn't reckon on it being so intense. I felt such a failure,' Alex said quietly, looking at the floor.

Leni felt a surge of sympathy at his candid admission.

He continued, 'Whereas for you, there was the shock of death, no time to prepare and no goodbyes. That's also very hard to come to terms with.'

'The shock was dreadful, but it was the lies that hurt, and

made me angry. I've wrestled with the thought that I should've foreseen things. I was too self-centred.' Putting the kettle on and drawing herself tall, she changed tack. She was not going to beat herself up any more on what she could, or should, have done differently. 'Time to look forward and make new plans.'

'Too right.'

'Coffee? Brandy?' Leni got out mugs and looked at the bottles in the cupboard. 'Or I've got Calvados?' She put everything on a tray. It was time to push the past away and enjoy the moment.

'Yes to Calvados. Let me carry that through,' he said, picking up the tray.

They drank their coffee, enjoying the last of the fire. She wondered how the next bit was going to work. She didn't want him thinking that she expected to sleep with him. Or vice versa but it was definitely what she wanted. The time felt so right.

'I'll show you your room.'

Alex collected his bag from the hall and followed her upstairs to the spare room. He pulled her close. 'I've loved being with you tonight, Leni.' He bent his head to kiss her.

Leni hungrily kissed him, feeling him harden as she tilted her pelvis into his hips. She led him to her room where they peeled off each other's clothes between passionate kisses. Falling onto the bed, Leni slid away the sheets and entwined her body with his. She cried out with pleasure as she felt him thrust into her.

Afterwards, she lay quietly, a blissful tingling in every nerve ending. Startled to feel so utterly at ease, she felt languid, like she needn't rush to the bathroom to clean up, or break the spell with words. Minutes passed and she felt his chest heave less deeply. Their breathing slowed.

Alex shifted position to face her and he stroked her hair.

'Do you plan on banishing me to the other room now?'

'I'd like you to stay.'

'Thank goodness. Kick me if I snore?'

'Do you?' She laughed, enjoying his unpretentious attitude.

'I sincerely hope not.' He kissed her.

In the morning, they made love again, discovering each other's bodies slowly and tenderly. Leni shed tears.

'What's wrong?' Alex stroked her back.

'I'm happy.' It was an odd feeling, euphoria and poignancy combined. How could she express that? 'It's bliss to feel satisfied. I've kept my sexual longings at bay and you've reignited them.'

'That's good, right?' He grinned.

'Very good,' Leni said, nuzzling into his chest.

After breakfast, they took Monty for a walk. The sky was cobalt blue and a hard frost made the pavements glisten in the sun. They took a path that led towards the river. Leni mentioned her first visit to the cinema.

'The nearest one is in Devizes or Andover. Jake was incredulous having to go in the car. He was used to walking to the multiplex.'

'I can imagine. There'll be other things like that, that he'll have to adjust to.'

Leni let Monty off the lead as they reached the field. 'You must've had to make huge adjustments when you and Heather split?'

'The worst thing was not seeing the kids every day. Missing little snippets of conversation about their friends, or what they'd done at school. I missed them, dreadfully.'

Leni squeezed his hand. 'That must've broken your heart.'

'It's better now, as we've all got used to the routine. I'm close to Jamie still, but Chloe is harder to read. She internalises a lot and doesn't talk as freely with me. But maybe, that's normal teenage behaviour?'

'I'd say so. As a girl I would always confide in my mum, before going to my dad,' Leni said, then whistled for Monty, who'd raced ahead.

'I'd love you to meet them,' Alex said. 'We could go to the cinema, or out for a meal together?'

'I think choosing a film may be hard with their differing ages, trying to find something that they'd all enjoy.' Leni kept the surprise from her voice. She'd introduced Jake to Alex when Alex was just a friend, but now that they'd slept together, meeting his children took on greater significance.

'Right. It's too cold to sail, and anyway, Chloe's totally bored with that.' Alex frowned. 'How about ten pin bowling? Do you think Jake would like it? More to the point, would you?'

'He went once, for someone's birthday. I can't say it's my thing, but I'll have a go. Where is it?'

'There's one in Swindon. We've been quite a few times.'

Monty returned and Leni put him back on the lead to walk home. 'Jake and I could get a train from Pewsey and meet you there?'

'I'd pick the kids up from their mum in Chiseldon. It's on the way from mine, or would you prefer to meet up first and get the children together?'

'Might be awkward for them, my meeting their mum at the same time as our first encounter?' This was going a little fast. They'd only just made love and now she was about to meet not only his children, but his ex-wife.

'Right. Didn't think properly.' He squeezed her hand. 'Bit flustered, to be honest.'

'It's OK,' she said. She wouldn't admit she felt nervous, too.

'I'll look into it,' he said. 'Let me know which Saturday works for you in January?'

They followed the groove in the path to return home.

Alex collected his things and as they enjoyed a prolonged hug, Leni revelled in his radiating warmth. He felt solid and dependable, and she liked the way he inhabited his clothes, not appearing self-conscious or trying too hard.

It was quiet after he'd gone. She could still smell him in her bedroom as she went to change for the interview. Her thighs ached and she smiled at the memory, idly wondering if she'd have cystitis after all that love-making. Just thinking about it gave her a warm glow in her belly.

It was an informal meeting with the gallery owner but she wanted to make the right impression. What to wear? Choosing studded biker boots and a bright, geometric scarf, she pulled on tight black jeans and fastened her red mohair jacket. With a slick of lip gloss, she was good to go.

# 17

After walking through town with a smile on her face, Leni reached the gallery. Michael opened the door, wiping his hands on a paint-spattered cloth. He wore old ripped jeans and his blue Guernsey sweater looked well lived-in, with patches at the elbow. When he spoke, his craggy face lit up and voluminous grey hair shook. His deep, gravelly voice reminded her of Richard Burton, reciting Dylan Thomas poetry. It was a joy to listen to.

'Hi, come in. I was just finishing off a canvas, didn't notice the time.'

'I hope it's not a bad time for you to stop?'

'It's fine. I'm changing the stock around after Christmas and want new canvasses out front. This needs to dry. Shall we go through?'

He led her into the back studio. There was newspaper all over the floor and cans and tubes of paint on every surface. Pots of brushes and bottles of turps were jammed onto a metal trolley in the corner. Canvasses leant against the walls and two were fastened on tall easels.

'I work rather frenetically, as you can see. I like to have one or two paintings on the go at once.' He pulled a swivel office chair towards her and sat opposite on an oak throne-like chair. 'Tell me a little bit about yourself.'

Leni launched into her story about moving to Pewsey, the one she'd rehearsed earlier.

Michael told her about his customers, the hours of work and pay.

'Will you need me on Saturdays?' She dreaded that he might and wondered if she should quickly say she wasn't readily available.

'That's negotiable. My wife sometimes comes in on Saturday and we're closed on a Wednesday, like a few other shops here.'

'I hoped to spend weekends with Jake, but he can go to his cousins if you need me occasionally.'

'Is four days a week what you had in mind?'

'It's perfect, as I am training as a silversmith, so Wednesdays can be dedicated to studying and practising my craft.'

'When does your son start school?'

'Tuesday 4th January.'

'Seems like I've found my new assistant then.' He stood up and shook her hand. 'So, would you like to start on 6th January?'

Taking in the room, its contents and atmosphere, she felt a rush of thankfulness. Michael seemed lively, an interesting character, and the studio literally dripped with creativity. She could walk to work and have time for her own creative endeavours. Money would be tight, though. She'd need to do her accounts to see about household bills and cost of living. Monty would need letting out during the day but maybe, in time, Michael might let her bring the dog to the gallery. He was well behaved and the customers might like seeing him. She wouldn't ask him now.

Back at home, she made a sandwich and sat at the table with the Radio 3 afternoon concert playing quietly in the background. She made notes and entered dates on her phone. She searched online for a Wednesday Pilates or yoga class and researched Stagecoach Performing Arts in Marlborough. She'd better check that Jake wanted to do it first. Maybe Mum would help out financially with that. In a minute she'd unpack the last few boxes then enjoy a long soak in the bath. Tomorrow she would leave for West Wittering at 9am to avoid Winchester rush hour. A few days with Mum and Jake, then the school holidays would be over and she and Jake would face their new challenges.

Jake slung his Star Wars rucksack over his shoulder and slammed the car door. Minibuses pulled into a bay at the front of the school and parents found spaces to pull up, away from the prohibited zone. A lollipop lady stood sentry beside the traffic lights ready to step forwards and shepherd her precious charges across the road. Leni put her hand on Jake's arm, but he shrugged it off.

'Hey Mum, I can cross by myself.'

'Sorry, old habit.' She had butterflies in her stomach as if it were her first day at a new school. 'I'll just come in to say hello to your head teacher, OK?'

'See you later,' Jake said, looking awkward, before jostling through the door with other pupils. The Reception and Year One children filing in looked so young in comparison.

The hallway was covered in bright posters and student art, stories and photographs. There was a strong smell of lino floor polish as she stood at Reception waiting to have a word with Mrs Grayling.

'You wanted to see me?' The head teacher came into the

hall and shook hands with Leni. 'Come in,' she said, holding the door open.

'Thank you. I appreciated your email. Jake sometimes appears to act strong, but I'm anxious about him settling in, particularly as the other friendship groups will be well-established by now.'

'We had some new students in the September term and will have another child joining us in the Summer Term. I've put him with David, who's a very caring boy, and he'll be his buddy to show him the ropes. I'll also ask Jake's teacher to keep an eye out and will let you know how he got on at the end of this week.'

Mrs Grayling stood, indicating that Leni's time was up and she had things to attend to.

'Thank you.' Leni walked back to her car. Further along the pavement she saw a group of parents talking and wondered if, in time, any of them would become her friends. She wanted to fit in, just like children do. It's the outsider, the child who is seen as different, who gets picked on and has a hard time. She'd read about the school's anti-bullying policies and knew that staff were better equipped these days, than in her school years, to spot anything suspicious. Jake should be fine. After all, he'd been used to a large mixed London school.

She reached her car just as a woman in a faux leopard-skin coat and beanie hat drew level. Wisps of blond hair rested on her collar.

'Hello there. I saw you coming out of Mrs Grayling's office. Are you the mum of the new Year 3 boy?'

'Yes, my son's name is Jake.'

'I'm Naomi, David's mum. Welcome to St Richard's. It's a great school with a thriving PTA, so if you're thinking of joining, it's a great way to meet lots of the other parents?'

'Yes, I probably will, thanks. My name's Leni.'

'Nice to meet you. David is Jake's buddy this week.'

Leni looked around her. 'Are those the herb boxes that the children planted up?'

'Yes. They grow all sorts.'

'Jake likes gardening.'

'He'll enjoy that then. They have Mr White in Year 4 and he's very popular. He initiated the school allotment where they grow larger veg. It's been a really good enterprise to encourage healthy eating – the kids love it.'

'We heard about that on our visit.' Leni sensed that Naomi wanted to get away. 'Thank David from me for being Jake's buddy.'

'I will. I've got to dash. See you at pick up?'

'Yes, see you later.' Leni sat in her car for a few minutes thinking about what Naomi had said and also about the house, Jake's new school, and possibly new friends for her, too. She supposed she could add a boyfriend into the mix, too. It reminded her to send Alex a text asking him for supper at the weekend, if he didn't have the children. It wouldn't be long before she and Jake were going to meet Chloe and Jamie, and it would help if Jake felt relaxed in Alex's company. She had a couple of days to herself then she'd start her new job. There was a knot of anxiety in her stomach and she recognised that it was the thought of doing something new, and wanting to do well in the post. She'd walk Monty to burn off some of her inner turmoil and research online jewellery courses. There was much to be excited about.

# 18

Pewsey station was busy on Saturday morning as Leni and Jake stood on the platform for the Swindon train. Once on, Jake bundled his puffer coat into her hands and bagged the window seat. She stowed it on the overhead rack and put her brown leather gloves and beret in her handbag. She began to thaw out after the freezing wind on the platform. The train lurched forwards.

'How long's the journey?' Jake said, fixing his gaze on his Nintendo.

'Just over an hour.' She put her magazine and his comic on the table and pushed his rucksack behind her feet. Her stomach was jittery already.

'How long will we be with them?'

'About an hour bowling, then we'll have some lunch, I imagine?' It sounded laid-back, in theory.

'Will we get Monty later?'

'Yes. I'm sure he'll have a lovely time at doggy day-care. The owner looked very friendly, didn't she?' It was a rhetorical question. 'We should be back around 5pm. Is that alright?'

'I suppose so.'

That response would have to do, she thought, finishing her coffee. It wasn't that he didn't want to meet Chloe and Jamie but he'd already asked why he had to. They meant nothing to him and he wanted to spend time with his new school friend.

Gazing from the window, Leni tried imagining how the get-together might go. She'd seen photographs of Alex with his children. He'd told her about their interests and characters, but she had only a hazy sense of their personalities. They naturally felt loyal to Heather so she understood they'd be wary towards a new woman. She hoped he'd prepared them sensitively for today. Picking up her magazine she resolved to be approachable and open-minded, but wouldn't try too hard, at this stage. Easier said than done.

As they approached Swindon, Leni pulled Jake's coat from the rack and zipped up her parka. Getting off the train, she clutched the train tickets inside her pocket, tweaking the edges repeatedly.

They reached the barrier and there he was. It was a cliché to say someone was tall, dark and handsome, but it ran through her mind as she saw him. Standing to one side of him was a tall, thin girl, her hands deep in her coat pockets and skinny legs ending in a pair of chunky Dr. Martens boots. Chloe's long, blond hair hung down in straight ribbons on either side of her face and matched the colour of the faux-fur trim on her coat. She was very pretty, but she wasn't smiling. On the other side of his father, Jamie looked like a little mini-me of Alex. With dark hair, a friendly, open face and cheeky grin, he'd grow into a handsome man, thought Leni.

'Hello Leni, Jake. Did you have a good journey?' Alex said.

'Good, thanks, and not too crowded.'

'This is Jamie.' Alex proudly placed a hand on the boy's shoulder.

'Pleased to meet you,' he said.

'Pleased to meet you, too,' Leni replied, smiling at his nice manners.

Alex turned towards his daughter. 'And this is Chloe.'

'Hi,' Chloe said, looking briefly at Leni then away into the distance.

'Nice to meet you,' Leni said. 'Can I introduce Jake?'

He stuck close to Leni and mumbled a hello.

'Shall we go? The car's just outside.' Alex ushered the group to the old Discovery Land Rover and opened the front door for Leni. Chloe sat behind Alex as Jamie and Jake climbed in the other side.

'Your turn to sit in the middle on the way back,' Jamie said to his sister.

'Maybe,' she replied in a sardonic tone.

'How are you, Jake?' Alex asked, clipping his seat belt. 'Are you settling into your new school?'

'Yes.'

Leni waited to see if he would expand about his experience at school but he remained quiet and shy. 'You like the football teacher, don't you, Jake?' she said.

'I play football,' Jamie cut in, 'at Crofts, for the Under 14s. I'm pretty good.'

'What's your favourite position?' Jake piped up.

'Winger, because I'm a really fast runner.' Jamie smiled.

Jake opened up as the boys boasted about their sporting prowess.

Alex drove towards the outskirts of town. 'That's the Leisure Centre where Chloe does trampoline classes,' he said, pointing to a modern brick building and then flicking a switch to get the windscreen blower started.

'That sounds energetic. Have you been doing that long, Chloe?' Leni asked.

'Not very long.'

Not very forthcoming. 'Do you do it barefoot?' Leni said, trying again to engage Chloe.

'No, we wear socks.'

'It must be fun to do somersaults. Have you got to that stage?'

'Of course,' Chloe replied, witheringly.

Leni felt like a fish floundering on dry land. Why didn't Alex say something? He can't be so absorbed in driving that he'd not noticed the staccato conversation she was trying to have with his daughter. She'd leave it.

'Do you have trampoline lessons too, Jamie?'

'No, just football, and I love karting. I'd like to be a Formula 3 driver when I'm older.'

'Cool.' Jake's eyes widened. 'I want to try that. How old are you?'

'Thirteen.'

Alex spoke. 'There are age or height limits at lots of karting sites. At the moment the Swindon Arena works well, but hopefully I'll take Jamie to some of the bigger, outdoor venues. The Mansell track in Honiton is on the site of an old airfield so it's really smooth to drive on. Perhaps we can have a day out there together.'

Leni made the boys laugh retelling her sand-dune buggy experience.

They reached the Tenpin Bowling site. Alex drove to a distant section of the car park as it was so congested.

On entering the building, Leni's senses were immediately assaulted. Clattering skittles occasionally overtook the noise of background pop music, and a bright patterned carpet and flashing gaming machines held her like a rabbit in the head lights.

'What a hive of activity.' She grimaced, wrinkling her nose at the smell of fast food.

'Don't worry, I've only booked one game,' he said, removing his shoes and putting them on the reception desk.

Thank goodness for that, she thought. The place looked so tacky. As she exchanged her boots for a pair of two-tone bowling shoes she tried not to think how many sweaty feet had worn them before her.

'Are these really necessary?'

'They're indoor shoes. They stop people tracking dirt, grit or water onto the lanes,' Alex explained, as he tied his laces.

They collected drinks, settled into a booth and he went to the console. 'Who's going first?'

'I will,' said Jamie, jumping up.

Alex typed his name on the keypad. 'Who's next? Chloe? Jake?'

Chloe didn't answer, seemingly absorbed in her soft drink. Jake stood shyly beside him. 'I'll go after Jamie.'

'Right, then Chloe, then Leni and last, but not least, me? I'll be the late starter who goes on to win, you just watch.'

'Yeah, right, Dad.' Chloe's tone was sarcastic.

Leni felt self-conscious putting her finger into one of the smaller balls. Yuk, the outside of the ball felt sticky. What sort of hygiene did they have in this place? Taking a run towards the lane, she let go of the ball too quickly and almost fell over, trying to disengage her finger. Oh God, that wasn't very cool. She watched a young bloke with a sleeve of tattoos jump in the air as he got a lucky strike in the adjacent lane. His teammates gathered around him, patting his back like a footballer after scoring a goal.

They took a few turns each. Chloe threw the ball half-heartedly, without direction or intention, and several times it went rolling along the side gutters, missing the pins completely. She didn't hide the fact that she wasn't trying. Jamie's roll was accurate and he leapt up and down when he got a half or full strike. Jake used two hands to roll the ball down the middle of the lane, hitting some pins on most of his attempts. He delighted in any going down and was mesmerised watching the bar remove all the pins to be reset again.

'Come on Chloe, it's your go.' Alex had to chivvy her. Leni caught his exasperated expression.

On the way to the restaurant, in the car, Jake got out his Nintendo. 'Do you have this game?' he asked Jamie.

'I prefer the FIFA game, but let's see it?'

They stopped at TGI Fridays for a meal. The boys talked easily while Chloe was noticeably monosyllabic. Alex tried different topics of conversation then gave up. Leni could see he was fighting a losing battle; Chloe was acting stubborn and obtuse.

At the train station Alex, Leni and Jake got out of the car. She leant back in. 'It was lovely meeting you both. I may be the current owner of the Loser's trophy but I plan to pass it on next time.'

'You're on.' Jamie laughed. 'Cheers, Jake.' He shouted from the window, his breath dispersing in the cold air. 'Practise those "keepie-uppies" and we'll have a competition next time to see who wins.'

'OK,' Jake shouted back and gave him a little wave.

On the station concourse Leni gave Jake money to buy a bar of chocolate from the adjacent booth.

Alex hugged her. 'I'm sorry about Chloe's behaviour.'

'It's OK, she's bound to be distant. It was great seeing Jake and Jamie hit it off so well.'

'Jamie's a peace-keeper. I don't worry too much about him. With Chloe, you'd think she'd prefer parents who are happier apart to dodging the emotional minefield they were in a few years ago. I wish I handled her better.'

'You're doing the best you can.' She turned to the Departures screen. 'Anyway, we'd better get our train. Come over for supper again soon.'

'Return match at mine? I can cook, you know.'

'I'd like that, but I've got Jake to consider.'

'Of course, I understand.' He kissed her and nuzzled her neck. 'I really want to see you again. Talk during the week?'

Leni nodded. Jake returned, clutching his chocolate. 'Can we go sailing again, in your boat?'

'It'd be my pleasure,' Alex said.

A voice on the tannoy announced the imminent arrival of the train. Alex squeezed Leni's arm, before she and Jake went through the barrier. 'Safe trip.'

Shivering as they stood on the platform, Leni turned briefly to see if she could still see him. 'Did you enjoy yourself? Jamie liked you.'

'He was brill. I hope he'll play football with me.'

'I'm sure he will, and it sounds like we may go sailing with Alex again.'

'Chloe was stuck-up, wasn't she?' Jake broke off some chocolate and devoured it in one mouthful. 'She didn't act very friendly.'

'I think underneath her sharp outside is a sad person, about her mum and dad not being together any more. We won't take it personally. She just wants her daddy to herself.' That was a bit tactless. Her words might rekindle Jake's loss. She must think more carefully before speaking, next time.

They boarded the train and Leni lay their coats and scarf on the seat beside her as Jake sat opposite her. 'We probably won't see them again for a while.' She sent a text to the dog-care agency saying they'd pick Monty up in ninety minutes, all being well on the journey home.

They settled into life in Pewsey. Jake slotted in well with his classmates, his contemporaries liking the cool, London kid, and he played football at weekends. They took Monty to get vaccinated at the vets' and looked at the notices for any litters of kittens available. Leni suggested they wait a couple of months so Jake could play with the kitten outside, and they'd be able to get it house-trained without needing a litter tray indoors. She'd never lived with cats before and wanted to avoid accidental upsets on her new carpets. Everybody knew that cat pee was a stink to be avoided at all costs.

The job at the gallery was going well, although it was less busy with customers than at Pie Boutique. During quiet moments Leni used her iPad to look up the original paintings of the shop's prints and learnt about the artists and their career history. She knew little about contemporary art and loved to hear Michael's stories of classmates from his days at Central St Martin's School of Art. Many customers were interesting to talk to and she found it fulfilling to source a print for them or to investigate recommendations of emerging artists. Michael was quite happy to let her reorganise the shop and she sourced an old cabinet via Alex which was perfect for displaying all the cards. Within a few weeks he allowed her to bring Monty in, and the dog sat quietly in his basket behind the counter. The customers often wanted to pet him and she loved having him keep her company, while Michael worked on a canvas in his studio.

She arranged with Alex to meet up with him and Chloe. There was the perfect opportunity during February half-term, when Jamie would be on a school rugby tour and Jake would be staying overnight with his Parsons cousins. Leni felt they'd have a good chance to get to know each other better, not being in a group and where Chloe couldn't hide behind Alex and Jamie's conversations. She suggested a visit to the theatre to coincide with the date of her solicitor's meeting in London.

# 19

Alex knocked on Chloe's bedroom door. She opened it, kicking aside a towel, and revealed heaps of clothes and discarded makeup strewn across the bed.

'Nearly ready? We need to leave in five minutes.' He didn't want to be late.

'Do I have to go?' She scowled. 'I don't want to see a show with that woman.'

'Her name's Leni, and she's looking forward to meeting you again.'

'Jamie's lucky to be on his rugby trip.' She checked her jumper in the mirror. 'It sounds like a lame musical, anyway.'

Alex took a deep breath. 'You'll probably enjoy it, if you allow yourself to.' He turned to go, trying not to get riled. 'Please make an effort tonight. Leni's treating us to the theatre.'

He collected a jacket from his bedroom then popped his head around Chloe's door before going downstairs. 'Could you leave your room a bit tidier, please? It's not a hotel.'

'This is tidy,' Chloe retorted. 'Anyway, there's no time, now.'

After switching off the sitting-room lights and picking out

a golf umbrella in case of rain, Alex went to the car. Chloe banged the front door behind her and stomped down the steps in bright green Dr. Martens and faux-fur leopard print jacket.

'That coat looks nice,' Alex ventured, holding the passenger door open for her. He got a grunt in reply. Nothing unusual there. He slipped into the battered seat of the car, checked the satnav, and they set off for London.

As they drove in silence Alex was thoughtful. He really liked Leni and it was crucial she and the kids got on if their relationship was to thrive. How could he get insight into his increasingly secretive daughter? With Jamie, he'd chat about football, how Oxford United were playing, and then personal or emotional issues usually seeped out, naturally. Alex was gratified that people warmed to Jamie's easy-going personality. He seemed to talk easily with peers and older people alike, and he'd yet to hit the grumpy phase.

'What's keeping you glued to your iPad?'

'Nothing. Just school stuff,' Chloe said, clicking off the page and putting the device in the pocket of the car door. 'Everyone's talking about the Prom. I think Sam fancies Shaz and we're sick to find out who Jed will ask. I expect it'll be Harriet – she's the prettiest.'

'You know boys like girls with a bit of spark and a good sense of humour. It's not all about looks.'

'Dad,' she said, grimacing.

'So, have you made your A Level choices yet?' he said.

'Really? Do we have to talk about it now?'

'Alright,' he agreed. 'What about summer holiday plans? After your exams finish?'

'Molly and I want to go to the Isle of Wight festival.'

'Where would you stay?'

'God, Dad, you're such a dinosaur. We'd camp. Some of

the boys are going too, so we'll have three or four tents. I've saved my pocket money, and the babysitting money I've earned.'

'What does your mum say?' Alex asked, imagining Heather wouldn't be too happy about the scheme.

'I haven't told her yet.' Chloe started picking at her flaking nail polish. 'She's in one of her black moods.'

'I'm sorry to hear that.' He paused, wondering how to proceed. He mustn't say anything negative. 'How's Bob handling it?'

'He's such a prick. Always telling us what to do and spouting his opinions when nobody asked for them.'

'Does he understand bipolar disorder?' Alex said, empathising with Chloe and remembering how fragile his ex-wife had been, in the midst of an episode.

'He's such a know-it-all. Says his mate's a doctor and keeps telling her what to take and how to deal with it.' Chloe turned away to look out of the window.

'It must be difficult.' Alex put his hand on hers.

'I wish I could make her feel better.'

'I'm sure you do, love. It's not your fault.' He squeezed her hand and switched the radio on, setting it to Radio 1, knowing Chloe preferred that station. They stopped talking and listened to a few tracks.

'When were we last in London?' Alex asked, slowing down as the traffic increased at Hammersmith.

Chloe calculated the year the family had spent a few nights in the city, then pointed out the V&A Museum and other landmarks they'd visited.

'I love these shops. The fashions are way better,' she said, gasping at the bright lights of Harrods.

Alex recalled the holiday but the memory also brought a stab of pain, as he remembered how much Heather had found fault with him. The hissed harsh words, berating him for his poor choice of restaurant and accommodation, and the barbed complaints. He'd felt desperate, and ashamed, about the breakup of their family but admitted to a feeling of relief, no longer being undermined. He reminded himself that she was ill, and needed support, for the sake of the children, as well as for herself.

Driving past the glow of lights from The Ritz he cheered up and chose to look forward rather than wallow in past sadness. Piccadilly Circus was heaving with cars and people, and he turned onto Shaftesbury Avenue.

'We're here,' he said, with an excited grin, and parked in the nearest NCP.

They side-stepped other pedestrians in the bustling theatre district to reach the restaurant where he'd arranged to meet Leni. It was a hive of activity as Alex spotted her waving from a corner table.

'Hi Chloe, how lovely to see you again.' Leni stood up and kissed Chloe on the cheek. Alex was relieved that Chloe didn't shy away.

Alex hugged Leni, and they sat down to study the menu and chat about the forthcoming show. Waiters whizzed past with trays of drinks and scooped notepads from apron pouches to take orders. Red and white gingham tablecloths and glass tea-light holders created a warm atmosphere and the buzz in the American diner increased as more people sat down to eat.

As Alex savoured a mouthful of red wine, he relished the warm glow he experienced from being in the company of these women. His adored daughter, and Leni, who snuck into his thoughts more and more, these days. It would be dreadful if either one found it difficult to accept the other.

'I like your necklace,' Chloe said abruptly, twirling pasta onto her fork.

'Thank you. I've found this amazing silversmith and I love her pieces.' Leni stroked her hand over the chain of her pendant. 'Do you like silver or gold?'

'Anything eye-catching, and long-drop earrings.'

'The ones you're wearing are pretty,' Leni said. 'Much as I love my job in the art gallery, I hope to run my own jewellery business in the future.'

'Cool. Will you have to study?' Chloe said.

'I've started a one-year online course, but I'll need to attend workshops for hands-on teaching, and networking.'

Chloe's phone rang. She jumped up, dropped her fork onto the plate and rushed away to take the call.

'Sorry about that,' Alex said. 'They can hardly go five minutes without their phones.'

'No, that's OK,' Leni said, putting her hand over his. 'That was kind of Chloe, showing an interest. I think we'll find common ground as we get to know one another better.'

'I'm sure you will,' Alex said, tingling at Leni's light touch on his fingers. He counted on Chloe adjusting to him having a steady girlfriend. 'Had we better go?'

He settled the bill and they walked to the theatre. Stepping forwards to cross the road, Leni reached urgently for Chloe's arm.

'I don't need help. I'm not a baby.' She jerked her arm away.

'Sorry,' Leni apologised. 'It's just that Jake once ran out between cars when he was little, and it's instinctive. I didn't think.'

Alex held Leni's hand as they walked to the Haymarket. Once they'd reached the Theatre Royal and joined the throng ascending the steps, he leaned in close. 'Thanks for this treat – it's really special.'

'My pleasure,' Leni said, beaming at him.

They reached the foyer. 'Shall I get a programme and order

interval drinks?' Alex said. It was the least he could do after Leni had bought the tickets.

'Lovely. I'll grab one now.' Leni waved to the programme seller nearby. She bought two and handed one to Chloe, who was staring at the decorative surroundings.

'Beautiful, isn't it? The theatre was built in 1720,' Leni said.

'Cool.'

'Have you seen other shows in London?'

'Mum doesn't like crowds. She has anxiety.' Chloe looked momentarily awkward, as if she'd said too much. 'We go to the panto and stuff in Swindon.'

'That sounds fun. My mum and dad were keen theatre-goers. Fran and I were often taken to see something or other. It was always an occasion, everyone got dressed up. It's good that it's not so exclusive now, and appeals to wider audiences.'

'Do they still do rush tickets?' Alex asked.

Leni nodded, then seeing Chloe look baffled, explained. 'That's when you queue in Leicester Square on the morning of the show and sometimes get lucky with a last-minute ticket at a knock-down price.'

They took their seats in the auditorium. Alex sat in the middle and switched his mobile phone off.

'I hope you enjoy it,' Leni said.

'I'm sure we will.' Alex smiled at her then turned to watch Chloe examining her surroundings.

Leni leant forwards. 'There was a dreadful incident in 2004 when the chandelier fell part way down and bits of ceiling fell onto the stalls. Luckily no one was seriously hurt, but wouldn't that've been a horrible shock?'

'It's not going to happen again, is it?' Chloe said, looking up, anxiously.

'No, no, it's been put right,' Leni said. 'Sorry, that was a bit doom-monger of me. On another note, how's Jamie?'

'Loving the tour, and they've been pretty successful, too.' Alex couldn't hide the pride in his voice.

'Don't you worry about broken bones? It's such a violent game.' Leni shuddered.

'Players at Jamie's stage usually only sustain minor injuries. I hope I haven't spoken too soon.'

'Jamie said Simon's got a broken finger.' Chloe blushed, biting her bottom lip.

'You've been in touch?' Alex raised his eyebrows. 'Isn't Simon the boy you like?'

Chloe shifted in her seat, looking embarrassed. 'Jamie rang 'cos Mum wanted to know what time they were getting back to school.'

The orchestra tuned up then the lights went down. They played the opening number as the immense, red velvet curtain raised to reveal the stage-set and actors in position. The spectacle was full of colour and vitality as the chorus began.

As she climbed the steep steps of the auditorium at the interval, Chloe gasped. 'That was brilliant.' She turned to Leni, her face flushed. 'I didn't expect it to be any good.'

They talked animatedly about the first half as they sipped their drinks.

'What did I tell you?' Alex beamed. 'I don't want to say I told you so.'

'Then don't say it, Dad,' Chloe said, cuffing him across the arm, with a smile on her face. 'Where's the toilet?'

'Along the landing,' said Leni, running her fingers through her hair. 'And just to warn you, there'll be a massive queue.'

After Chloe left, Alex hugged Leni. 'This is wonderful,

very well chosen.' He kept his arm around her waist, wanting to inhale and bottle the smell of her scented skin.

'I'm so happy she's enjoying it. I looked across and she was mesmerised.'

'Yes, it's opening up another world. She's sometimes as stubborn as a mule about what she thinks she dislikes.'

'Where does she get that attitude from?' Leni laughed and squeezed his hand. 'Isn't it normal for a teenager to say they hate things that adults like?'

Chloe returned, and they took their seats again. When the curtain went down after the final show-stopping song, they clapped and cheered repeatedly. The actors took their bows until the curtain remained down and the house lights went up.

Standing on the pavement outside the theatre, Alex looked at his watch. 'Fancy a post-show drink?' It was a wrench that he wouldn't be able to kiss Leni, but this wasn't the right time, with Chloe there.

'I'd better not,' Leni said. 'I'm staying at a friend's and told her I'd be back around 10.30pm.'

'Can we drop you there, on our way out of town?' He really didn't want the evening to end yet, despite knowing he should get Chloe home.

'She's in north London and you've got a long enough journey as it is, but thanks for the offer.' Leni kissed Alex on the mouth.

Chloe twisted her leg and fiddled with her hair. 'Thanks for taking me to the show, Leni.'

'I'm glad you had fun.' Leni kissed her cheek. 'We'll do it again, and maybe take Jamie and Jake to something, in future.'

'Do you reckon they'd like *Thriller*?' Alex asked.

'Cool,' Chloe said. 'I'd like that, too.'

'Great,' Leni said, pulling her scarf closer and tilting her beret to one side. 'Or we could have an outing in Oxford or Salisbury? There's some great regional theatre.' She kissed Alex again. 'Talk soon.'

'Enjoy half-term with Kat and Mike.' He held onto her for another few seconds before she pulled away.

'Safe journey home.'

Alex watched her walk away then put his arm around Chloe. 'I'm so happy you had fun.'

When Kat and Mike came to stay with Leni, they went to Stonehenge. The weather was sunny and cold, and the boys relished being together again. They ran from the car to the Visitor Centre as Leni and Kat walked and talked behind them. Wandering past archaeological treasures of pottery and jewellery, the boys fell upon the exhibit of human remains. They were fascinated looking at the reconstructed face of a man, based on bones found near the site.

Outside the centre, Jake chased Mike around one of the Neolithic houses. 'Hurry up, Mum. We want to see the stones.'

Leni looked at the open-sided shuttle buses, ready to take visitors to the historic site. 'Are you happy to walk, Kat? I could do with it.'

'Yes, it'll do the boys good to let off some steam,' she said, pulling her beanie hat over her ears.

They walked to the stones, gasping at the sheer scale of them, close up.

'They're bigger than I thought,' Mike said.

Leni craned her neck to look at the top of one. 'They're so iconic. Do you know they're 4,500 years old? It would've been a masterpiece of engineering getting them here.'

'Where did they come from, then?' Jake stood open-mouthed.

Kat blew on the tips of her fingers sticking out from her colourful Fair Isle wrist warmers. 'Hundreds of people would've been involved. They think they came from West Wales.' She brought her scarf up to cover her mouth as a gust of wind blew across the open plain.

They stopped to watch a demonstration of rope making and grain grinding. After getting back to Leni's house, the boys had tea and sloped off to watch television. The women sat in the kitchen, talking about relationships and how fulfilled each one was, in their respective jobs.

'How's the shop?' Leni sipped her tea. 'Are you happy with Rachel?'

Kat stretched back against the chair, clasping her hands together. Her hair was windswept and there was colour in her cheeks. 'Look, it's not the same as when you were there, natch, but she's capable. She's willing to learn, that's the important thing. And you? How are you getting on at the gallery? What news of your plans for a jewellery business?' She rattled off questions as she gobbled the coffee cake that Leni had made the night before.

Leni told Kat about her online course. 'That's going OK, and I've got a weekend workshop coming up soon. I'll have to beg a bed from you.'

'You know you're always welcome, and Jake too.'

The women compared the progress of their sons and Leni asked about Kat's fitness programme.

'I'm training for the Dublin marathon in October. Connell's said Mike and I can stay, and we're going over for May half-term.'

'That's fantastic news. I'm so happy for you.'

'It's just for a few days,' Kat said, looking distinctly bashful.

'That doesn't matter. He's obviously serious or he'd only ask you to visit. It's a good sign that he wants Mike to come too.'

They got up and started preparing supper.

'It would be great for the four of us to do something together?'

'I wonder how that would make Connell feel? Seeing me with someone other than Will?' Leni said, taking chicken breasts from the fridge and vegetables from the rack. 'It's a lovely idea, as far as I'm concerned.' She handed Kat a knife and chopping board. 'You OK to prep the veg?'

'Whatever you like. You know I can't stand cooking, so give me a task and I'll try not to spill blood.'

The women laughed. Kat looked about the kitchen, taking in the bright kilim rug that came from Chiswick, red lacquer cabinet doors and huge Smeg fridge. 'I've got house envy, again. You've made it so welcoming. It's less stuffy though, I'd say.'

'Thanks, Kat.' Leni browned the chicken breasts in a heavy Le Creuset iron skillet. 'I suppose it reflects my own style now. I haven't kept any of the things that Will liked but I didn't. Those hideous gifts from his aunt all went, in the move.'

Clocking the time, Leni smiled. 'Is it too early for wine?'

'I thought you'd never ask.' Kat held up a carrot stick, one end twice as thick as the other. 'Oops, not exactly a baton. And to hell with ugly things that don't make you happy.'

Leni laughed. 'That's what I love about you, dear friend, you speak your mind.'

'Think we share one or two of the same vices.'

After taking Villeroy & Boch crystal goblets from the cupboard, Leni poured two large measures and handed one to her friend. 'We've got a lot of catching up to do. Cheers.'

# 20

It was the Easter school holidays and Alex's house was full. Leni took two days off work and she and Jake were staying with him for a long weekend. Chloe and Jamie arrived on Friday night and they enjoyed supper then sat in front of the fire. When Alex suggested a game of Scrabble, Chloe rolled her eyes and said she'd rather stick pins in them, and disappeared to her bedroom. Jamie accepted the challenge. Jake said he didn't want to play on his own, so he and Leni played together, against father and son. They laughed at silly words and Alex told bad jokes.

The next morning, Jake spooned his cereal with one hand as the other reached down to fondle Monty's ears. He was engrossed reading the back of the cereal packet as Leni pulled tins from the cupboard and positioned weighing scales on the granite worktop. She assembled ingredients as Chloe came into the kitchen wearing baggy, checked sweatpants and a hooded top with the sleeves pulled low over her hands. Remains of yesterday's kohl makeup smudged her eyes. She pulled a new box of cereal from the cupboard.

'Sleep well?' Leni said, measuring out a slab of butter. 'I'm making a cake. Any particular favourites?'

'I don't really care either way.' Chloe's head went down towards her spoon.

'Chocolate for me,' Jake said.

Leni weighed flour, sugar and cocoa.

'Any coffee on the go?' Alex came in and kissed Leni's neck. 'Shall I make a pot?'

'Not for me, thanks,' she said.

'I don't like coffee,' said Jake. 'Can I have a hot chocolate?'

'Sure.' Alex nodded and looked to Chloe, who made no reply.

'Does anyone know if Jamie's up?' Leni asked.

'I've just woken him. He's gone for a shower,' Alex said, measuring coffee into the glass jug. 'I thought we'd ask the neighbours over for drinks tomorrow.'

'Is Simon coming?' Chloe's head raised, spoon suspended and slurping noises temporarily on hold. She caught Leni's eye and looked down. 'Not that I care. I may have other plans.'

'We'll invite the whole family.' Alex sat opposite her with his coffee and a biscuit.

Chloe blushed.

Leni thought Chloe's smile made her look so much prettier than her usual sulky face. A rebellious attitude was to be expected in a teenager, but she wished the girl had more of her brother's sunnier disposition.

'So, have you thought any more about A Levels choices?' Alex asked.

'Dad, I don't want to talk about it now.' Her spoon clattered into the bowl. 'I'm stressed enough doing revision. I'll think about it when I get my results.'

'It's just that you may want to consider the subjects you

enjoy most, as you'll be studying them in depth at A Level. How's the revision going?'

'Leave it out, Dad,' she groaned, pushing the empty bowl away.

''Scuse the noise.' Leni switched on the mixer. She likened Alex to a terrier on the scent of a rabbit and not giving up until he had his quarry. It would be hopeless trying to get information from Chloe now. She poured chocolate mixture into the two tins, handing the coated spatulas to Chloe and Jake to lick clean.

'This'll be ready in twenty minutes. What time do you want to leave?' Leni stacked the dishwasher with mixing bowl and utensils. 'I can take butter icing in a tub and put the cake together on the boat.'

Alex drained his coffee and put the cup in the dishwasher. 'I'd like to be at the marina around 11.30am for high tide. I've got to sort the tools I need.' He kissed Leni's cheek. 'Will you be ready to leave in twenty minutes, guys?' he asked, leaving the room.

'Huh, thanks for warning me.' Chloe's sarcastic reply was accompanied by an eye roll.

Leni cleaned the work surface, comparing father and daughter. They both had a strong nose and full lips but Chloe's golden hair was a complete contrast to Alex's messy thatch of dark hair. Her colouring must come from Heather's side. Jamie's dark hair was straight and sleek, cut fashionably short at the sides with a long wave across his forehead.

'Pack swimmers and towel.' Leni weighed icing sugar into a bowl. 'Your dad says we'll get to Little Cove. We can enjoy a refreshing swim and it shouldn't be too crowded.'

'I'm not swimming – it's far too cold,' Chloe said, leaving the table and casting a withering look at Leni.

'Bowl in the dishwasher, please.'

Chloe sighed theatrically as she plonked the bowl in the machine.

'I'll swim.' Jake grinned. 'I don't get cold. I swim at Granny's even in winter, don't I, Mum?' He stacked his bowl and rushed from the room to get dressed.

'Take an extra sweater. You may feel the cold afterwards,' Leni called to his departing back. She fished a tablet from under the sink and set the machine to wash. It probably looked a bit stereotypical, the woman baking and the man fiddling about with some tools. It didn't upset her. She acknowledged that she was happy being involved in Alex's family life and sharing the novel experience of bringing up a girl. She wondered if Jake would become surly and monosyllabic at Chloe's age and although it was likely, she hoped he would retain his current cheerfulness.

Jamie dashed into the kitchen for breakfast as Leni went to find Monty's life-vest. Within the hour, Alex had packed everything in the car and they were ready to go. It was a warm spring day and they set off in good spirits, looking forward to a day's sailing ahead.

A month later and the two families were together again, as it was Alex's turn to have the children for the weekend. When Leni went to his bedroom to get a cardigan, she heard a scrabbling noise. Chloe spun around to face her, looking guilty.

'What are you after?' Leni crossed the wooden floor to the cupboard, glancing at her jewellery box on the Georgian mahogany chest of drawers.

'Nothing, just a hanky,' Chloe said, defensively. 'We're doing an art project at school. I'm borrowing one of Dad's.'

'They're in this side.' Leni noticed the high colour in

Chloe's cheeks, as she handed her a clean, white square from his top drawer. Running a brush through her hair, she waited for Chloe to leave. 'Supper will be ready in a few minutes.'

She gently closed the door and checked her jewellery. It wasn't her house, but she still felt like her space had been invaded and she couldn't help feeling suspicious. Leni didn't quite trust Chloe. Touching a pair of her earrings, Leni was reminded of the occasion when she'd been given them. They stirred up unhappy memories. Those sapphires may be pretty, but they'd been a guilty offering from Will after he'd confessed to a liaison. It was all water under the bridge now. Perhaps she should sell those; she wouldn't wear them again. They didn't make her feel happy. She sighed as she shut the door to go downstairs.

After tasting the puttanesca sauce and adjusting the seasoning, she pulled the pan off the hotplate and checked the spaghetti was al dente. She wiped a spill from the lid of the Esse. She was getting used to Alex's oven, relieved she had experience of cooking on a range at her mother's house.

'Can you put your toys away, please?'

Jake gathered up his Lego models, and spare pieces, throwing them into a big black box and pushing it to one side of the tartan armchair by the window.

'Go and wash your hands, too. They'll be covered in dog hairs and dust from playing on the floor.' She drained the pasta, steam temporarily enveloping her face.

'Food's ready.' She opened the door of the snug where Chloe and Jamie were lounging, each plugged into their laptops, watching music videos and YouTube clips.

Alex was pruning a fruit tree at the end of the garden.

'It's ready, my love,' she called.

A noisy few minutes ensued, with chairs being dragged

across the tiled floor, Alex washing his hands and Monty weaving around their feet.

'Can someone please shut the dog in the snug?' He poured a craft beer.

Jamie cajoled Monty to the other room with a dog treat then everyone sat at the table.

'How's your project coming along, Chloe?' Alex forked pasta with gusto into his large, shallow bowl. He passed the serving dish to Jamie and gave the black pepper grinder an energetic twist across his food.

'You haven't got anything of use here.' Chloe scowled. 'All my materials are at Mum's. I'll have to do it there.'

Leni heaped salad onto her plate. She wouldn't interfere or offer advice, but watched Alex's reaction to his daughter's criticism.

'If there's anything I can get for you in town, let me know?' he said, sounding positive.

'It's a bit late then,' Chloe said sarcastically, 'and we're going back to Mum's, anyway.'

He turned to Jamie. 'Any news on your match next weekend?'

Leni took a sip of cold, crisp Sauvignon Blanc as Jamie replied. He and Alex discussed the sporting prowess of one of Jamie's friends and the likely availability of tickets for a match they wanted to see.

'This is awesome sauce, Leni.' Jamie grinned as he confidently swirled pasta around his fork and loaded it, in one movement, into his mouth.

Jake watched the older boy and tried to copy him to get his spaghetti onto the fork in the same way. It all fell off, splashing sauce onto his tee-shirt.

'Here, like this.' Jamie demonstrated his technique once again.

Jake laughed. 'I like using my spoon.'

Chloe looked scornfully at the boys. 'Molly and I have booked our Isle of Wight tickets.'

'That sounds good, when is it?' Leni poured mineral water and offered some to the others.

'Ninth June. After our exams finish. I can't wait.'

'Did you talk to your mum about it, yet?'

'No, but we're going,' Chloe said defiantly. 'We've got it all arranged with the others.'

'I'm sure it'll be fine, if you're going in a group.' Alex put his fork and spoon into his bowl and wiped his mouth on his napkin. 'I need to talk to her about something else, so we can discuss it when I drop you back tomorrow, if you like?'

'There's nothing to discuss. I've finished my exams then, and it's my sixteenth birthday a week before.'

'I'm not sure what that has to do with anything,' Alex said, 'but let's not worry about it just now.'

'Jake's going to a festival, too, aren't you?' Leni interjected.

'Where?' Jamie asked him.

'I'm going to Scout camp, in the summer. We can build our own fires and we're going to canoe on a river.'

Alex collected up the pasta bowls. 'Could someone bring the other things over, please?'

Jamie got up from the table and carried the used dishes to the worktop.

'There's a tiramisu in the fridge, if anyone's got any room?' Leni said.

'I'll get it.' Jamie was over to the fridge in a flash. 'I love your puddings.'

The dessert was demolished with speed and it was Chloe and Jake's turn to clear the dirty dishes. The family tidied up and pushed chairs back under the table, holding a lively discussion as to which DVD film they should put on. Jake went to let Monty out as Jamie checked the log-burner.

Leni went upstairs with Jake to read him a story. When she'd finished, he put his arms around her neck.

'We're almost like a real family, aren't we?'

'Yes.' She kissed him. 'It's beginning to feel like we fit together.' She smiled as she stroked his head and turned off the light.

After the film, she and Alex went to bed. She held him close. 'I think this evening went quite well, wouldn't you say? We're getting better at this.'

He kissed her. 'You're bloody marvellous. Jamie's thoroughly enchanted. Your tiramisu helps,' he teased. 'And I think Chloe's beginning to relax. She's definitely warming to you.'

They quietly made love. They heard Chloe and Jamie say goodnight to each other, and it wasn't long before all the bedroom doors closed and the house was quiet.

# 21

Leni became aware of heavy stomping overhead, then expletives, as Chloe clattered downstairs, dragging something that sounded like a dead body. Leni wiped her hands, checked the chicken pie in the oven and went to see what was going on, glad that Jake was with a friend today and wouldn't hear the swearing.

Chloe dumped her rucksack on the hall floor then crouched over it, pushing an acid-yellow top into a bulging side pocket.

'Shit. I can't fit it all in.'

'Want any help?' Leni hesitated. She got no answer, so tried another approach. 'What sort of weather's due at the festival?'

'I don't know.' Chloe shrugged, regarding Leni with cynicism. 'Who cares?'

'When I went to Reading the only thing you took was your sleeping bag. Now you've got mobile phones, wet-wipes, and heat pads for your wellies.' She realised she must sound ancient.

Chloe grunted as she buckled the straps of the bag, heaved it to the front door then grabbed her parka from the coat rack.

'What time are you off? I could use a little help with the lunch for you all.'

'The boys'll be here soon.' Chloe put her jacket on the bag and bit her lip. 'Molly'll look really hot – she has cool clothes.'

'Oh well, that's good. You can share hers if it rains?'

Chloe rolled her eyes. 'I've got to text some friends,' she said, disappearing into the snug and pointedly shutting the door.

Leni returned to the kitchen, calculating how long the pie would take to brown and wondering when Chloe would drop the sarcasm. She was different when she was in front of Alex. Why couldn't the girl offer some help? She remembered how as teenagers, she and Fran had always laid the table, and put out glasses and water. What made today's teenagers so entitled? Not that she had much experience of this age group. Perhaps it was more that she and Fran had been afraid of their father's temper and keenly felt their parents' expectations.

The doorbell rang as Leni swept carrots into a waiting pan and onto the hob.

'They're here.' She rapped on the door of the snug as she crossed the hall. A tall, sandy-haired boy, with the beginnings of a beard, jumped out from the driver's side of the car, while his passenger remained engrossed on his mobile phone.

'Hi.' She hadn't met any of Chloe's friends yet and thrust out her hand, marvelling at this tall, rangy lad who looked older than his seventeen years. 'I'm Leni, Alex's friend.'

'Sam.' He grinned. Cool and confident, he wore low-slung black jeans and frayed festival bands on his wrists.

The other boy finished texting and came into the house, pushing shades onto his head. 'Hi, I'm Jed.' He fixed Leni with a dazzling smile. 'I heard about you from Clo. Nice to meet you.' He kissed her cheek, charm personified.

She briefly wondered what Chloe had been saying about her.

'We're almost ready to eat.' Leni led the way into the kitchen where rays of sunshine strafed the wooden floor. 'Can I get you a tea or coffee, or anything?'

'Yeah, coffee would be great, one sugar.' Sam put his sunglasses on the counter. 'Nice of you to give us lunch before we go, thanks.'

'You're welcome,' Leni said, watching Jed's thumbs whizz about on his mobile phone. 'It's a pleasure to meet some of Chloe's friends. Sorry Alex couldn't join us.'

'Hi everyone, here I am.' Chloe burst into the kitchen, jumping into Sam's arms, wrapping her legs around his thighs.

Leni noticed Sam's momentary embarrassment before she turned away and loaded a Nespresso capsule into the machine. 'We're having coffee if you'd like one, Chloe?'

'Naw, it's festival time,' she said, turning her back. 'Want a Beck's, Jed?'

'Cool.'

'If that's OK?' Chloe hesitated, holding the fridge door open.

Leni handed Sam his drink, hiding her surprise at being asked permission. Chloe usually helped herself to anything she wanted, at any time. Perhaps she wanted to impress the boys?

'Are you sharing the driving?' Leni asked.

'Nah, Jed's not got his licence yet. They're in my safe hands.' He held his upturned palms out.

'So where's Molly?' Leni stirred milk into her coffee.

'She's meeting us here,' Chloe said. 'She needed to go into town for something. Hope she won't keep us waiting. I want to get a good spot.'

The friends talked about the headline bands before a sing-song voice resounded in the hall.

'Anyone home?' Molly staggered into the kitchen weighed

down by her rucksack, a long plait interwoven with fake flowers swinging across her face. She dropped the heavy pack and excitedly hugged each friend in turn.

'Is your mum still here?' Leni prodded the carrots.

'Nah, she dropped me at the gate 'cos she had to pick up my brother,' Molly said.

Deeming them ready, Leni drained the carrots, put them in a serving dish and set it on the table. She handed Chloe five plates from the warming drawer then triumphantly carried the steaming pie towards the seated group.

'Wow. That looks amazing.' Jed's eyes widened.

'Help yourself to everything. There's water in the blue jug.'

Forks and knives clattered on the plates as the friends became more animated. Chloe looked love-struck towards Sam, as he teased the girls about their GCSEs now that he and Jed had sat the superior AS Level exams. Leni watched with interest until they'd all finished.

'Time to go.' Chloe gathered up the plates and put them on the counter. 'We can't stay any longer or there'll be massive queues.'

Sam and Jed took other tableware to the side and binned the empty bottles in the recycle unit.

'Thanks for your help.' Leni wiped down the table, incredulous at how long it had taken her to make that chicken pastry pie and how little time it had taken to consume.

The girls heaved their rucksacks on as Sam aimed the keys at the Vauxhall Corsa, plipping the doors open. Jed grabbed Chloe's pack and squashed it on top of the kit already in the boot.

'Send a text to me, or your dad, to say you've arrived safely?' Leni whispered to Chloe. 'Your dad won't expect you to check in every day. Just the once.'

'OK,' Chloe said, pulling away.

The two girls squeezed their long limbs into the back seat, clutching oversized tote bags and shoving their parkas beneath their feet. With shouts of goodbye, Sam revved the engine and the blue car pulled out of the drive.

'Have fun.' Leni's words hung in the air, as Jed's hand came out of the window for a final wave.

It was very quiet in the house after they left. Leni felt a pang of sadness, memories of going to boarding school as a teen reminding her of earlier partings. Thank goodness for Monty's company. She stroked his head and mulled over the rite of passage of attending a music festival. It was all raves in her youth, big warehouse parties and massive gatherings in unknown countryside outside London.

She took a load of washing from the machine and pegged it on the line. Blossom blew about the garden as clouds scudded across the sky. Her spirits lifted, loving the sight and smell of clean washing drying in the sun and being blown about by the wind. It gave her a sense of accomplishment, for some reason.

Monty got up from his sunny spot by the back door to follow Leni into the house and after making a couple of rotations, lay down on the hall rug.

Leni gathered up a pair of Chloe's discarded shoes at the bottom of the stairs and took them back to her room. The smell of Daisy perfume hit Leni's nostrils as she regarded the rejected festival clothes and jewellery. She wouldn't tidy up. After all, it wasn't her place in Alex's house, and would make Chloe cross. Collecting a damp cloth from the bathroom, Leni decided it wouldn't be breaking any boundaries just to run the cloth over the bookshelves and windowsills. As she lifted assorted mementos, and photos in frames of all shapes and sizes,

Leni tried to understand Alex's daughter a little better. Their relationship was moving in the right direction but she intuited that Chloe felt unhappy about the plan for Leni to move in with Alex. She felt sudden guilt for being in the room and went to drop the cloth into the sisal basket by the sink.

Sitting with a cup of herbal tea on the sofa, which was piled with tapestry and old velvet cushions, Leni reflected on her position in this new family. Jamie seemed more accepting of the status quo and found it easy to communicate with her, but then he wasn't as complicated as Chloe. It was great that he loved Leni's food and they played card games like 'poohead' and whist, together. Both had a competitive streak to win at backgammon and chess, bouts of which lasted hours. He'd been surprised by a 'girl' liking the game.

Returning to the kitchen, Leni longed for Alex to be home. He would hold her in his strong arms and reassure her that it was all going OK, and she would try to stop second-guessing whether their two families were ever going to bond.

Chloe didn't like the way Sam's talk was heading. She scrolled through her Instagram account.

'I'm definitely going to get laid this weekend.' He smirked.

'Ten pounds says you won't,' Jed countered. 'Look at that bum-fluff. Call that a beard? The girls'll run a mile.'

The boys amicably slagged off each other's looks for a few minutes. Chloe squeezed Molly's thigh as she raised her eyebrows to the roof.

'What's new guys?' she said. 'Same old, same old, with you two.'

'What about you, Chloe? Is someone going to pop your cherry over the festival?' Sam leered at her in the rear-view mirror.

'Shut up, Sam, I've heard it all before.' She continued texting. 'Can you promise we're leaving at lunchtime on Monday, as my dad is asking what time we'll be back?'

'Yeah, the roads will be shit any later and with Bristol commuter traffic on top of that. Anyway, I've got work in The Plough at 6.30pm. Don't be late or I'll go without you.'

'Thanks, Sam,' said the two voices in unison from the back seat.

'You're the dog's bollocks,' said Molly.

Jed opened a can of lager. 'Girls?'

'No thanks,' said Chloe. 'The suspension's crap in the back and the way Sam's driving it'll go all over my new Zara top.'

'I'm up for one,' said Molly, taking a can from Jed and pulling the ring on it.

They arrived at the back of a long queue of cars and slowed to a snail's pace. A snatch of bass drifted from another car and the four joined in with the lyrics at the tops of their voices. Their car jolted as it hit an indent in the grassy track.

'Oh, Molly, you've spilt on my new top!' Chloe looked aghast as she fluttered the wet patch back and forth. 'Did you pack wet-wipes?'

'Sorry, Clo.' Molly rummaged in her bag, pulled out a striped scarf she often wore turban-style around her head, and pressed it into her friend's hands. 'Jeez, I'm so excited, but a little bit scared too.'

That admission set the boys off with ribald teasing. They inched past different car park signs until they arrived at their allocated place.

'What if I lose you and there's no signal? The Wi-Fi's going to be shit.'

Chloe and Molly made contingency plans if they got

accidentally separated. Sam and Jed discussed tent location and security.

'Last year we brought an old fishing rod of my dad's and tied a pink feather boa to the top. Did you bring that red boa, Mol?' Sam asked as he locked the car.

They staggered with all their kit until they spotted a pitch they liked. Unfurling the two tents and laying out all the rods, the four friends wrestled with the parts until eventually one tent was erected. They started on the second tent.

'Bet someone will come between us, and them next door. All very well having chosen this spot, within a couple of hours you won't be able to see the grass.'

Noise of bands starting their sets drove the four to abandon their gear and zip up the tent compartments. Molly taped her feather boa to the top of the rod and Jed pushed it hard into the ground. The soft mud yielded to the spike.

'Front and left at the barriers, if we get separated?' suggested Sam.

'Woohoo,' Chloe cheered. 'Now I'm ready for a drink – who's coming with me?'

The group set off, cans in hand, Chloe adjusting her money belt around her waist as she craned her head around, making a mental picture of their pitch in relation to the odd trees in the vicinity. Chloe linked arms with Molly and they skipped along together for a few yards. Chloe abruptly jumped in front and spun around to face her friend.

'How do I look?' She made a pirouette, a froth of lager flying from her can.

'You'd look good in a bin liner. You're totally rocking those denim shorts and, personally, I like a bit of bum showing.' Molly laughed.

'Your plait looks cool, and where'd you get those spangly wellies, anyway?'

'I told you, I found an ace vintage shop in Frome last weekend.'

They came to a signpost and made their way to the Main Stage and threaded their way towards the front of the rocking crowd. Over the following hours, the swell of audience grew, the bright sunshine gave way to a mellow sunset, the bands cranked up the volume and thousands of revellers started to party hard.

Chloe felt wrecked. Her brain couldn't compute that it was Monday already. Four bleary-eyed and hungover friends got tetchy with each other, commands and insults flying back and forth as they packed up, and loaded their gear into the car.

Hunkering down in the back seat, she felt really grubby as she made a pillow of her beer-stained and muddy sweatshirt. The seat belt irritated her neck so she undid it and let her lanky hair fall over her face as she started to zone out, oblivious to her friends laughing and joking about the mishaps they'd overcome.

Sam gripped the steering wheel. 'You're gonna have to keep talking to me, mate. I'm shagged out.'

'Literally, you dog!' said Jed. 'I hope you're not going home with more than you went with.'

'What's that supposed to mean?'

'You know. Herpes, chlamydia, crabs.'

'Euwwgh, don't be disgusting,' Molly said, leaning forwards. 'He's probably already got something from his recent Tinder hook-ups?' She sat back, clicking the seat belt into place. 'You're grossing me out.'

There was silence in the car. Sam struggled to stay awake as the others fell asleep. After swerving onto the hard shoulder he slapped his thighs to stay alert. Immense relief flooded through him when he saw the south Bristol junction. Nearly there, he thought. Almost home. His eyelids drooped. Not far now.

As the car struck the lorry in front, there was a colossal sound of crunched metal and the young friends were catapulted forwards. Chloe crashed headlong onto the windscreen. The damaged car veered off the road, ploughed into the bank, and came to a violent stop. Drivers in cars behind stopped and called the emergency services. Police vehicles and ambulances arrived at the wrecked car to alleviate the devastating result of a lad falling asleep at the wheel.

# 22

Alex bombarded the policeman with questions.

'We've taken eyewitness statements and you'll be informed as soon as we know any more. Both boys have left hospital with minor injuries and our colleagues are talking to them individually, in order to compile our report.'

'How's Molly?' Leni reached for her phone to see if she had Molly's number. 'I'd like to speak to her, or her parents?'

The policeman spoke. 'She's being kept in for observation, we believe.'

'We're wasting time. Let's just go to the hospital.' Alex grabbed his wallet and the car keys. His face was ashen and drawn. 'We can speak to the others later. It's Chloe I need to see. Now.'

They drove to the hospital in numbed silence and rushed to the Trauma Unit. A calm, quietly spoken nurse met them.

'She's in a coma but she's stable. You can see her for a few minutes then the doctor will come and talk to you.' She led them along a corridor. Leni glanced into side wards, some of which had their doors open, where patients were hooked up to lines and monitors in the dimly lit rooms.

The nurse stood aside as they entered the room. Alex gasped and made small whimpering noises.

'Oh God.' He kissed Chloe's forehead. 'Not my little girl, please.' She wore a regulation gown, looking small and fragile between the white sheets with her shoulder and arm immobilised. A mask covered her mouth and nose, and a drip fed drugs via a peg into her slim hand. Leni gently stroked Chloe's other hand on the far side of the bed as Alex pulled up the visitor chair as close as he could, without physically getting onto the bed.

'It's Dad, my love. Can you hear me? I just want to tell you how much we love you and that you're going to get better very soon.' He brushed tears away.

They sat in the hushed room. Chloe's breathing apparatus emitted a regular beep. Alex rested his elbows on the bed and, with his chin in his hands, stared in disbelief at his daughter. The door opened and a doctor and nurse approached.

'Hello, I'm Dr Singh.' He put his hand out. 'You're her father and mother?'

'Yes, I'm Alex, Chloe's dad, and this is my partner, Leni.' They shook hands.

'Her blood pressure and vital signs are good. She's sustained a fractured shoulder and humerus, most likely from the impact of hitting the front seats on impact. We can't set the arm until the swelling goes down. The most important thing now is to find out if there's been any damage to her brain as she hit the windscreen with force, it appears. We're going to keep her in an induced coma overnight and we'll do an MRI head scan once the oedema has settled down.'

'Is she going to be OK?' Alex's reedy voice caught in his throat. 'Will there be any damage, do you think?'

'We'll know after the scan, but she's comfortable and stabilised now so that's all good.' Dr Singh closed Chloe's notes on his clipboard.

'What time's the scan and when will we know anything? Should we wait here?' Leni distractedly pulled at strands of her hair, an anxious habit she hadn't done for months. 'How long will it take?' Her mind was a maelstrom of emotions. Could Chloe have brain damage? Would Alex cope with that devastating possibility? Their relationship would suffer. Oh God, how selfish she was, thinking how the outcome of the accident would impact on her, when Chloe had recently escaped death's clutches.

'There's nothing you can do right now.' Dr Singh's gentle voice interrupted Leni's muddled thoughts. 'Go and get some tea. You're welcome to sit with Chloe for a while but then I suggest you go home and get some sleep. She'll need all your support when she's out of the coma tomorrow. There's a quiet prayer room if you prefer to remain on-site and a nurse can come for you if there are any changes in her situation.'

'Thank you, Doctor. It's been such a shock, it's impossible to take in.' Alex appeared to have diminished in stature, his head hanging to one side and shoulders slumped downwards. He looked a lost, defeated, shadow replacement of the strong, athletic man of yesterday.

Leni felt her mobile vibrating and quietly slipped from the room.

'Hello?' she said, inhaling the institutional smell of cleaning chemicals as she walked to find a quiet spot. It was Sam's mother, enquiring after Chloe. Leni gave a brief outline then asked about the crash, from Sam's point of view. As they talked, she watched drivers park their cars and was struck how odd it was, that life appeared to be going on as normal for other people while she felt as if she was in a bubble.

'Thanks for calling, Lauren, but I'd better go. Alex needs me. Best wishes to Sam.' Leni went back to the ward. The beautiful evening hues of green and blue sky dwindled to an inky indigo in the distance.

'That was Lauren. She sends her love.' Leni put her arms around Alex's shoulders. 'Shall we have that coffee?'

She led him away, supporting him along the corridor the way they'd come. Fishing in her purse for change she stopped at the vending machine. They found the quiet room and Alex sank down heavily in an armchair, appearing oblivious of everything around him.

'Here, my darling, have this. I won't be a minute.' Leni handed him a plastic cup of steaming coffee and placed hers on the low veneer table in the middle of the room. She went to find another vending machine for a bar of Dairy Milk chocolate.

'This'll make the coffee more bearable, I hope. It's just coloured water, isn't it?' She broke off a chunk and put it in Alex's hand.

They sipped their drinks and ate chocolate in silence. On the table lay old magazines beside a handful of leaflets advertising the Samaritans. On the walls hung a variety of watercolour landscapes and posters displayed in cheap clip frames. One picture showed Jesus in a white robe, arms spread wide, with a quote from the bible reminding onlookers that his death ensured humanity's endurance. She flinched. If there was a God (if such a deity existed), was he really merciful? What about all those innocent children stuck, through no fault of their own, in war zones, or those unlucky ones, across the globe, dying from malnutrition and lack of access to clean water?

Leni scanned her mobile for a number.

'I'm sorry to ask this, Naomi, but is there any chance you could keep Jake overnight after his playdate?' Leni whispered, while looking over at Alex. His eyes were closed and his head rested on the back of the armchair. 'I'm not too sure how long we'll be at the hospital.'

'No problem. How is she?'

'She's been made stable. We'll know more tomorrow.' Acid reflux created a pain in her oesophagus. 'Tell Jake I'll pick him up after school tomorrow. Can he borrow some underwear?'

'Of course. Don't worry about him.' Naomi's calm voice soothed Leni's jittery anxiety. 'I'll call you if I need to.'

Leni put her phone on silent and sat beside Alex. It was peaceful for a few minutes then a loud commotion in the corridor broke into her thoughts.

'Where's the doctor? I demand to see him, right…' The volume of a high-pitched voice increased as the door flew open. Heather stood transfixed, spitting out the word 'away' as she glared at Leni.

'Why is *she* here?' Striding towards her ex-husband, Heather's aggressive tone continued. 'This is *our* daughter. I haven't seen a doctor yet. Where the hell is he? Whose fault was it? Is the boy in custody?' A torrent of questions gushed from her tight, angry mouth.

'Leni drove me.' Alex stood up. 'I was in a bad way. I wasn't in a fit state to drive.'

'I'm going to get Bob.'

'Where is he?'

'Outside, having a cigarette. I didn't think it would be helpful for extra people to be here.' Heather stared pointedly at Leni.

'We're all involved, so please sit down and I can tell you what the situation is.'

'Well, I want to see her as soon as possible.' Heather sat down, stuffing her scarf into a ratty-looking bag.

Leni gasped. Her gold pendant was hanging around Heather's neck. She was quite sure it was the one that Will had bought her in Dubai. How could she be wearing it? She bit her lip to stop herself from blurting out an accusation.

A different doctor came into the room and announced himself as Dr Prince.

'Chloe's mother?'

'I am.' Heather frowned. 'And I demand some answers. What are you doing for Chloe? Is she alright? Is her face OK?'

Dr Prince sat down and indicated to Heather to do the same. He placed the tips of his fingers together.

'Well, first things first. We stabilised her in an induced coma to do an MRI scan on her brain. She has concussion and may suffer repercussions from that. There'll possibly be some amnesia but that should fade. It will take time though, and you need to understand the seriousness of her condition. She needs a calm environment in order to recuperate and it's likely she'll make a good recovery.'

As Dr Prince spoke Leni stole glances at her necklace. Had it been taken? It was impossible that Heather had exactly the same one as her.

'Can I see her now?'

'Of course. Don't be alarmed by all the equipment she's hooked up to.' Dr Prince stood up. 'Either Dr Singh or I will see you tomorrow,' he said, as he left the room.

They filed into the side ward. Heather let out a wail when she saw Chloe. Leni touched Alex's arm, leaving him and Heather on either side of the bed. She waited in the corridor, thoughts jumbling as to when she'd last worn the pendant, or even seen it in her jewellery box.

Alex soon came out and they took the lift to the ground floor. Leni held his hand as they walked to the car. They saw Bob draw on his cigarette and amble towards the entrance, hands deep in his pockets.

'How is she?' He avoided looking at Alex, concentrating his gaze on Leni. They spoke about Chloe's diagnosis and prognosis.

Leni drew a deep breath. 'Can I ask you a question, Bob?'

'Fire away.'

'Where did Heather get the pendant necklace she's wearing?'

'Can't think which one it is?' He stubbed out his cigarette under his heel.

'A heavy gold link chain with a large filigree ball hanging from it.'

'Oh, yeah, that one. It was from Chloe and Jamie. They clubbed together for Heather's birthday. Wasn't that nice?'

'It's my necklace.' As Leni spoke she heard Alex gasp. 'Will bought it for me just before he died.'

'Well, you must be mistaken. Jamie'll tell you. Now if you'll excuse me, I'd like to see Chloe.'

'I'm not mistaken,' Leni said, clutching Alex's arm. 'It must have been stolen.'

'Are you calling me a liar?' Bob thrust out his chest, his seventeen stone and wide neck creating an image of a buffalo about to attack.

Alex squared up to him. 'Back off, Bob.'

'Says who?' he snarled, taking another pace towards Alex.

'Look, it's perfectly reasonable. Leni wants to know where Heather got the necklace.'

'And I already told you, so you back off.'

Alex took Leni's arm. 'Come on. We'll ask Heather directly. It's got nothing to do with him.'

'You think you're so superior.' Bob's eyes narrowed and his lip curled, as he blocked their way. 'You're a real knob.'

'Is that so?' Alex sneered.

'Stop this,' Leni said. 'Let's deal with it another time. Please?'

Alex's aggressive fight-or-flight attitude wilted. 'You're right. We'll talk to the children when Chloe's stronger.'

Bob turned on his heel towards the hospital entrance, muttering obscenities about them under his breath.

'I'm exhausted. Let's go home,' Alex said in a dejected voice.

'I'll drive.' Leni opened the passenger door and watched his sloped shoulders and weary frame fold into the seat.

They arrived at the house. He went to call his sister on the phone as Leni made tea and toast, and let Monty out for a pee.

'I'll call my parents tomorrow. I'm not going to call them this late or they'll be in a dreadful state.'

'And Jamie'll want to see her. Can you take him tomorrow?'

'Yes, I'll ask Martin to hold the fort at the shop.'

'I'll check my jewellery once I've collected Jake and got home.' She rinsed her mug and put it in the dishwasher. 'But I know it's my pendant, I just know it.'

Alex got up, put his mug into the machine and held her tight. 'I'm sorry.'

'No, I'm sorry to even mention it, with Chloe and everything. It's not a priority.'

Alex stepped back, appearing stunned. 'What were they thinking? I'm astounded.'

'Perhaps you could have a quiet word with Jamie so you

don't have to question Chloe? He might know something?' Leni said, opening the back door to let Monty in. 'Time for bed. It'll be a long week, I imagine.'

'Rest assured,' Alex said, with a weary voice, 'I'll get to the bottom of it, and your necklace will be returned.'

# 23

It was mid-August when Alex, Leni and Jake went to collect Chloe from hospital. Leni picked up the small suitcase of clothes and toiletries that Heather had dropped in, as Alex supported Chloe around her waist.

'This is for you. I bought it with my pocket money.' Jake shyly presented her with a rabbit pompom on a chain, to hang from her bag.

'Thanks, Jake.'

'Are you better now?' he asked.

'I'm better than I was, after the accident. To be honest, I just can't wait to get out of here and feel normal again.'

With a pale face, limp hair and faltering steps, Chloe reached the car and sat in the back next to Jake. Leni wrapped a travel rug around Chloe's thin frame.

'You're bound to feel anxious, but your dad will drive really carefully.'

'Let's get you home,' Alex said, reversing from his space.

For several minutes they were silent, each looking out of the window. Leni recognised the gastropub at Ogbourne and recalled having a meal with Alex there. That had been a fun night. It was on one of their early dates, and she thought about how much their relationship had developed over the past year. It troubled her that Chloe didn't fully accept her, but she understood that the girl must feel insecure. She'd need lots of loving support, not only from her father.

'I've been thinking, while I was in hospital.' Chloe's small voice broke the silence. 'I want to come and live with you, Dad.'

Leni's gut tightened. This wasn't how she envisaged things going. Chloe was only due to stay with Alex for a couple of weeks, while Heather and Bob were on holiday. Jamie would be arriving too, in a day or so, after his holiday with a school friend. The house will be heaving, she thought. How would that work for them all?

'What's brought you to that decision?' Alex kept facing forwards with both hands on the wheel.

'I can't stand Bob, and I'm fed up with Mum's black moods.'

'Is she going through a bad patch?' he asked.

'She's so unpredictable.' Chloe's voice whined. 'Sometimes she bites my head off before I've even said anything.'

'What about Jamie? How would it be for him, on his own, do you think?'

'I know. It's not fair.' She sounded close to tears. 'But he can decide for himself when he's sixteen?'

'There are several things to consider, not least your school,' Alex said.

'I don't want to stay on, anyway? I want to go to Swindon Sixth Form College.'

'It's further away from mine than from your mum's house.'

'I can get the bus.' She sniffed. 'I've looked at the timetable and there's an express from Marlborough.'

They drove past the entrance to the Golf Club and arrived at Saxon Green.

'Let's talk about it later – we're home now.' He parked close to the house.

Leni retrieved the case. 'Could you take Monty into the garden while we get Chloe settled, please, Jake?'

'OK. I'll play ball with him.' Jake rushed to hug the dog.

Alex took Chloe up to her room while Leni made tea.

He came into the kitchen. 'What do you think about her idea?'

'Jamie would be very upset.'

'That's what I was thinking.' He sipped his tea. 'But perhaps he could move in too? There's the third bedroom. The boys would have to share, when Jake comes over. Or I might be able to reconfigure the loft and put in a Velux window?' Alex looked cheerful as he spoke.

Leni considered the idea. They'd talked about her moving in with him soon, but that wouldn't be easy now. 'I can stay in my cottage and review the situation at Christmas?'

Alex nodded. 'If Chloe does two years at college, she'd finish as Jamie does his GCSEs. He might also like to go to Swindon College, or there's St John's here.'

'What about Heather? She won't want them to leave? Both at the same time?'

Alex sighed, looking remorseful. 'When we split up, we agreed that the children would live with her until they finished school. We thought that would work best for them. But it's different now that she's with Bob.'

'Let's mull it over and talk again in a few days' time.' There was a lot to consider, not only what was best for her and Jake.

She loved this man, and she accepted he came with baggage; the whole thing just needed some clear-headed thinking.

Leni tapped on Chloe's door. There was no response and she wavered momentarily whether to knock harder and wake her up, or try later. She had to find out about her pendant. Jamie had known nothing about it. He'd only seen his mum try the necklace on when it was her birthday. The mystery had been like a festering scab these past weeks. Would Chloe steal her stuff, and did she think she'd get away with it? Perhaps it was a cry for help. Leni took a deep breath and rapped her knuckles on the door.

'Can I come in? I've brought you some toast.'

A muffled voice replied. In the dark room, Chloe hunkered beneath her duvet. Leni pulled the curtains open, allowing some light in, and drew the armchair closer to the bed.

'How are you feeling?'

'Tired, and I'm still sore.'

'I wondered about a massage? I know a good therapist in Pewsey if you'd like one?'

'Maybe,' she replied in a non-committal voice. She poked her head from the duvet and shuffled up the bed, reaching for her plate of toast.

'I don't like jam.'

'Oh? You liked it in the summer.' Really, she was so irritating. Leni tried another tack. 'That's alright, I'll get you another piece. I'm happy to eat that one. What do you want on it?'

'Peanut butter.'

Leni went downstairs and returned with a fresh piece of toast and two mugs of tea. She sat, without talking, as they drank their tea. She wanted answers, but knew she had to tread carefully. She would take her time.

'I hope Molly's better. Have you spoken to her?'

'She's OK. She went back to school on Monday. It's weird not being there with everyone.' Chloe licked her fingers then wiped them on the duvet cover.

'Won't be long for you now, the physio's nearly finished, I understand. Your dad says you've spoken to Swindon College about a place?'

'Yeah, they've accepted me on the photography and philosophy course, starting in September.'

'That's good news.' Leni put her empty mug on the bedside table. She paused. 'I hope I've always been welcoming and kind to you. I've never tried to replace your mum.'

'I know that,' Chloe snapped back.

Leni took a deep breath. 'Your father and I are serious about each other. I hoped you'd be happy for him. When he and your mum split up, he put on a brave face because you were so young. He loves you and Jamie very much, you know.'

Chloe groaned and hid her face behind her mug.

'If there's anything bothering you about our relationship, it would be good if we could talk about it.'

'You've got everything,' Chloe blurted out. 'You've got Dad, and everything as you want it. Mum's got Bob. What about me? And Jamie? It's not fair.' She pulled the duvet up to her chin and looked away as tears spilled over.

Leni resisted the urge to hug her, knowing Chloe wouldn't like it. 'You and Jamie will always be paramount to your mum and dad. They're your parents. We'll just be a bigger family, that's all.' She waited for a response, but getting nothing, she said with a small smile, 'Jake's looking forward to having a brother and sister. It's what he's always wanted.'

'Stepbrother. Stepsister,' Chloe snapped back.

'Yes, you're right. But fractured families can heal, you know. Jake and I will stay at the cottage and your dad is settled here, so, for the time being, that's the way we'll work it. Not living with your mum and Bob will feel different, but change can be good. It can be empowering.'

'You don't understand. My mum won't cope without us.' She tore a tissue from the box by her bed and blew her nose. 'I feel guilty.'

'I am trying to understand, Chloe. New challenges help us to grow and develop. I know from experience. If you want to go back to your mum's, you can.'

Chloe bit the inside of her cheek. Leni imagined she was trying to picture what it would be like living with her dad and lessening her supporting role to her mum.

'Try it 'til Christmas? It could be fun.' Leni got up to leave. 'I'll cook some breakfast and we can talk more downstairs?' She picked up the mugs and plates and closed the door behind her. That didn't go so badly, she thought.

While grilling bacon, mushrooms and tomatoes, Leni reflected on Chloe's concern for her mother. Heather suffered with depression, but there was nothing to suggest she wasn't coping. If anything, wouldn't it give her a bit of respite from the responsibility of having the kids most of the time? Alex said he knew that she bad-mouthed him in front of the children and often seemed irritated by them. Jamie had ruefully let this nugget slip out.

She made a pot of coffee, humming along to a track on the radio. She hadn't mentioned the necklace, but felt relieved to have opened up dialogue about Chloe's feelings. Slowly, slowly, catchy monkey, as the saying goes.

Her phone pinged with a text from Alex saying he was minutes away. Would it be better for Alex to question Chloe without her being present? She'd get his opinion. She didn't feel qualified on how best to handle his daughter.

'That smells good.' Alex came in and kissed her.

'How was your meeting?'

'Went really well. The client wants a huge ash table. He's a regular host, so we've got a few weeks' work on that. It's a bit of a logistical headache how we'll get it to him in one piece. I'll need to borrow a bigger trailer.' He removed his jacket. 'How's Chloe?'

'She's in the shower. We had a chat about her staying here and my remaining in Pewsey. It didn't feel the right time to mention the pendant. Do you think she'll feel interrogated? Would it be better coming from you, without me here?'

'I think she'd deny it. With you in the room, she'll be forced to confront her behaviour.'

Chloe came into the kitchen wearing her old tracksuit, pink nail polish chipped and fingernails ragged where she'd obviously been chewing them. Huge fluffy Dalmatian slippers made her look childlike, and her hair, usually straightened with military precision on a daily basis, was now lightly dried and tousled. Leni liked this unsophisticated look.

'Hi Dad.' She sat down and gulped down her orange juice.

'Hi Chloe. Are you feeling rested?'

'I got woken up by someone,' she said, pointedly looking at Leni, 'banging the front door.'

'That was probably me, going to my early meeting.' Alex jumped in before Leni could admit she'd made quite a din getting Monty and Jake out of the door, to take Jake to school.

'I went back to sleep, anyway.'

Leni put the cooked mushrooms and tomatoes into the bottom oven. It was ridiculous to feel guilty about making some noise earlier. They shouldn't have to tiptoe around the house during daylight hours.

Alex looked serious as he regarded his daughter. 'Chloe, I want to talk about the necklace you and Jamie gave your mum for her birthday. Where did you buy it?'

'I got it in a little place in the Brunel Centre.'

'I don't think so.' He shook his head from side to side. 'It's a designer piece, and the shops there don't sell that kind of thing.' He paused and folded his arms. 'I believe you took that necklace from Leni's jewellery box.'

'No I didn't,' she denied vehemently. 'Is that what she said? She's lying.'

'It belongs to me, Chloe.' Leni spoke in a quiet, firm voice.

'That's ridiculous – why would I take your stuff? I don't even like you.'

Alex gasped. 'That's not nice. Please apologise to Leni.'

Chloe looked shamefaced, but remained silent. 'Sorry,' she said eventually, her face all red and blotchy, and bottom lip trembling.

'What possessed you to take Leni's jewellery?' Alex went over to Chloe and put his hand on her shoulder.

'I felt sorry for Mum.' She burst into tears. 'She was feeling so shit and I wanted to cheer her up. You've got so much stuff, I didn't think you'd miss one necklace.'

'But it's wrong to take something that isn't yours. You know that.' Alex frowned.

Leni pitied Chloe, whose tears now ran freely down her face. 'Will gave me the pendant just before he died, so it's very special to me. I don't wear it often, but it's something I treasure and keep, in memory of him.'

Alex knelt beside his daughter, and put his arm around

her. 'Try to imagine how Leni feels, Chloe? It was the last present he ever bought. She lost her husband and Jake has lost his dad.' He stroked her hair off her face and spoke quietly. 'You'll need to ask your mother for it back, so you can return it.'

Leni pulled paper towel from the roll and handed it over. 'I'm sure she'll understand, once she knows?'

'She won't,' Chloe shouted. 'She'll be furious. It'll tip her over the edge.' She picked at her nail polish.

'Does Jamie know where you got it?'

'No. I just told him to cough up £20. He wouldn't have a clue how much a necklace costs. He was happy to leave it to me.'

'It's up to you, then, to ask for its safe return. You can't involve him.' Alex went to pour some coffee. 'You'll need to find another gift with his contribution.'

'Can't you just get another necklace?'

'It was bought in Dubai,' Leni said. 'It's not something you can buy on the High Street.'

Alex looked at the clock as he handed a coffee to Leni. 'Can I help with anything?'

'No, everything's ready.' Leni busied herself getting the food out, and put three plates of cooked breakfast on the table. The theft of the necklace would have to be put aside, for now.

'I'm not hungry.' Chloe pushed the plate away and scraped her chair backwards.

Alex remonstrated. 'Come on, now. Leni's gone to the trouble of making it.'

'I don't want any—'

'Don't worry about it,' Leni cut in. She wasn't going to pander to Chloe's childish behaviour, or cajole the girl into eating. She would take a lesson from her dog-training classes: reward good behaviour and ignore the bad.

'I'm not staying here any longer,' Chloe yelled. 'I'm packing my stuff.' She tried flouncing out, but the giant slippers slopped off each heel as she crossed the room.

Alex raised his eyebrows and exhaled loudly. 'I'll go and speak to her in a minute.'

Leni sat at the table, drinking coffee. 'I'm not surprised by her reaction. It's humiliating having to own up.' Sinking her knife into the egg yolk, she watched the runny liquid spool over the plate. 'Give her some time to let the reality sink in.'

'I don't think she really wants to move back full-time into her mum's.' Despite the emotional turmoil only moments before, he tucked into his breakfast with relish. 'I love this black pudding. Is it from the butcher off the High Street?'

She smiled. He'd vowed to her, when they got together, that he'd try to be less of an ostrich when faced with difficult issues, and he was learning to wear his heart on his sleeve. He didn't like upsetting his daughter, and why would he?

As Leni rinsed out her mug, she appraised her cottage garden. There was nothing flowering in November but even the bare bones of the site gave her pleasure. The fruit tree at the bottom of the garden and the stone walls on either side created structure, while two clumps of *Cornus alba* gave a bit of colour.

Her landline rang. That'd be Mum. She was about the only person who preferred it to using a mobile.

'Hello Leni, how has your week been?'

Leni related a story from her job, and the talk with Chloe. 'Heather wants proof that the pendant's mine. Can you believe it?'

'Oh, really, that's ridiculous.' Imogen tutted. 'Once Chloe confessed to taking it, then that should be the end of the matter. Heather should return it, immediately.'

'I know, and it's not as if Will gave me a receipt. It was my birthday present.'

Imogen was silent for a moment.

'Are you still there, Mum?'

'I just had a thought. Have you got a photograph of you wearing it, while you were with Will?'

'Mum, that's a brilliant idea. I'll check, after our call.' Leni wrote 'photo' on the notepad beside her. 'I'm signing up for that weekend jewellery course I told you about. I'm so excited, I can't wait.'

'Will it repeat what you've learnt during the online course?'

'I think it'll consolidate everything I've done so far, but it'll be great having an expert to hand, and learn special skills from her. I imagine the equipment will be good, too.' Leni took the roving phone into her sunny sitting room. 'Enough about me. How are your Christmas plans shaping up?'

Imogen gave a run-down about her forthcoming choral concerts and the dates she'd be at Fran's house. 'When will I see you and Jake, and Alex?'

'We're in Venice for Alex's birthday, as you know, so would you like to come and stay here after that, before going to Fran's?'

Imogen didn't answer the question. 'When are you away? Have you got Jake's childcare sorted?'

'We're off on the 1st and back around lunchtime on 5th December.' It was a relief not to ask her mum for any more favours. 'Jake's with Naomi.'

'Ah yes, that's David's mum? Isn't that kind of her?'

'They're best buddies now. I have David every Wednesday after school while Naomi's on her gardening course. It all evens out, eventually.'

'Hang on, darling, I'll get my diary.' Imogen delved into

her handbag. 'I'm staying with my friend, Betsy, in Cornwall for a few days, and I've got some other things on, so it may be best to wait and see you all on New Year's Day. Can you still make it?'

'Absolutely. It'll be special having Alex there, this year. Can you fit Chloe and Jamie in, if they're with us? Of course, they may be busy with friends. I'll find out.'

'I'm looking forward to meeting them.'

When the call ended, Leni went to her study area. She hadn't put any photographs into albums for years, but there may be one or two uploaded to the computer. She logged on, clicking on the pictures folder. It jolted her, seeing photographs of Will. An ache came into her belly. Perhaps if she'd been less self-absorbed, and tried harder to understand him, they might have been happier, but she couldn't have foreseen his heart problem. She flicked through pictures of Jake as a baby. Where had those years gone? It seemed like only yesterday that they were a young couple, starting a family. She took a deep breath, scrolling until she found the Dubai folder. There they were. The photo showed them standing on the hotel balcony. That must have been when they had cocktails before dinner, and a waiter took the shot. The pendant shone bright against her white linen sleeveless dress. She remembered the heat and how warm her skin had felt as they sat there, drinking and laughing. Not so long ago, really.

She printed out a copy for Chloe to show her mother and emailed it to Alex, feeling vindicated. There was the proof. Hopefully, Heather would relinquish the necklace, and Jamie and Chloe could make it up to their mother this Christmas with an extravagant present, something she really needed or wanted. Leni banished a fleeting thought that she'd send Heather a bouquet of flowers once she had the necklace back. Madness. That wouldn't be tactful. She'd like to do something though, to thank Chloe for owning up and getting it back. Presuming it did come back. There was nothing more she could do about it now. She'd get on with her life and, after getting her credit card out, she paid the jewellery course fee.

Alex brought his toolkit when he came over to Leni's house the following Sunday. He'd offered to make her a compost bin. Leni showed him the planks of wood she'd bought and they stood at the bottom of the garden, deciding on the best location. Jake jumped up and down, excited to be Alex's assistant on the project.

'Wow, I'm impressed,' Leni said, bringing hot drinks and biscuits out to them. 'It's looking good in such a short time.'

'It'll take another hour, or a bit more. Jake's been helpful keeping the planks straight and handing me the tools.'

'Alex let me use his drill.' Jake beamed with delight.

'Please be careful.' It was great that Alex was teaching him such a useful skill. She could do with a lesson herself; she'd be using tiny drills for her jewellery, in future. 'I'm drawing necklace designs. I'll give you a shout when lunch is ready.'

When they came in, Jake went to retrieve a pack of cards from his bedroom and Alex washed his hands.

'I've been learning some magic tricks.' Jake pulled his chair out and proceeded to practise with the cards. 'I'll do them for Granny, and my cousins, at Christmas.'

They'd just finished lunch when there was a knock at the front door.

'That'll be David.' Jake jumped up. Leni and Naomi stood chatting on the doorstep for a few minutes, as the boys rushed off upstairs to play.

'Shall I pick him up around 5pm?'

'That'd be great, see you then.' Leni closed the door and

returned to the kitchen where Alex had cleared the dishes and was making coffee.

They went into the garden, wrapped up against the cold. 'Maybe a couple more hours of daylight, so should easily get it finished,' Alex said. 'With your help.' He kissed her.

They talked as they worked to complete the compost box.

'Chloe thinks she wants to move back to my place at Christmas.'

'How's she doing?'

'She's not getting on with Heather. They're having a lot of rows. Jamie says the atmosphere's been tense since she returned. He'd missed her, of course, but was happier because Bob was less bossy with Chloe out of the house.'

'Would you like her to move back in with you?' She needed to know.

'It would provide stability and I think it's what she needs.' He stood up and faced her. 'I don't know how that would affect us, but I want you to know that you're the best thing that's happened to me in years. I want a future together.'

Leni tucked a strand of flyaway hair behind her ear and smiled, her heart filling with affection. 'I lost one love, I'm not going to lose this one.' She kissed him. 'We'll work it out.'

She handed him another plank of wood and held it straight as he drilled holes for the screws. A grey squirrel ran along the edge of the wall and down the branches of the apple tree, foraging for nuts dropped from the bird feeder hanging in the tree. She should have put gloves on; her fingers were getting cold.

'How was Heather about returning my necklace?'

'OK, I think. She recognised that Chloe's been disturbed about many things, not least the accident. My relationship with you was one thing to contend with, but Chloe was also stressed about boyfriend issues, the usual adolescent stuff of fitting in, FOMO, and so on.'

'FOMO?'

'Fear of missing out. Jamie filled me in.' Alex hammered the last nail and stood back to view his handiwork.

'I'm just relieved she got it. She'll hand it over next time she comes.'

'Hopefully the worst is behind her, now.' Leni realised that she'd have to wait longer before moving in with Alex, as Chloe would need to settle there, first. It hit her that she'd put Chloe's feelings before her own. She could wait until the spring and Forsythia Cottage would be easy to rent out, then.

The light faded as Alex sanded off a few rough edges. 'Just give it a couple of coats of preservative, to help protect the wood.'

'It looks brilliant, thank you.'

'It's great to be appreciated,' he said, gathering his tools and following her into the house.

'Shall we look at diaries to firm up our holiday and Christmas plans?' Leni wanted to confirm the nights that Jake would stay with Naomi. She made tea as he unlaced his boots and got out his phone.

'Looking forward to Venice?' he said, face glowing from his labours.

'I can't wait. All that stunning art and architecture.' Leni sipped her Earl Grey. 'What are you hoping to find?'

'Glass chandeliers and mirrors from Murano, and possibly a little something for you?' He grinned. 'I hope you won't get bored trudging around warehouses? You may prefer an afternoon to yourself.'

'Not at all. It'll give me decorative ideas for when I have my own shop.' She went around the table to hug him. 'I just love being with you, whatever we're doing.'

'Likewise.' He kissed her gently. 'It'll be fantastic if it's crisp and sunny, and there should be fewer crowds, in early December.'

She picked up her Filofax and they agreed commitments for the following weeks and confirmed going to Imogen's for New Year's Day. Putting the diary back in her bag, she asked, 'What time do you need to leave in the morning?'

'I'll go around 8am and head straight to the workshop for an hour.'

Two weeks later packed luggage stood sentry in Forsythia Cottage, Jake's small duffle bag beside Leni's carry-on case.

'Nearly ready, Jake?' Leni called upstairs then clipped Monty's lead to his collar.

'Coming.' Jake raced downstairs and gave her a hug, handing over a card. 'I did this for Alex's birthday.'

'Thank you, darling.' Leni smoothed his scruffy thatch of hair. 'He'll be so pleased you created it 'specially. Now, let's get Monty to the kennels and you over to David's house.'

When they arrived at Naomi's house, Leni knelt down and hugged Jake. 'Have a good time, and remember to be helpful to David's mum.'

He gave her a quick kiss and rushed off to see his friend.

'Thanks, Naomi,' Leni said. 'Call me any time, if you need to, otherwise I'll call Jake tomorrow night.'

'Off you go, and don't worry about a thing.' Naomi waved her off. 'Have a great time.'

# 24

'Hey, you.' Leni held Alex's hand, resting it on her thigh. 'Have I told you how excited I am?' she said, grinning as the engines roared and they were pressed into their seat-backs as the plane tilted skywards.

'Yes, here we are, back where it all started. Just twenty months since we first met, and you shared your dreams en route to Dubai.' Alex lifted her hand and brushed his lips across it.

'A lot of water under the bridge, hey? So much sadness then and so much to be thankful for, now.' She squeezed his hand, her heart filled with love for this gorgeous man beside her.

The trolley service got underway and they ate and drank, and talked. Leni then started her new book and Alex scoured the sports section of the newspaper.

After arriving at Venice airport they went to find a taxi.

'I've got a surprise for you.' Alex ushered Leni towards a man holding a placard with their names on.

'Oh my God, really?'

'*Buon pomeriggio*, follow me.' The chauffeur guided them to his water taxi, and put their luggage inside.

Leni stepped carefully down into the sleek vessel. From the inside glass-walled cabin they watched the industrial buildings fade into the distance behind them and took in the unfolding view ahead.

'It's spectacular.' Leni pointed to the ancient city. 'Is that St Mark's?'

'Yes, that's the Campanile, the bell tower. We'll go exploring tomorrow. We can take a lift to the top.' He pointed to other buildings. 'There are so many beautiful churches. It's incredible, isn't it?'

'Like nothing I've ever seen.' She gazed in awe at the soft pastel-coloured buildings all appearing to float.

After gliding through the murky water the boatman tied up alongside a quay and made the boat fast. Leni accepted his hand and stepped ashore, the floating sensation still making itself felt. She wrapped her pink mohair coat close as a chill wind whipped through the labyrinth of canals. Alex passed over the suitcases. The wheels bumped noisily along the cobbled street as they made their way to the hotel.

Leni stepped into the reception area and looked around. The walls were jammed with contemporary art and a ceramic log-burner glowed in one corner. 'How did you find such a gem?' Modern sofas, scattered with bright velvet cushions and elaborate trims were grouped around a huge tree trunk and glass coffee table. 'It's so quirky – I love it.'

The suave receptionist picked a key from the board. 'Please find your room on the first floor. Breakfast can be taken in the salon, or in your bedroom, if you prefer.' Leni swooned hearing his accent, making the English words sound so seductive. Had she always been a sucker for a smooth foreigner speaking her language?

They walked up a flight of stairs and Alex held open the

bedroom door. Clear evening light flooded onto a cream and pink silk rug. The king-size bed had a mound of pillows piled up against the satin striped headboard. Going straight to the window they admired the view of a canal below and ornate buildings facing them across the water. Alex pulled the narrow doors inwards, revealing a wrought-iron balcony, where a table and two small chairs filled the space. To their left was a small, arched bridge, and to the right, the vista opened up to a wider cross section of canal. A vaporetto water taxi was plying its business and a gondola cruised below carrying two couples pointing at the magnificent sights.

'Tea here or an exploratory walk straight away?' Alex stepped back into the room and opened his suitcase.

Leni circled his waist with her arms and lay her head against his back. 'Let's not rush anywhere. I just want to hold you first.'

Shedding their shoes, they lay on the bed and kissed. He stroked her hair and caressed her cheek, then his hand moved up and down her back as he pressed her close. She stood to undress. She enjoyed watching him, watching her. She slid off his jeans and boxers while he unbuttoned his shirt, flinging it onto a chair. Pushing the bedspread and duvet down the bed he held his arms open and their bodies entwined in an aroused clinch. Leni's joy of giving and receiving sexual pleasure was profound. Skin on skin, with sweat mingling, their desire heightened until they both felt the release of orgasm. Alex pulled the duvet close and they lay contentedly in each other's arms.

'So how much sightseeing will we do, after all that exertion?' Alex laughed.

'Talk about getting sea-legs, how about sex-legs? Mine are like jelly now.' She leant up on an elbow and kissed him. 'You're gorgeous. And we're such a good fit together.'

Alex looked into her eyes. 'I'm a very lucky man, to have found you.'

They lay quietly for a while. Leni's stomach gurgled and she clutched her belly with one hand. How embarrassing.

'Time to eat?' He chuckled. 'You have the shower first.'

Leni enjoyed a long soak under hot water. She wrapped herself in a fluffy robe and wasn't surprised to find him fast asleep, hair tousled and one muscled arm dangling over the side of the bed.

She sat down and touched his shoulder. 'Are you staying put or coming out to see the sights?' She watched him rouse. 'Your turn in the shower.'

Dropping the key to Reception they set out to explore. Referring to his guidebook, they found St Mark's Square. 'A drink in the Square or shall we saunter down an unknown alley, and take whatever we find?'

'I'd really like to see the Square. We'll need a vaporetto, won't we? It's too far to walk.'

They waited at the stop, standing next to a chic Italian couple conversing in their rapid native tongue. They boarded a busy boat. Motoring along the highway of water, Leni stared entranced at the splendour of the buildings on either side. The stucco-fronted properties were painted in complementary shades of ochre, terracotta and sand. After passing small landing stages and gliding under bridges they reached their stop at St Mark's. The sun was dipping in the sky and windows shimmered in the water's reflection. It was cold, but they decided to take outside seats at a café on the edge of the Square, and ordered olives and an aperitif.

'I've heard these cafés charge an arm and a leg?' She rested her bag in her lap. 'Not surprisingly, given its location.'

'Worth every penny. It's an experience everyone should have, once in a lifetime,' he said, sipping his drink. 'I love watching your expression taking in the sights.'

'Isn't it heavenly? I just love people-watching. You can almost guess who is Italian. They're so sophisticated.'

She felt blessed to be in this beautiful place with her loving man and all expectations of the city surpassed.

'Tomorrow I've booked a tour of St Mark's and the Doge's Palace with a canal cruise,' Alex said, popping an olive in his mouth. 'We'll skip the queues and see some of the most important sites. It'll be a reminder of our date on Regent's Canal.'

The sky was dark as they finished their drinks and went to find a trattoria.

After waking to find a cold, dry morning, they walked from the hotel to join the tour. Afterwards, having accidentally left the guidebook behind, they wandered the streets, enjoying interesting alleyways and choosing any intricate bridge to cross and weave their way around the watery city. They stopped for a reviving *aperitivo* in a small bar.

'We're acclimatising,' Alex said, raising his glass. 'I almost feel like a local. These Aperol spritzes are *perfetto*.' He waved his arm with a flourish, putting on an Italian accent as he spoke. *'Molto buona.'*

Leni laughed and clinked her glass against his. 'Happy birthday.' She pulled a small box from her handbag and watched him pull away the navy ribbon. 'First attempt. Hope you like them.' Her stomach fluttered. She hoped they didn't look too naïve.

Alex picked out a pair of heavy silver cufflinks which he lifted to the light and twirled in his fingers. 'They're beautiful. Thank you, my darling Leni. I'll crow that I was gifted your first pieces when you're selling your designs at International Jewellery Fairs.'

Leni blushed, basking in the pleasure that he liked her present, then changed the subject. 'So, where are we? Will your sense of direction get us back to the hotel? I'd like a quick shower and change before the concert.'

In the evening, Leni and Alex listened spellbound to a Baroque concert in San Vidal Church. She squeezed his hand, tears welling in her eyes as the musicians played Bach in front of Carpaccio's magnificent painting of *San Vidal on Horseback with eight saints.*

The next day, they took the advice of Alex's friend to visit one of the city's great Renaissance palaces, Palazzo Grimani. The ceiling frescoes and stucco work had been beautifully restored and sumptuous artworks adorned the rooms. Bad weather saw them hurry back to the hotel where they spent the afternoon making love, and watching the rain splash at the windows and on the canal.

'*Perfetto*, for me.' Leni stretched languidly. 'A city break shouldn't be all history and culture, should it?'

Alex traced his fingers over her breasts and belly.

'What do you want to do tomorrow, apart from our trip to Murano?'

'If there's time, I'd like to see the Peggy Guggenheim Collection. Do you like modern and surrealist art?' Leni still didn't really know about his wider taste in art, and imagined it might be quite conservative, thinking of the antiques he sold. This was the chance to challenge herself too, and possibly introduce something different to them both.

'Sounds a good plan. Why's it so remarkable?'

'There are works by Picasso, Magritte, and Max Ernst.

252

He was Peggy's husband, by the way. And I'd like to see Jackson Pollock's radical paintings.'

After waking early the next day, they boarded a vaporetto for the hour-long journey to Murano. They toured two glass factories and a showroom to look for authentic glass pieces to sell in Alex's shop. After lunch they returned to the city taking a water taxi to Accademia, alighting beside the Guggenheim Museum, housed in an eighteenth-century Palazzo. They circled Marini's *The Angel of the City* sculpture. Alex angled his mobile to get a full shot. Leni took advantage of the deserted terrace, resting her hand on the bronze sculpture, close to the horseman's erect phallus.

'Take a photo,' she said, putting on a silly face.

'Cheeky.' He took pictures as she posed. 'What would Jake say?'

'He'd laugh. Anything about body parts is ridiculed.'

'Maybe with school friends. Perhaps not where his mother's involved? A bit too close to the bone?'

Leni fell about laughing. 'Sorry, it was your choice of words.'

Alex pulled her close. 'Let's see.' He showed her the photographs.

'You're right.' She groaned. 'Delete, delete.'

They went in, spending a couple of hours looking at the artworks and learning about the artists. They found a small bar where they had a drink and discussed the paintings they'd seen.

Leni drained her glass of wine. 'I'd like to find things for the children.'

'For Christmas?'

'Yes. You're an experienced shopper.' She reached for his hand across the table, marvelling at how smooth and dry it was. 'You source things for your shop, so you must like present shopping, right? Could you bear it?'

'Of course. Do you want to go alone?'

'Ha, you think I'm getting yours here?'

'Aren't you?' He gestured to the waiter for the bill then referred to the guidebook.

'Let's not go to the touristy ones listed. I saw the shops that I like, yesterday, when we walked back from Palazzo Grimani.'

Alex checked his watch. 'Shops close at 7.30pm so we've a bit of time.'

They left the restaurant and walked hand in hand, crossing canals and regularly checking the map. She stopped at a shop selling masks where they amused themselves trying on the highly decorative and ornate guises.

'I'm going to buy a couple of these. They'll look gorgeous on my sitting-room shelves and be a reminder of our wonderful trip.'

It was late when they went out for their last meal. Leni chose pasta vongole while Alex had a traditional Venetian dish of salted cod with anchovies. They made their way slowly back to the hotel, reluctant to face they'd come to the end of their holiday.

Leni woke with whirling guts. Her teeth felt furry. Just making it to the bathroom in time, she heaved into the lavatory bowl. After running cold water over her face and taking a few sips, she stayed in the bathroom until she was sure she wouldn't vomit again. She brushed her teeth.

'Those mussels last night must've been off – I've just thrown up.' She groaned, sitting down on the bed.

'Get back into bed. I'll pack our stuff.' He put their suitcases on the far side of the bed and pulled clothes from the wardrobe. 'No breakfast for you.'

'I couldn't face it. Maybe just black tea?'

'See how you feel when you're dressed. We've got about an hour before we need to get the water taxi to the airport.'

Subdued on the journey home, Leni hoped she'd feel well enough to go to work the next day. Then there was Christmas to think about, with its attendant carol concerts, nativity play, present shopping and cooking, and Jake's two-week school holiday. She needed to be well. Planning to introduce Chloe and Jamie to her mum on New Year's Day, she just couldn't afford the time to be ill.

# 25

Imogen opened the front door to see both her daughters arrive at the same time. Car doors slammed and Hugh, Fran and their children came forwards to kiss her. Rosie yapped and turned circles around the hairy labradoodle. Cecily knelt down to hug and kiss the smaller dog.

'Go on in.' Imogen shooed Fran and Hugh towards the door. 'Don't get cold.'

Alex and Leni stepped forwards and from the rear seats Imogen watched two youngsters jump out, their heads together in an animated conversation.

'You can't say that about Ronaldo. He's awesome – he's scored loads already this season.'

As they approached, the older boy stopped talking and stepped shyly to say hello to Imogen.

'You must be Jamie,' she said. 'It's very nice to meet you. I've heard a lot about you.'

'Really?' He shook her hand.

Imogen turned to her grandson, grasping both shoulders. 'My, how you've shot up, Jake. Is it country living that makes you grow so fast?'

He hugged her then ran off to join the other children playing with the dogs.

Alex held a bouquet of flowers. 'Lovely to see you again, Imogen. Can I introduce you to Chloe?'

Imogen took the flowers. 'That's so kind, thank you.' She turned to the pretty girl standing in front of her. Clothed from head to toe in black, Chloe had heavily kohl-rimmed eyes and the bottom two inches of her blond hair had been dip-dyed inky blue. She wore a shiny green nose stud and every finger, including her thumbs, was covered in silver rings. Leni had forewarned her that Chloe was going through a 'goth' phase.

'What a fabulous house. I love it.'

'Well, thank you.' Imogen was surprised by Chloe's first words. 'It's better in the summer. You're not seeing it at its best.'

'It's picture-book perfect. I'd like to photograph it.'

'You're welcome to.'

Imogen ushered everyone into the sitting room. A flaming log-fire burned in the hearth and candles scented the room with bay leaf and vanilla. At the far end of the room, a bushy Christmas tree was adorned with strings of twinkling lights and feathered birds. A fairy, with a wand and shiny gold hair, held court from the top.

The children piled onto the long sofa, squashing plush cushions as they jostled for space. The adults took seats on armchairs and an ottoman. On the central coffee table, one tray held champagne flutes, hi-ball glasses and two bottles, encased in cooler sleeves. The other tray held bowls of nuts and crisps, which the younger visitors were eagerly eyeing up.

'There's sparkling elderflower there, or you can help yourself to Coca-Cola from the utility fridge.' Imogen gestured to the glass jug of pale green liquid.

Luke jumped up. 'How many for Cokes?' He counted hands and left the room.

Hugh popped a cork and poured champagne.

'Jake.' Leni raised her eyebrows, watching him scoop a huge handful of peanuts. 'You're welcome to pass those around?'

'How did your concert go, Mum?' Fran said.

'It was magical. They turned all the church lights off and the whole place was candle lit. The pedestal flowers were a triumph, considering the time of year. We sang our pieces interspersed with traditional carols which the congregation joined in with. We raised the roof.'

'Was it a fundraiser?' Hugh asked.

Imogen beamed with delight. 'We collected £400 for the Alzheimer Unit at the cottage hospital. It's marvellous. Robin would have benefitted from the unit, had he lived. They're offering a programme of activities, dancing and singing. It's a really lovely place.' She sipped her champagne. 'Enough of me. How are you liking sixth form college, Chloe? I hear you're studying photography. It was a particular hobby of Robin's. I'll lend you some books on the subject, if you want?'

'Yeah, that'd be nice.' Chloe peeped out between long strands of hair, twisting her feet, clad in black Dr. Martens boots. 'College is good. Better than school, as you can pretty much do your own thing? I'm in with a cool bunch of girls.'

'What about boys?' Jamie piped up. 'You're a rugby supporter now, aren't you?'

Chloe's cheeks flushed. 'Yeah, I'm learning about it. I wasn't interested in sports before, I left that to Jamie.'

'Has a certain forward got something to do with it?' He teased his older sister.

'Shut up, Jamie.' She laughed, colouring deep red as she flicked her hand at him.

Jake looked with intrigue from one to the other sibling. Luke returned with cans of drink and noise escalated as the group of adults talked together with the children breaking off into their own animated conversations. Cecily followed Chloe's every word and gazed adoringly at the older girl, holding court.

Fran asked Alex about the shop and how well Christmas sales had gone. Imogen requested Hugh and Leni's help in the kitchen.

'Someone keep an eye on the fire, please,' she said, leaving the room.

In the kitchen, Imogen handed bottles of wine to Hugh. 'Could you deal with these, please, dear?' She peered into the oven. 'I may need your strength to get these out.'

'I'll do it, Mum. Have you got a stand to put them on?' Leni dragged two large fish pies from the oven, put them on the side and covered both with foil.

'Chloe seems quite self-assured.' Imogen passed Leni the colander and two large pans of vegetables. 'She's recovered from her injuries?'

'Pretty much,' Leni said, draining veg and piling them into hot dishes. 'Her fractured arm's healed completely but the damaged ligaments and muscles from the shoulder break give her a bit of pain.' She put the dishes into the bottom oven. 'Physically, she's healed well but I'm still concerned about her. Despite her ups and downs with Alex, she decided to stay put at her mum's. She feels a great responsibility to help care for her.'

'That sounds mature. I hope she had counselling after that dreadful accident?' Imogen retrieved dinner plates from the warming drawer and counted them. 'And Heather sees a psychiatrist, surely? Chloe shouldn't have all that burden.'

'You're right. She just felt she'd be abandoning her mum, and she didn't want to live at Alex's without Jamie.' Leni filled two jugs with water. 'It may change again, of course.'

Hugh put the opened bottles of wine on the table. 'How do you get on with them? They seem delightful.'

'Jamie's very easy-going and Jake adores him. Since Chloe's had more of Alex's attention, it's better all round. The accident was a catalyst for improving our relationship. She accepts I'm not a threat, after all.' Leni lit the candles in the central flower arrangement. 'Anything else, Mum?'

'Just call everyone in. It's ready, and I don't want any of it to go cold.'

Hugh and Leni returned to the sitting room, requesting everyone carry their glasses to the kitchen. Alex scooped up the empty snack bowls and Fran secured the handle on the log-burner.

Luke ordered the others to put their empty cans in the recycling bin and they filed into the steaming kitchen to find a seat.

'Dogs into the utility, please. I don't want them tripping me up,' Imogen said.

Leni led the three dogs out of the room and Alex joined her.

'Are you feeling OK? It seems to be going well.'

'It's wonderful. All the people I love best, gathered together. I'm very happy.' She enjoyed a long, slow kiss in Alex's arms. 'Come on, or Mum'll be wondering where we've got to.' She pulled him by the hand.

They walked into the kitchen to find everyone sitting down, except Imogen and Fran. The children were playing with their napkins, making them into boats and silly hats.

'I hope you all like fish pie?' Imogen plunged her large scoop through the brown, crispy potato layer and pulled out chunky pieces of assorted fish in a béchamel sauce. 'Fran, can you start on the vegetables? It's easier serving it this way.'

Chloe looked embarrassed. 'I am a vegetarian, but don't worry, I'll eat a little fish.'

'Oh dear, I am sorry. Leni, you didn't warn me.' Imogen looked fiercely at her daughter. 'I'd have made something else for Chloe,' she remonstrated.

It was Leni's turn to look embarrassed. 'I thought you'd reverted, Chloe? Didn't we all enjoy bacon butties the other day?' She looked to Alex for confirmation.

'It's a recent thing.' Chloe twirled the ends of her blue hair. 'Since Christmas.'

Alex harrumphed. 'A week? Come on, Chloe, you liked fish in the past.'

'OK, but I'm never eating beef again. Or lamb. Or anything with a furry face after watching a horrible film about the way the animals die.'

'I'll have her share,' Jamie said. 'It's my favourite.'

Fran finished putting vegetables onto each plate and Leni placed them in front of each guest. Imogen hung up her apron and sat between Jake and Cecily.

'This is excellent, Imogen,' Alex said, with fervour. 'I'll have to bring you freshly caught mackerel, some time. I often hang a line from the boat.'

'Can I freeze them?' Imogen dabbed her mouth and sipped white wine.

'I did a school project once, that said you can freeze mackerel whole, but it must be cleaned thoroughly and best vacuum sealed,' Leni said, turning to Alex. 'Mum loves lobster, if you get any?'

'A mate in the Solent has some pots. I'll get one for you in the summer.'

'Put me down for one too, please,' Fran joined in.

Hugh piped up. 'I'll swap you for a river trout. A client offers me fly-fishing on the river Dun.'

The fish theme continued for several minutes. The children got bored and talked about other things. Cecily plucked up the courage to ask Chloe whether the ends of her hair would be permanently blue. It was obvious to everyone around the table that Chloe enjoyed the attention of the younger girl, as she smiled and laughed, and bent her head towards Cecily to share some secret.

The main course was devoured and plates were cleared. Imogen leant in towards Leni. 'What a catch. Alex is a dish.' She laughed at her own words. 'I like the way he tells a story. Such a self-deprecating manner. He looks like a keeper.'

'He is. He's gorgeous. I can't believe my luck.' Leni finished loading the dishwasher, then washed and dried her hands. 'Oh, I meant to tell you last week. You remember Kat?'

'Of course,' Imogen nodded, 'and her lovely boy, Mike, who was Jake's best friend?'

'Well, she and Will's old friend, Connell, have got together. I'm so pleased for her. We introduced them last year at the rugby.'

'That's lovely news. She was such a support to you. I'm glad you've managed to stay friends since you left London.'

'Yeah, it's great.' Leni put an arm around Imogen. 'Things have worked out for both of us,' she said, with a smile.

Fran brought a large bread and butter pudding, and a glass bowl of trifle, to the table and served everybody's chosen dessert. 'There's ice-cream if you'd prefer, kids.'

Luke got up from the table and pulled out a tub of Ben & Jerry's from the freezer. He waved the scoop about for requests.

Leni tapped her glass to get everyone's attention. 'I think this is a good time. There's something we'd like to tell you, now that the children know.' Alex came and put his arm around her shoulder.

Everyone went quiet and looked towards them.

'I'm pregnant,' she said, a wide beam of delight on her face.

Imogen gasped. 'Oh my goodness, that's incredible news, darling.' Her eyes welled up with tears.

Jake whooped with delight. 'Mummy told me yesterday, but I had to keep it secret,' he said confidentially to Luke and Cecily.

There were smiles all round, and lots of questions and congratulations.

'How far along are you?' Fran asked. 'When did you know?'

'I felt unwell in Venice, but I put it down to food poisoning, and then I was feeling generally tired, which I thought was the effort in the weeks leading to Christmas, and so on. We're still in shock, aren't we?'

'Happily so,' Alex said and kissed her gently.

'I know you don't all know me so well, but thank you for welcoming me into your family.' He gestured to Imogen and Fran. 'I'd like to toast Chloe and Jamie. They've coped with a lot of changes. I'm very proud of all you've achieved, these past few years.' Chloe buried her face in her napkin, embarrassed, while Jamie looked proudly towards his dad. 'Leni came into my life when I least expected it and she captured my heart. We're thrilled to bits.'

Leni stood up and put her arms around his waist. 'I want to thank my family, too, for all the support you've given me and Jake. We're overjoyed to join Alex's lovely family.' She picked up her glass and raised it towards Chloe and Jamie. 'We'll do everything to show that it is possible for two fractured families to heal and become one.'

'Cheers to that.' Alex raised his glass. 'Here's to a fabulous future, to each and every one.'